MAN AND WIFE

ANDREW KLAVAN

MAN

and

WIFE

A Tom Doherty Associates Book | New York

MAN AND WIFE
Copyright © 2001 by Andrew Klavan

All rights reserved, including the right to reproduce this book, or
portions thereof, in any form.

This book is printed on acid-free paper.

A Forge Book
Published by Tom Doherty Associates, LLC
175 Fifth Avenue
New York, NY 10010

www.tor.com

Forge® is a registered trademark of Tom Doherty Associates, LLC.

Book design by Richard Oriolo

Library of Congress Cataloging-in-Publication Data

Klavan, Andrew.
    Man and wife / Andrew Klavan.—1st ed.
       p.   cm.
    "A Tom Doherty Associates book."
    ISBN 0-765-30215-2
    1. Psychotherapist and patient—Fiction.   2. Suicidal behavior—
Fiction.   3. Married people—Fiction.   4. New England—Fiction.
I. Title.

PS3561.L334 M36   2001
813'.54—dc21

                                                        2001033553

First Edition: October 2001

PRINTED IN THE UNITED STATES OF AMERICA

0   9   8   7   6   5   4   3   2   1

THIS BOOK IS FOR ELLEN.

MAN AND WIFE

PART

ONE

ONE

MAYBE IF I HAD LOVED HER less there would have been no murder. Maybe if there had just been less devotion in the love. Plenty of men have happy marriages. Affection, partnership, earnest conversations, shared pursuits. If they begin with any blinding passion it fades in time. Their minds get sharp again. Maybe if I hadn't adored her so I would've seen more clearly. Maybe if I had seen more clearly no one would have died.

———

SO I GUESS THIS IS a confession of sorts. Which is something I know a little bit about. I've spent most of my adult life listening to confessions and I can tell you something—I mean you whom I imagine reading this—I can warn you right at the start. A man who confesses may swagger for awhile. He may come at the truth at an angle, try to dress it up to preserve his dignity. But in the end he'll give you the worst of himself. He has no choice. Guilt and solitude are driving him on. They've got him in a gonad-lock, tighter and tighter, until finally he's beyond even the civilizing influence of hypocrisy—it's no good to him, like money to a dying man. You hang around long enough and he'll tell you everything, done or dreamed. Never mind the big vices, the romantic ones, the ones he's secretly proud of. He'll saddle you with the whole scurvy little human enterprise, take you right up the asshole of his drooling fantasies, hit you with every sniveling, poisonous dream of envy and malice in his weak and unfaithful heart. Which, if nothing else, believe me, can make him an awkward sort of narrator to listen to. Because like any narrator, he wants your sympathy. He wants you to identify with him. He wants you to acknowledge that he's not all that different from you.

SO THAT'S ONE THING. And then there's me personally—because I'm no one's idea of a hero anyway. Physically, to begin with, I'm on the short side, narrow, soft. With a bland face under thinning darkish hair. My eyes are dull brown, baggy even at the best of times. They make me look older

than my forty-two years, make me look more serious too—
and a hell of a lot wiser—than I am. I'm not particularly
strong. I've never been fast or agile. I've never been any
good with women at all. My virtues, if I can call them that,
are of the sort generally considered suspect in the red-
blooded American male. That is, I'm intelligent and well-
educated. I try to be honest. Try to be compassionate with
the suffering people who come to me. Having been given
so much in life—money, privilege, position—I try to be
generous with the less fortunate. What else? I'm faithful to
my wife. I love my children. I'm a decent enough guy, in
other words, but no one's idea of a hero.

All the same, if you want to know what happened I'm
the narrator you're stuck with. It's my sin so it's my confession, my story to tell. If it's any consolation I probably
know more about the whole business than anyone. Because
whatever else I am, I am the man who loved Marie. And
I'm the psychiatrist who treated Peter Blue.

PETER BLUE. NINETEEN YEARS OLD. Gentle, dreamy,
hard-working, religious. And one Saturday night toward the
end of August, he beat up his girlfriend then drove out Oak
Ridge Road and set fire to the Trinity Episcopal Church.

The girlfriend, Jenny Wilbur, called the police right
after Peter left her house. Her voice, on the 911 tape starts
out loud, frantic. Sloppy with tears:

"He'll kill himself! Oh God! We had a fight! He's going to get a gun!"

"Did he threaten you? Did he hit you?" asks Sharon

Calley, the civilian dispatcher. "Are you hurt—did he hurt you in any way?"

Instantly, Jenny's voice becomes small and sorrowful. "He didn't mean to," she says. "You have to help him. Please. He says he's going to get a gun."

By then, the alarm had sounded at the Recycling Center—the garbage dump—on Fair Street where Peter sometimes worked. The patrolman responding was met at the dump's office by Jason Roberts who ran the place.

Roberts reported that his office had been broken into and his safebox broken open. Sure enough, the only thing missing was his old Smith & Wesson Model 10 revolver.

BUT IT WAS HIGHBURY'S POLICE chief, Orrin Hunnicut, who stumbled on Peter himself. I'll pause here to describe Hunnicut. He's worth describing both for his own sake and because he has a major role in the story.

The man was gargantuan, first of all. Had to be six foot four or five at least. He'd played football in college and at sixty-three he still had the build for it. Huge shoulders, massive arms, an aggressive barrel of a chest, an even more aggressive dome of a belly. No neck. His head just sat on top of his giant frame, just plunked there, blocky and solid. The face was somehow fleshy and rock-hard at once. Pallid, pinkish skin on his jowls. Thin lips, small flinty eyes. He wore his hair cut to the nub and upstanding like an angry white fire coming up from his brain.

He was a hard case, is what I mean to say. And recently he'd gotten even harder still. His wife of thirty-five years had died that winter. A mild, fretful little creature, she just wasted away. My own wife, as part of her church work, had helped nurse her through the end. And Hunnicut, she said, loved the woman sincerely in his own ham-handed fashion. Since her death, anyway, his face had become even more rock-like than before. And the flinty eyes seemed to have grown even smaller until they were now no more than black points flashing from deep within the pinkish stone.

AND SINCE HIS WIFE'S DEATH—and despite the fact there's not much crime in Highbury—Chief Hunnicut had taken to spending almost all his time at the police department. Which is why he was driving home so late that Saturday, around midnight as it happened. He was tooling his official Blazer slowly over the leafy stretch of Oak Ridge that led to his neighborhood. It was a warm, humid night. A solid cover of clouds across the sky. No stars but a bright patch of black and silver in the southwest where the full moon was hanging hidden. The steeple of Trinity stood against that patch, its belfry and clapboards visible in the outglow. The rest of the church was sunk into the darkness of the surrounding trees so it was easy for Hunnicut to spot the strange rose-colored gleam wavering at the eastern windows.

With a squeal of tires, he brought the Blazer to the curb. One meaty hand hoisted the radio mike to his lips even as he stepped out of the four-by-four.

"This is Chief Hunnicut, get the fire department out to Oak Ridge. We got the goddamned church on fire out here."

As to what happened next, I got some of it from the

police report, some from Hunnicut himself and some from a hilarious but possibly apocryphal account given to me by the state attorney. The way I heard it was this:

Hunnicut strode thunderously up the front walk to the building. He tried the double doors. No good; they were locked. So—get ready, here comes the exciting part—he hauled off and rammed into them with one prodigious shoulder. A single blow. The doors went flying in. Hunnicut went flying in after them.

Well, I'll tell you, the sight that greeted him would've made a lesser man quail. A pair of banners draped down two of the front columns were burning so that there were towering pillars of flame framing the central aisle. Between them, the immense gold cross on the wall above the altar caught the firelight and blazed scarlet. Thick smoke churned out beneath it, spreading over the pews, rising into the rafters.

For a moment, our chief stood still, hulking just within the threshold, frowning the fire back. Then, from underneath the fiery cross, from within the depths of the smoke, etched now in the heaving darkness, now by the crackling blaze, there emerged the figure of a man. Tall, lean, erect, Peter Blue stepped through the flaming portal. Hunnicut could see the wild expression on his face. He could see the pistol he was clutching in his hand.

"Get away from here!" Peter shouted. He lifted the gun. "Just get the hell away!"

That did it. Hunnicut stomped up the aisle to him. Muscled through the fire. Snatched the revolver out of Peter's grip. Slapped the boy twice—*whack, whack*—forehand, backhand, across the mouth.

"You pull a piece on me, you little prick?" he shouted as the flames whiplashed around them. "I'll wipe your god-damned ass with it!" He seized Peter by the hair at the back of his head, hoisted him to his tiptoes. Marched him back up the aisle toward the door. "You're under arrest for arson and all kinds of shit, you dumb fuck! The time you get out of jail, everyone you know'll be fucking dead!"

And he hurled Peter pinwheeling from the burning church out into the open air.

HUNNICUT WAS AS GOOD AS his word. The police charged Peter with arson, assault, burglary, larceny, theft of a firearm, threatening a police officer and reckless endan-germent. In theory, the kid was looking at more than fifty years in prison that Saturday night.

So the cops booked him. Then they locked him in one of the department holding cells. The plan was to take him to Gloucester Superior Court on Monday for a formal ar-raignment. Bail would've been set, court dates and so on. Only it didn't work out that way.

Peter had declined to make a phone call but Father Michael Fairfax, the rector of Trinity, had been told of his arrest. The moment he was sure the fire at his church was out, Fairfax hurried over to the department and demanded to see the prisoner. A Highbury officer escorted him into the cell block.

The two of them found Peter there wearing only his underpants and a T-shirt. The nineteen-year-old had taken his sweatpants off. He had climbed up on his cot and tied one leg of them onto the gratework over the high window.

Then he had knotted the other leg around his throat. Then he had stepped off the cot.

As the officer and the priest rushed shouting into his cell, Peter twisted in the air, first this way, then that way, strangling slowly.

T W O

THERE ARE TEN CHURCHES IN HIGHBURY. Two are Episcopalian. It's an accepted though unspoken fact that Trinity—the church Peter burned—serves the working and middle classes in the west of town while Incarnation, smack on the Town Common, is mostly for the wealthy and socially elite. That Sunday morning after Peter's arrest and attempted suicide, I was at Incarnation with my wife Marie. Now when I'd first met her nearly fifteen years before, Marie had not been religious in any formal sense of the word. Mostly she was just an orthodox Kook from the First Church of Kookiness. Any faddish, outlandish spiritual hoodoo then on the market—*bang*, she bought right into it. The healing power of pyramids, the wisdom of the lost city of Atlantis, aliens in Eden, druidic leylines in Stonehenge—I can't remember half the stuff she believed in. It was part of her inappropriate charm at the time. But almost the instant we got engaged, she ditched it all. Just like that. She went straight from looney-land to a complete, untroubled, and I would even say joyful faith in the rituals and tenets of the high Anglican church. That was Marie, that was her devotion. That was what love and marriage meant to her. My God became her God—which was pretty funny since my God hadn't even been *my* God since I was a little kid.

But never mind. Marie started going to church and I generally tagged along. It made her happy to have me there for one thing. For another thing, I kind of liked it—it warmed my cockles with childhood memories. Plus, to be totally honest, it did no harm to my position in the town or the reputation of my clinic for me to be seen as a regular churchgoer. But none of those was the main reason. The main reason—the real reason—I usually went to church with my wife was that I found it incredibly sexy to watch her pray.

She was thirty-six now, no longer the sylph of twenty I'd taken such a tumble for. But oh man, she was a ray of sunlight in that place. That old stone imitation-English church I knew as well as I knew anywhere. Packed to the walls every Sunday I could remember with the very crustiest of Connecticut's upper crust. One solid self-contented mass of ladies' hats and gentlemen's high-priced haircuts—

and then simple, true-hearted Marie. She just shone. When she was singing especially. Standing so I could see the shape of her in her flowery summer dress. Holding her hymn book open in her slender fingers. She lifted her eyes—and she had blue eyes, light blue eyes—and they were still so kind, so faithful. And her straw-colored hair was even paler now that there were strands of silver in it. And she had the sweetest smile-wrinkles at the corner of her mouth. And she sang in this high, thin voice, "Abide with me, fast falls the eventide: the darkness deepens; Lord, with me abide . . ." And I thought of the little gasping cry she sometimes gave when I was inside her, a little fading cry as if she were falling, falling away. And from the corner of my eyes I watched her thin lips shaping themselves around the words and I thought of the mornings she would bring me coffee and then, giggling, murmuring, kiss her way down my belly so that the coffee steamed untouched on the bedside table and grew cold. "When other helpers fail and comforts flee," she sang. "Help of the helpless, oh abide with me."

I was getting a little cramped in my jockeys by the time the hymn was over. When the congregation rumbled to their seats I used the moment to shift closer to her so I could sit with my thigh pressed against hers, so I could steal an occasional whiff of her perfume and her shampoo.

There was a pause of coughs and clearing throats. The Reverend Andrew Douglas climbed into the oaken pulpit. He smoothed out the pages of his sermon, preparing to begin.

Marie tilted her head toward me. I felt the touch of

her hair on my cheek. I caught a sidelong glimpse of her smile and her bright eyes glistening.

"I know just what you're thinking, Mr. Calvin Bradley," she whispered.

And when I moaned the old lady behind me raised her eyebrows so high they damn near knocked her hat off.

WE CAME OUT OF CHURCH squinting into the sudden sunlight. The humidity of the night before had been washed away in a series of thundershowers just before dawn. The day was bright and dry and there was even the faint fresh chill of autumn in it. Holding Marie's hand, I paused at the top of the church steps to look around. The sky was very blue. The grass on the Town Common was very green and the maples were still very lush and heavy. The five churches that surrounded the Common gleamed white through the leafy branches. This was the heart of Highbury, downright Arcadian.

And there, at the center of the scene, was Father Fairfax. Dressed in his clerical black, ominous as an undertaker. Looking straight at me, beckoning.

"I'll go collect the kids," said Marie. She headed off for the basement Sunday School. And I went down the stairs to join the rector of Trinity.

"Let's take a walk, Cal," he said. We started along the sidewalk toward the center of town.

I'd already heard about the fire. Father Douglas had told the congregation. Said a kid had been arrested, the church's part-time gardener and handyman. He assured us it wasn't a hate crime, not a religious attack. Just a troubled boy from a broken home. Banners and pew cushions took most of the damage from the smoke and flames, he said. It didn't sound all that serious.

But as we walked together I could see Fairfax was upset. Which surprised me because normally he was a pretty solid character. A trim, fit, compact figure in his fifties. Silver hair, jutting chin. The Muscular Christian type. Always starting up committees, heading up charity drives, that kind of thing. An expert politician with a knack for making contacts and using them well. A genuine power in the town.

Today though, as I say, he looked rattled. Unshaven, his eyes rheumy, his features lax with sleeplessness.

"It's all been blown way out of proportion," he said. We strolled slowly shoulder to shoulder past fine old white clapboard homes. "Because of Chief Hunnicut, that's why. He's just furious because Peter—the boy, Peter Blue—he pulled a gun on him."

"Yeah, well, that was a bad idea," I said. "A nuclear device might slow Hunnicut down but a gun's just gonna piss him off."

"Oh . . . Hunnicut!" Fairfax's lips worked fretfully. "Ever since his wife died he's just—an angry man, that's all. He's practically breathing fire. 'Any punk who burns down a church in my town, pulls a gun on a law officer . . .' on and on. He makes it sound as if civilization as we know it will come to an end unless this one—poor, troubled nineteen-year-old goes to prison."

"Well, the fall of civilization would certainly put a crimp in my afternoon . . ."

Fairfax didn't laugh. "He can't go to prison, Cal," he

said. He stopped. Touched my shoulder as I stopped too. He looked deeply at me with those exhausted eyes. "He can't go to prison. He'll kill himself. He will. He damn near did it last night. It was only luck that we got there in time to save him. He's in the hospital now but he swears if they put him back in jail he'll be dead within the week. And I believe him."

I lifted my shoulders. "Michael, he set fire to a church, pulled a gun. . . . How can you keep him out of jail?"

"I can't," said Father Fairfax. "You can."

It was awfully pleasant on State Street just then. The sky so clear, the birds all singing. Churchgoers strolling home and the occasional driver waving to us as his car eased past. We'd come nearer the business district now, were standing in front of the old house where Paul Cummings had his used bookstore, one of my favorite places. I can't say I remember any sense of foreboding, not even a twinge. I was just a little taken aback, that's all.

"Me?" I said. "What can I do?"

But Fairfax, in his usual fashion, had it all worked out. David Robertson, an excellent trial lawyer, was one of his parishioners. He'd agreed to serve as Peter's public defender. The state attorney—the prosecutor—was Hank O'Connor and he played golf with Fairfax every other Saturday. And he'd agreed to recommend that the court withhold judgement if Peter went into some kind of treatment. Then finally the circuit judge this year was Robert Tannenbaum, who not only served on several of Fairfax's committees but was also an old pal of my father's. They still played e-mail chess sometimes.

"The only problem is," Fairfax said, "Hunnicut's such

a popular man with the law and order crowd. He always
has been. Lots of friends, lots of contacts. And he's tough.
When he's on the warpath like this, he can just be tough
as nails. He'll play up the church-burning thing, make it
sound like a hate crime in the press. Make it sound as if
Peter really would've shot him."

"Well . . ."

"Without some support, it's going to be impossible for
Peter to get a break. I can't ask Hank O'Connor to go easy
on a cop-killing church-burning psychopath. Hank wants to
run for Congress in a couple of years . . ."

His voice trailed off and I could see the political chess
game working itself out behind his tired eyes. "Yeah?" I said.

He blinked, straightened. "You," he said. "Cal, you're
one of the most respected men in town."

"*Pshaw,*" I said. "Keep talking."

"It's true. People respected your father. Everyone's
crazy about Marie. Everyone knows you're straight as an
arrow."

"All right, all right. I'm buttered up. So what?"

"If *you* talked to Peter. Interviewed him, assessed him,
whatever. If it was you who recommended that Peter receive
treatment instead of jail time. Maybe offered to take him in at
the Manor for a while. O'Connor could use that. Even Hunnicut might back off if the recommendation came from you."

"Woof! I don't know. I mean, I'm flattered but . . ."
But now I was figuring out the angles too. The Manor—
my clinic—depended on fundraising. I wasn't sure I wanted
to risk Hunnicut stirring up ill will against me either. And
all for a boy who, let's face it, sounded like he'd earned a
little time behind bars.

Fairfax seemed to know what I was thinking. "Cal," he said, leaning close, so close I could feel the heat of his breath, "you know me. I wouldn't just ask this for anyone. This boy, this Peter Blue—there's something extraordinary about him."

"Extraordinary? What do you mean?"

"I ... I don't know how to describe it. It's just—like an aura he gives off. A *spiritual* aura. Really. Anne and I have both felt it. It's—not like anything I've ever experienced before. I mean, sometimes, when he was doing odd jobs around the place, working out in the yard ... I'd find myself just going out to him, you know? Just to talk to him. Just to be around him ..." He broke off with an embarrassed laugh. Looked away. "I shouldn't be saying this to a psychiatrist. God knows what you'll think."

What I thought was ... well, I thought I didn't have much choice. If the kid was such a great guy, if he was just mixed up, just made a mistake—and if he was a suicide risk to boot, if his life was in danger, well, what else could I do? To hell with Hunnicut.

"Sure, Michael," I said. "I mean, of course, I'd be happy to talk to him."

The way his face relaxed, the way he pumped my hand—this one mattered to him all right. "That's great," he said. "That's just great."

"I mean, I can't promise anything ..."

"No, no. That's all I ask. Just talk to him, make your assessment, let the chips fall where they may. That's great. Thank you. Thank you."

"Well ... I figure you must really care about this

kid. You seem to've called on every contact you have except God."

"Oh, believe me," said the priest, still pumping away, "believe me, God was the first call I made."

NOW OF COURSE WHEN I said "God," I meant that ironically. What with all the churches and priests involved, not to mention Peter Blue himself, there's a lot of talk about God in this story so I want that understood from the start. When I was a child, a little child, I was quite a believer. My father was a priest, the rector of Incarnation then, so of course I was. But by the age of twelve—by the time I understood him and my mother both—I was a dedicated scientist complete with microscope, chemistry set and sweeping philosophy.

"Everything that happens has a physical cause," I announced to my sister Mina once around that time. She was seven years my senior, already in college, and the height of sophistication, the font of earthly wisdom to me. She was home for some holiday or other, lying on the sofa browsing through the *Book of Common Prayer*. That's what got me started. "Everything's just a chain of matter," I declared. "That's all."

"Mm—Materialism," she murmured into the book's pages. "It's a great idea—but what's it made of?"

I ignored this. Mina was always making mysterious statements like that and I was busy working out my attitude. "There's no action at a distance, that's what I'm saying. No miracles or—or God or anything."

Mina lay the book on her chest, looked over at me affectionately. "Everything has a reasonable explanation, baby, if that's what you mean," she said. "Everything has a reasonable explanation—and that's the one some people choose to believe."

Well, what I'm saying here is: the reasonable explanation is the one I've chosen to believe all my life. I'm still a scientist, after all—of a sort, at least. I want this clear because I want you to know that that's the way I approached the case of Peter Blue—as a scientist. And I held to that approach to the end in spite of the shivery sense of sheer *weirdness* that frequently went up me during my dealings with the boy; in spite of that taint of coincidence and the unexplainable that seemed to seep into the texture of everything—not only during the nightmare that followed but from the first moment I met him, late that Monday afternoon.

T H R E E

HE WAS STANDING DEJECTED IN THE center of the room

when I came in. He was standing motionless. Shoulders

slumped, head bowed. As if he hadn't been rescued in his

jail cell at all. As if he were, in fact, a hanged man.

The moment I stepped across the threshold, he straightened,

raised his eyes to me. Spoke, it seemed, directly into my

thoughts.

"Welcome to my suicide," he said. "Join the crowd." And

he smiled brilliantly.

He was a striking person to look at. Tall, lanky but with a

fluid grace of movement. A sensitive face of fine features, almost feminine under the long black hair, almost beautiful really when he unleashed that dazzling smile. But there was a fierce, challenging, masculine wit in his gray eyes. Something knowing, something tragic and hilarious at once. *Welcome to my suicide.* There was something about him that felt unnervingly familiar to me. I couldn't place it at the time.

I stepped forward, offered my hand. "I'm Dr. Bradley."

He smiled again, the same bright smile. Shook my hand, fluttered his other hand carelessly in the air—a dismissive gesture, as much as to say, *How ridiculous this all is, don't you think?*

"And I . . ." he announced with a comic flourish, "I am Peter Blue."

WE WERE IN ONE OF the consulting rooms in the psych secure unit at Gloucester State Hospital. Very depressing place. They'd actually hired a consultant psychologist to come up with the decor and she seemed to have felt she could use it to somehow bludgeon the patients into a state of serenity. There were these lemon yellow walls which were supposed to impose calm. These horrible paintings—scenic woodland pastels—which I guess were supposed to make you forget you were locked in the nuthouse instead of gamboling free as a fawn. Then there was the enormous mock-wood desk to convey authority. Powerful high-backed doctor chair, ridiculously low-slung patient chair. And all of it washed into a deathly pallor by the unbearable fluorescent lights in the ceiling. There was a window too but it had a grate over it—and anyway it let onto a narrow hospital courtyard. There was no direct sunlight. The place was just grim.

I rolled the chair out from behind the desk. That was the most I could do. I set it so I could face Peter directly while keeping my notepad on the desktop by my right hand. He, meanwhile, sank his long body into the armchair before me. Crossed his legs protectively. As I arranged my papers, I noted how his hand wafted to the collar of his sweatshirt, an absentminded attempt to hide the fading contusion on his throat. He seemed to will the hand back down to the chair arm. After that, gazing blankly into the corner, he appeared to drift off into his own thoughts.

I settled back, gave a preliminary cough. "Do you understand why I'm here?" I asked him.

The dreamy way he glanced up, he seemed surprised to see I was there at all. "My lawyer sent you, didn't he? You're the one who's supposed to find out if I'm—treatable." His suicide attempt hadn't left him hoarse at all. His voice was mellifluous, low and mild. "Y'know, it's always been one of the great ambitions of my life to become treatable," he went on quietly. "When I was a boy, I used to say to myself, 'One day I want to grow up to be treatable.' "

"Well, then this may be that lucky day."

I surprised him with the joke—and he surprised me with his laughter. It was a sudden, wonderful sound. Deep and rich and almost childlike in its spontaneity. "The lucky day. That's very good. The lucky day."

"Okay, so that's why I'm here," I said. "What's a nice guy like you doing in a dump like this?"

"Ah well...I beat up my girlfriend and stole a gun

and set fire to a church. Tried to hang myself in prison. Where else would I be?"

"Want to tell me how it happened?"

There was a pause—a deciding moment: *Did* he want to tell me? A state shrink had already had a crack at him that morning so he was bound to be feeling wary. The shrink—Dr. Seymour Rankel—had diagnosed a Major Depressive Episode on axis one—an easy enough call to make on a guy with a noose around his neck. But on axis two he'd suggested Peter had Antisocial Personality Disorder. That's not a good thing. We generally reserve that category for real die-hard bad guys. It means violence, crime, probably drug use. In Rankel's preliminary report the words *No Remorse* were underlined three times.

Well, I knew Rankel. A lazy, small-spirited drone. His diagnosis was crap. I was certain of that already.

The pause went on. Peter Blue examined me with his pale eyes, with their expression of doomed hilarity—as if he were looking not only at me but at the whole sad, silly panorama of life. That expression really did remind me of something—of someone. It bothered me.

Now he uncrossed his legs. Shifted in his chair to present himself to me more directly. He had made his decision.

"Hurting Jenny was unforgiveable," he said softly. He raised his chin with a touch of defiant pride. "I know you won't believe me but it was an accident. She's going away to college next month, to that place in New York, in Ithaca—Cornell. And that breaks my heart because I love her so much, you know. I know she's going to meet people there and they'll be educated and sophisticated. And she won't want to go out with a man who does odd jobs for a living. Who works at the garbage dump."

I listened, impassive; continued to observe him closely. I can't say he struck me as "very spiritual" right off the bat. But for someone who "did odd jobs for a living," he was certainly intelligent and articulate.

He went on. "Jenny and I had one of those—*discussions*, you know, that turns into an argument before you realize it. I didn't want her to go. Jenny took my arm to sympathize with me. And of course I didn't want that either. So I—raised my arm to get her off." He showed me how he'd raised his arm—sharply. "My hand, the back of my hand, banged into her face and she fell over and her shoulder hit the edge of the table." He shuddered, frowned. "Anyway, I know you won't believe me but you can ask her: there's never been anything like that with us before. It was unforgiveable."

"Okay," I said. "So then what? Is that when you went to the dump and stole your employer's gun?"

"Yes. I was thinking about shooting myself." He said this with a sigh, with studied indifference. "I hadn't actually decided yet but I was thinking about it."

"Because Jenny was going to college."

"Because she was leaving me—all right, to go to college, yes. I know I'm supposed to think what a wonderful thing that is for her, what a wonderful opportunity, and I guess I do. I guess. I mean, really, I think, when it comes to what a person really is, college is pretty much bullshit. In fact, while we're on the subject, I think psychiatry is pretty much bullshit too." He laughed pleasantly. "By the way."

I answered with a brief smile. "What about religion? Is that bullshit?"

"Why do you ask me that? Oh, of course, I see: because I set fire to the church. No. No, it had nothing to do with that. I don't think religion is bullshit. I just think it's kind of sad, that's all. I mean, I can stand in the woods anytime I want and God will flow into my veins all through me and He and I are totally connected." He told me this so naturally it was a second or two before I realized what he'd said. He told me as another man might tell me he could draw well or sight-read music. He could stand in the woods and feel God flow into his veins. It was just something he could do. I had no time to consider it then; he was already going on. "But in church . . . I mean, I've *gone* to church. From time to time. I mean, church has got to be, like, the one place on earth where I *can't* feel God's presence at all. I mean, you pray and you sing and you sit and you kneel and you stand. And I mean you're thinking: Gimme something here. Anything! *Pleeeeze!*" That laugh again, full of pleasure. "It's almost spooky it's so empty. It's like being in a coffin. Except . . ." He raised a finger, pressed it to his lips. "Except when Annie sings sometimes."

"Annie. You mean Anne Fairfax, the rector's wife."

"Yeah. Yeah." He smiled broadly, fondly at her name. His affection appeared to be like his laughter, spontaneous, childlike. "Poor Michael, you know, Father Fairfax, he's up there on the altar, working away. He's chanting the magic words and arranging the magic chalice and drinking the magic wine. Just hoping for some little pat on the head from Jesus. Nothing. Right? Nothing. Then his—frumpy little wife gets up there, right? Looks like she's nobody. Just taking time out from baking some horrible tuna casserole for the church bazaar. Then she gets up to sing her solo in the choir. And, suddenly, it's like—*barrrannggg!*—*heeere's God! Live and in person! Chariots, angels, trumpets* . . . It's like a parade!" I had to smile too now to hear him laugh the way he did, with such delight, his eyes so bright, his hands—large, powerful workman's hands—describing God's arrival in the air. "She's like this radio tuned to the God channel. When she sings, it just plays right through her." Which made him laugh again. And then slowly, his laughter trailed away. He shook his head at the absurdity of it. "I set fire to the music really, not the church."

I shifted in my chair. "All right. What does that mean?"

"Well—I was sitting there, you know. That night. With the gun. Trying to figure out whether to kill myself. I mean, all right, I don't suppose I would've really, but I went to the church to think about it because . . . well, I guess it was too dark to go into the woods and I knew I could be alone in there. I was sitting in the choir. Smoking a cigarette. Sort of playing with the lighter—*flick, flick*, you know. And I guess I just started thinking about sweet Annie— sweet nobody little wife little Anne, how beautiful it was when she sang the hymns. And I sort of took out one of the hymnals from that—little pocket, you know, in front of the pew. And I started to read the songs—the lyrics to the hymns she sometimes sang. And it was, like . . . oh no! Oh no! They were *awful!* You know? I mean, you'd hear Annie sing them and you'd think, oh, this hymn, it's so wonderful and spiritual and alive and full of God. And then there were these words on the page. And they were—*pathetic!* They were *beggar words! Abide with me! I'm so helpless! Abide with me, pleeeeeze!* I mean: vomit."

Right there, I think, that was the first time I felt it. A little shiver, a little synchronistic thrill of the mysterious. You know, just the coincidence, the fact that it was the same hymn Marie had been singing.

"So I don't know," Peter Blue continued. "I don't know what I was doing, thinking. I was just upset, I guess. I started tearing these—horrible, horrible songs out of the book, you know. And then . . . then I'd light each page with the lighter and just—toss it away. Just toss it away because it was so terrible." He shrugged. "What can I tell you? It was stupid. The—whatchamacallit—the drapery caught before I even knew what was happening. Then before I could do anything that . . . the policeman came in."

"Chief Hunnicut."

"Mm."

"And what happened then?"

He sniffed, shrugged. "You know what happened. I'm sure you read the report. He arrested me."

"He also hit you a couple of times, didn't he."

"Yes."

"Slapped you in the face."

"Mm."

"That must've pissed you off."

He stretched his arms out, gave a little yawn. The picture of weary unconcern. "Not really. I'm not really the sort of person who gets angry very much. I mean it about

God. When you actually feel God, you know . . . When you actually feel how we're connected in His love—I don't know—after that, you don't have room for being angry or hating people. It's just a waste of time."

Oh boy, I thought. *Oh brother.* "Okay," I said. "So he hit you and it was swell."

"Well, I'm not saying I *liked* it. I mean, I feel sorry for the guy. He must be carrying an awful lot of rage around inside him to act that way."

"Well, you did pull a gun on him, Peter. Policemen don't like that. It's kind of a sore point with them."

He tried another laugh but this one didn't quite come off. Behind the lofty wit in his eyes I caught a glimpse of the fear, the turbulence. It came back to me—as if I had forgotten—that he was only nineteen. Just a boy, really. Just a boy, and miserable. "Not like it helped me much, did it? Having a gun."

"No," I said. "No, it didn't. You had a gun and the chief slapped you anyway."

"Like I was . . ."

"What?"

"Nothing."

"Go on, Peter. He slapped you like you were what?"

"Ach. No. Nothing."

"A woman. That's what you were going to say, isn't it? He slapped you like you were a woman."

"I should've . . ." His mouth twitched into a frown. "I had the damned gun."

"That's right. You had the gun and the bastard bitch-slapped you. How did that make you feel?"

"Great!" snapped Peter Blue. "It was a regular summer pick-me-up!"

He turned in the chair, turned his face away. I sat still, waited. The moment stretched out, stretched out. Then, with a heaved breath, he came back around. A complete transformation. The fear, the turbulence—gone. The high-minded tragic irony back in its place again. And the smile too; he gave another fond smile, only the affection in it was for me this time.

"So I guess maybe I was a little angry about that," he said.

"I guess maybe you were."

"You're pretty good."

"Thank you."

" 'Bitch-slapped.' That was excellent. Where'd you get that?"

"I work with kids a lot. You pick this stuff up."

He laughed his delighted laugh. "All right. Well, anyway, that's the story. I'm sorry I set fire to Michael's magic God-house. I really am. He and Anne have been very nice to me. I'm sorry."

"Why did you try to hang yourself, Peter?"

Still smiling, smiling sadly, he shook his head, gestured dismissively. Answered mild and calm. "I'm not going to let them lock me up. When I'm locked up like that—I can't feel God anymore. I can't feel God at all and that's just worse than death to me. If they send me back to jail . . . well, I won't stay. I'll die instead."

"What about here? You're locked up here."

He thought about it. "No. It's all right here. I mean,

I can't get out, I can't get into the woods the way I like
to . . . But here, God comes in sometimes. Last night, I mean,
I had this beautiful dream. It took me right out of here,
out into the woods. I dreamed I was on this hilltop out
there. I was standing up on this hilltop in the woods, on
this flat stone, this—ancient altar of some kind. And I could
hear this—this whispering. All around me. Very soft, very
soft but, like, drowning out everything else, so there was
nothing else. Just this whispering, whispering, whispering
everywhere. And I turned—I guess I wanted to see what it
was—I turned and right in front of me, there was a wooden
cross. And there was this . . . this brilliant, blinding white
light behind the cross. The whispering was coming out of
the light so I sort of—stepped up to the cross and sort of—
peered, you know, peered into the light. And slowly, slowly,
I saw this thing taking shape. It was this owl! This—incredible—beautiful white owl. The most beautiful . . . It
was looking right at me. And its wings spread, you know,
opened . . . beautiful . . ."

And now he sat very still. His lips slightly parted, one
hand lifted up. His gaze was a million miles away and his
features were soft with the delight of longing. The glare
from the fluorescents played dingy on the yellow walls, dead
and dingy on their despairing serenity. But I don't believe
he saw that. He saw the forest around him. The forest and
the wooden cross and the beautiful white owl spreading its
wings. . . .

When he finally noticed I was there again he blinked
and straightened in his chair, refreshed.

And then he smiled—radiantly.

———

I WAS SURE OF ONE thing anyway: if they put the kid back in jail he'd die. He'd hang himself just as he said he would. There wasn't a doubt in my mind. Not to be too dramatic, but it's fair to say that at that point Peter Blue's life was pretty much riding on my report to the court.

So it was going to have to be a good one. Chief Hunnicut had heard about my involvement and he was well and truly furious. He was telling anyone who'd listen that our churches, our police officers, the very fabric of our society for the love of God were in danger because delinquents like Peter were being treated too leniently by the courts. He— or someone—leaked Rankel's "antisocial" diagnosis to the area's biggest newspaper, the *Dispatch*, and they then dutifully issued a story making Peter sound like a genuine menace to society. That was Tuesday. By Wednesday some of the town's religious leaders were starting to grumble. "If it'd been a black church that was burned," one of them told the paper, "you can bet we'd see justice done in a hurry." Caught between Father Fairfax and Chief Hunnicut, Hank O'Connor, the state attorney, was said to be fretting about his congressional aspirations.

On Thursday, I handed in my report.

Peter Blue is intelligent, sensitive and articulate. Despite the fact he did not complete high school, he reads extensively—primarily books on religion, philosophy and natural science—and is relatively well educated. Though he claims to be satisfied earning his living through manual labor, it seems clear his life is restricted more by emotional and practical considerations than by his own potential.

Peter's father abandoned his family when he was five years old, leaving Peter and his mother without warning and ceasing all communication. Peter continues to live with his mother. He describes her as sexually promiscuous and says she often becomes over-emotional and manipulative when under the influence of alcohol and prescription drugs. Though trained as a hair stylist, Mrs. Blue doesn't work enough to support herself and is dependent on Peter's income. Peter must therefore put in long hours at the recycling center and as a freelance gardener and handyman as well.

All of which was my way of saying: Hey, the kid's had a hard time here—cut him some slack.

The report went on:

Peter tends to form intense attachments to people and then reject them with equal intensity when he fears they've betrayed or abandoned him. This pattern is directly related to his feelings of rage at his father's abandonment and his mother's failure to adequately fulfill her parental role. Because it's difficult for Peter to face this powerful and painful anger, he tends to disassociate himself from its consequences, a reaction which might be mistaken for remorselessness. For instance, Peter deludes himself that striking his girlfriend Jennifer was an "accident," as opposed to an act of fury at her "leaving him" for college. Likewise he feels the church fire was almost an unimportant byproduct of his aesthetic displeasure at the lyrics of certain hymns. In truth it was a cry of anger and pain that Father Fairfax and his wife could not protect him from Jennifer's abandonment and had therefore failed in their role of idealized parents. In either case, there was absolutely no anti-religious or "hate" motive involved in the arson, and I deem it extremely unlikely to recur . . .

Which was to say, this was a personal crime not a political or religious one—everybody be cool.

I continued:

Peter's behavior fulfills at least five of the criteria for a diagnosis of Borderline Personality Disorder. While I confess this category is something of a catchall, it is eminently clear to me that the alternative diagnosis offered of Antisocial Personality Disorder is not indicated in any way whatsoever.

Translation: Rankel's an idiot.

And I concluded the report like this:

If he is returned to jail, Peter is almost certain to carry out his threats of suicide. Conversely, if put in treatment, he is likely to make enormous strides in a relatively short period. Peter is fully capable of forming an attachment to a caring therapist provided the therapist behaves with sufficient compassion and integrity to justify his trust. Given that circumstance, I am confident Peter can become an extremely worthwhile and productive person.

In other words, if you put him in jail you'll kill him. If you don't, I'll take the responsibility for fixing him up.

As icing on the cake I offered Peter my clinic's Cooper Bed for thirty days. This in itself was no small thing. The Manor was expensive—close to a thousand dollars a night then—and Peter was uninsured. Even with insurance he'd be unlikely to get reimbursed for more than ten or eleven days of inpatient care. But the so-called Cooper Bed was subsidized by a bequest of my maternal grandfather. It was assigned at my discretion, generally for short terms to handle needy emergency cases. To give it over for thirty days of nearly free treatment was unheard of. Plus I promised to work with our Utilization Review staff to find funding for Peter's outpatient care after that.

The report did the trick. Or maybe it was the fact that Chief Hunnicut grew up on the wrong side of town while my dad was playing e-mail chess with the judge. I can't say for sure. But in either case, Peter was released from the hospital without having to return to jail. He agreed to check into the Manor the second Friday in September—the first day our subsidized bed could be made available. Judge Tannenbaum said he would ask for another report on the matter in thirty days and make a final dispensation of the case at that time.

"You did a wonderful thing, Cal," said Father Fairfax when he phoned to congratulate me. "You put your reputation where your mouth is. The judge really appreciated that. The ball's in your court now. What you do in the next thirty days is going to spell the difference between life and death for that boy."

"Oh, well, that's a very relaxing notion, Michael, thanks a lot," I said.

And after I hung up, I laughed and thought: *Welcome to my suicide.*

F O U R

EVERYTHING THAT FOLLOWED GREW OUT OF a chain of
thought. It came to me on an evening in early September.

It was just coming up on the dinner hour. I was in the
armchair in the living room. Marie was in the kitchen with
Eva, our eleven-year-old daughter. I could hear the two of
them giggling over something, the pots and silverware
clanking as they prepared the meal. At my feet, Cal Jr.—
J. R.—our nine-year-old son was splayed prone on the rug
slaughtering monsters in a video game on the TV. Our

three-year-old Dorothy—Tot—was on my knee playing with my face while I tried to read the newspaper.

Our house is a sort of fusty old place on the outside. The usual white shingle, black shutter colonial favored by the area's old families. Three stories with gables up top and a screened-in breezeway below. Inside, though, Marie had an architect open up the rooms, make them more contemporary, warmer. The red tile of the kitchen floor flows right out into the polished oak of the dining area which opens in turn into the living room, a vast expanse of overstuffed furniture and colorful rugs. From where I was planted with my daughter and my *New York Times* I could—whenever Tot removed her fingers from my eye sockets—both follow J. R.'s progress against the alien invaders and catch glimpses of Marie and Eva when they passed by the kitchen door.

"Lettuce, lettuce, lettuce," I heard Marie say. "Why do you let me forget to buy these things?"

"Me?" said Eva, still in a laughing fit. "You have a pad right there on the refrigerator that says, 'Things to Buy.' "

"Oh," said Marie, laughing too. "And I suppose you think I should write things I want to buy on it."

Tot had now grabbed hold of my lower lip and was trying to see how far it would stretch. "I kent weed web u do dat," I said through tears of pain. Tot squealed in delight at the funny noise Daddy made.

"Mo-om! God!" Eva laughed harder. "That's not how you spell lettuce! I mean, even, like, Tot knows that!"

"Ah, put a sock in it," J. R. muttered to himself. He was a knightly lad and he loved his mother. He hated when Eva teased her about her lack of education.

"Gee, thanks smarty-pants," Marie said. "If I'd known I was going to have such brilliant children, I'd have had a dozen of you." I could see them at the door now. Marie placed a bread basket in Eva's hands and propelled her gently into the dining area.

"Well, we must get it from Dad," said Eva laughing over her shoulder. She was dark and pretty and a holy terror sometimes—just as my sister had been. "Lettuce! Gawd!"

"What makes you so smart, ya dimwit?" said J. R. a little louder.

"Stay out of it, buddy," I told him as Tot seized my nose. "Leave your sister alone and just blow the nice zombie's head off. Ouch!"

"Eva's about the least dimwitted person I know," said Marie. She was carrying a pitcher of lemonade to the table. Eva, setting down the bread there, preened at the compliment. Marie paused to look at the TV. "Wow, J. R. Look how good you are at killing those spacemen. I'm surprised there are any left."

J. R. rolled his eyes but he was pleased. Which of course set Eva off.

"I don't see why all those games have to be about *killing*," she said as she flounced back to the kitchen.

"What do you want them to be about?" said J. R. "Ballet?"

I cracked up. "I like that. That's good. *Bloodbath at Swan Lake*."

Marie lingered another moment, smiling over at me and Tot now. "Is she bothering you, sweetheart? Do you want me to take her so you can read?"

"What, this horrible creature?" I said—and I tickled

Tot into a fit of laughter. "I want you to take her and put her in the soup!"

Laughing myself, I glanced up for a second. Marie was still watching us. Watching us with such an expression of— I don't know what to call it—*warmth* on her face that the same emotion welled up in me suddenly and I felt it leap between us like an electric arc.

I adored her. *And God*—the words went through my mind—*she wasn't even supposed to be my wife.*

That was how the chain of thought began.

SHE WASN'T SUPPOSED TO BE my wife. When I was twenty-eight, I was more or less engaged to a woman named Sarah Cabot. Her family knew my family and they arranged for us to meet at a party and so forth. She was the sort of girl I'd always figured I'd end up with. Pretty in a sort of angular way. Self-assured, well-educated, accomplished. She worked at a public relations firm in Manhattan. I was in Manhattan too, in the first year of my psychiatric residency at Bellevue.

I was very unhappy. Not because of Sarah. She was all right. We went to good restaurants together and chatted about all the people we knew and made love with the playful abandon that was recommended by the magazines she read. Given my ineptitude with women, I was grateful to be making love at all. So that was fine.

No, it was the work that was getting to me. I don't know what I had expected. Somewhere in my mind, I guess, was the idea that my father's Religion had failed to help

my miserable mother so I would sally forth armed with
Science to help the miserable everywhere. That was what I
concluded later in my training analysis anyway. But whatever idealism I might have brought to the trade was pretty
well blown away the first time I participated in a session of
ECT—electroconvulsive therapy; shock therapy. Man, I
didn't even know they still did that stuff. But sure enough,
one fine day I found myself putting the juice to a patient
of mine named Edgar.

Edgar had been institutionalized after barricading himself in his apartment for three weeks to keep an imaginary
army of transvestites from spiriting him away. I was new
at the game and had no idea what to do with him. One
supervisor was telling me to stick to psychoanalysis, another
supervisor was insisting I experiment with medication. They
were rivals—the two supervisors—they hated each other.
At one point the medication guy actually shouted at me,
"I'll fix that Freudian son-of-a-bitch!" The life of the mind,
right? Meanwhile, of course, Edgar kept getting crazier and
crazier. So finally I was more or less ordered by the unit
chief to "zap him," to give him ECT.

Well, it was dreadful. There's just no other word. Up
on the tenth floor. A green cinderblock room. Painfully
bright fluorescents flickering, buzzing. All these wires and
tubes hanging from hooks in the ceiling. I felt like the
Grand Inquisitor. The nurse wheeled Edgar out from behind a curtain. Lying on a gurney. His mad eyes wide with
terror. "Is this it?" he kept whimpering pitiably. "Is it happening now?" I mean, Jesus Christ. The anesthesiologist
knocked him out, thank God, and paralyzed his muscles

with succinylcholine. That way the seizure induced by the current would only be visible in his right foot—which was left alone so we could test his reflexes. The resident who was teaching me the procedure kept singing to himself through the whole business. Just tuneless singing, "Dum de do, de do de dum." The nurse rubbed some gunk on Edgar's temples, strapped the metal contacts on him. Plugged in the electrodes. It was up to me to press the red button on the black box that would send one point five millivolts into Edgar's brain. "Dum diddle ee dum, diddle ee dee," my instructor murmured. Outside, through the dusty window, I could see snow falling. I pressed the button.

The life of the fucking mind, I remember thinking as Edgar's right foot clenched and leapt around making the gurney rattle. *The life of the fucking mind.*

It worked by the way. The treatments left Edgar much improved. Much happier. No more transvestites after him. He was released from the hospital a little while later.

I, on the other hand, became depressed as hell.

"Just get through this, sweetheart," Sarah Cabot said to me gamely, "and in a few years you'll have an office on Park Avenue and I'll be green with jealousy at all the rich beautiful women coming to you to solve their watchems, their neuroses."

I took a walk alone one afternoon. Slate gray skies. Sidewalks piled high with filthy snow. Streets swimming in slush. February. I hated the city.

I came upon a diner. The Glass House it was called. A rectangle of dull light in the gathering dusk. A couple of people hunched at the counter, a couple more at the tables.

I went in. Found a place in the corner. Ordered a cup of coffee and stared into it.

I guess I looked as depressed as I felt. The waitress came over and tried to cheer me up. She just plunked herself down across from me and opened her copy of the *Post* on the table. When she glanced up from the paper I was gaping at her.

"I'm going to read your horoscope, okay?" she said. "Something really good is gonna happen to you. Soon. I'm sure of it."

Normally I'd've been tongue-tied with a girl as pretty as that but I was so startled by the whole business I blurted out, "But—you don't even know when I was born."

"Oh—yeah." She hadn't thought of that. "Right." She scanned the paper. "Well, maybe we should find a good one first and then decide."

That was Marie.

SO I REMEMBERED THAT ALL in a flash. Sitting in my chair those many years later. I remembered the oddly muted sense of discovery I'd felt on seeing her: *Ah, there she is.* As if I had found some misplaced something—a book, my glasses, my heart and soul—before I even realized I was looking for it. And even then I couldn't acknowledge what had happened. She was too unlikely; a thoroughly inappropriate woman. Without knowing why, I simply found myself returning to the Glass House for coffee—more often— every day. Listening—sardonic but entranced—to her goofy chatter: the lives of celebrities, the predictions of seers, maudlin stories about rescued children in the news. And then I found myself murmuring back to her: my disillusionment about the usefulness of the intellect, my disappointment in my chosen profession, my sense that I had lost my way. Confiding everything so effortlessly into her simple, accepting, sweet, sweet, sweet blue eyes . . . I tell you I thought the coffee in the Glass House was the best goddamned coffee I had ever drunk. I recommended it to my colleagues. I'm not joking. I was that self-deceived. I thought there must be some extra ingredient in the stuff that made me feel so incredibly good after a cup or two. Because what else could it have been? The waitress? A girl from nowhere who hadn't even finished high school? Who rattled on about how the stars shaped our destinies and how angels were the secret authors of our dreams? No one could have been more surprised than I the night I walked her home and found myself suddenly naked against her naked skin; suddenly with her arms around me and her breasts against me, all of her white and warm; suddenly in the throes of something so alien to my youth I couldn't even put the name of passion to it until weeks had passed.

Weeks had passed . . . My chain of thought—my memories—continued. And suddenly I was thinking about my sister, about Mina. I had gone to visit her not long after Marie and I became lovers. It was a rainy evening in April.

Mina was thirty-five then. And close to despair though you'd never have known it to look at her. She cut such a grand, graceful figure. She looked like our mother, was slender and long like her. Wore her dark hair short and shaggy, flopping unkempt on the same noble brow our mother had.

It was a noble face altogether really. Chiseled and handsome, elegantly pale. The nose was turned up, the lips thin, the expression haughty, faintly amused. She seemed to watch even the tragedy of her own life unfold with an irony bordering on disdain. Her literary hopes had been disappointed, her love life was a disaster. And now alcoholism—which she also had in common with Mom—was closing around her like a fist. It was all combining to destroy her—and yet she seemed to observe every stage of the process from a great height, wryly.

As for me, by the time I came to her that day I was in absolute confusion. "Mina!" I practically wailed. "What'm I gonna do?"

"Tell all, baby," she said. She slapped two whiskey glasses on her kitchen table, splashed some cheap red wine into each.

She had only one pretension: poverty. She had the same trust funds I did and yet she'd lived in the East Village, in this rundown studio for years. The bedroom was so small we had to sit in the kitchen and the kitchen was just a narrow rectangle of peeling linoleum. We faced each other across a card table by the window, crammed between the refrigerator and the wall. Outside, the miserable little rain fell on the courtyard, a patch of dying grass. Inside, a bare bulb glared down on us.

"I met her in this diner," I said. "She's a waitress there."

"In a diner?" Mina laughed. "Oh my stars and garters! Mom and Dad will kill you in your sleep. She isn't black is she?"

"No—you think they'd mind that?"

"No—but it'd be fun watching them *not* mind."

"She's just a sweet, simple, loving person . . ."

"Oh well, then you're fucked. No one's really like that. She must be a gold-digger."

"She's not a gold-digger! She's just from Missouri."

"Oh."

"Or Oregon orginally. She just hasn't had time to become like everyone else in this crappy city yet."

"Okay. So she's sweet and simple." Mina leaned back in her metal folding chair, glass in one hand, bottle of Mateus in the other. She splashed herself another drink. "Exactly how simple are we talking about? And don't go all WASPy and coy on me. I mean, are we at moron level here?"

I laughed in spite of myself, shook my head. "No, Mina! Jesus. She's just—uneducated, that's all. She left home when she was fifteen. She had to fend for herself."

"Ah ha! Because of her twisted and unsavory upbringing."

"Yeah, her parents—they were apparently pretty bad. Violent. She won't tell me much about it. She never talks to them anymore . . ."

"And yet they've left their hidden, horrifying scars on her secret soul."

"God, you're awful. I'm trying to tell you something here: I've met this woman who's just . . . She's sweetness and light. Personified. I mean it." I leaned forward, elbows on the table, close to her in the constricted space, shaking my head. Mina was looking down. Smirking, observing her hands pour a third glass of wine. "She has this beautiful, gentle whisper of a voice..." I said.

"Alright, let's not get sappy. I've got my own problems."

"Well, you should see her. I mean, customers come into this place. You wouldn't believe it. Nasty. Crazy some of them. And I've never once seen her so much as lose her temper. Not with any of them, not one time. She's so patient with them; kind. I've never even seen her stop smiling."

"She sounds like a psychotic."

"Agh!" I ran my hands up through my hair. I was laughing—Mina always made me laugh—but I was young too and this was real anguish for me. "Don't do that! I hate that! That attitude, this city! This whole city! The life of the fucking mind. You get a goddamned superior intellect on every goddamned street corner! Everyone knows the right theories and the right political positions and the right movies to see—and no one has an ounce of real human kindness to share out among them. I swear to God, Mina, I don't care about smart people. Smart people stink. Smart people are the stupidest people on earth. She's worth a hundred of them, easy. Easy."

"Well!" said Mina affectionately. "My oh my. I'm chastened. You may consider me well and truly chastened. I'm the picture next to the word *chastened* in the dictionary."

"Oh shut up."

She swirled the wine in her glass a moment. "Okay. Okay, baby, let's start again. Let's stipulate you've latched on to some kind of idiot saint here. So where are we? Have you cheated on the Coathanger yet?"

The Coathanger—that was her nickname for Sarah Cabot. And I'd done worse than cheat. I hadn't even mentioned Sarah to Marie. The whole thing—the *fever* of the whole thing had caught me so completely off guard. There'd been nothing like it in my life before. I was terrified of losing it.

I didn't answer. I sighed, turned to stare out at the drizzle on the grass.

Mina snorted softly. "Don't take it so hard. Why should you be different than any other man?"

"Okay. I deserve that."

"Aw shit. No you don't." The alcohol was beginning to get to her. Her enunciation was growing expansive and lazy. I could smell the wine on her breath as we leaned toward each other again. "You're right, I'm just a bitter old bitch. You're a beautiful guy. A fine beautiful guy and we all know it."

"I love her, Mina. I mean, it's like a truck hit me. I mean, it's bliss—genuine bliss. Just smelling her skin, just watching her eyes. I mean, shit, Minerva, just listen to me! I'm an Episcopalian, for Christ's sake. I never talk like this. This is a—an actual, *bona fide* life crossroads here."

Mina paused, her drink at her lips. Set the glass down. Studied me a long time. She had these powerful, powerful green eyes. "Okay," she said more soberly. "Then that's what it is. So what do you want from me? I mean, you want me to state the objections."

"Sure. No, don't. Okay, go ahead," I said.

"Well, I mean, for one thing—God only knows what you two'll talk about after your prostate goes south."

"Thanks. I was hoping to sneak in a couple of years before that happened."

"She'll never feel comfortable around your peers," Mina went on. "The men'll patronize her, the women'll—ah, despise her. You'll have to get her someplace she can have friends, y'know, a world she can be in. That means the suburbs probably, maybe even the country. Hey, you won't be troubled by the life of the mind there, baby, that's for sure. Then—Jesus—then she's gonna start having kids on you. And I mean, it's not gonna be like the Coathanger would have—one little New York Dexter-type with sixteen nannies who's so grateful to have you say hello he'll behave like an angel. This is a full-time mom you've got here by the sound of it. So that means all kinds of little monsters running around, all souped-up and energized on love and kisses. And you know you—you love kids. You're not gonna want to go off every other day to some conference or symposium where you could be making a name for yourself. I mean, that'll be your life, Cal. Forget Park Avenue, forget King of the Shrink Hill. It'll be like . . . Well, it'll be like what you used to pretend our family was like before you found out it was all bullshit."

I nodded slowly. "Well, all right," I said. "Well, maybe that's the answer, maybe that's what I'm looking for. I mean, maybe I'm nuts, Minerva, but that just sounds great to me. As long as I get to do it with her."

"Fine. Then what's the problem?"

"Oh, I don't know." I sagged as a long breath came out of me. "It's just all so—blissful somehow."

"Yeah, that is tough."

"No, I mean . . . I keep hearing Dad in my mind. I keep hearing him say that—that bliss is shallow, y'know? I'm afraid he'll say that to commit your life to bliss is just—shallow."

Mina narrowed her eyes drunkenly, swaying a little in her chair now. "So the hell what? You're no Hercules but you've never been a *moral* coward. You've never had any problem standing up to Dad."

I frowned down into my drink, still my first drink, almost untouched. "I'm just afraid I'll agree with him," I said.

Mina's laugh—her full-blown laugh—was a high, fluty trill, very feminine and pretty. She reached out and patted my hand—a surprising gesture; we never did touch much. Then she swept up her glass, swigged the last of her drink. Started to pour herself another.

"Anyone who thinks that bliss is shallow doesn't understand the tragic nature of bliss," she said.

Another of her oracular pronouncements. I had no idea what it was supposed to mean. None. But I guess I understood that she had given me her blessing in some way. And I guess that was what I had come for. Aside from that, really, my decision had already been made.

TOT HAD CLIMBED DOWN OFF my lap now. She was sitting over on the sofa watching J. R. kill his monsters. I gazed at her absentmindedly out of my memories. Such a beautiful little girl—Marie's creature, gentle and cherubic—ringlets of yellow hair spilling over her full cheeks, her deep blue eyes. It made me sad somehow to see her there so fresh and new and to remember Mina.

My sister had killed herself seven years ago. Seven years ago this month, this September. She had drowned herself in the waters off New York Harbor. She was forty-two, just the age I was now.

Welcome to my suicide, I thought again.

And that's when it dawned on me, that's when I finally figured it out: the look in his eyes. That look in Peter Blue's eyes of humor and sadness combined, that lofty detachment. It was Mina's look. It was the very same. I knew he had reminded me of someone. He had reminded me of her.

"Supper's ready," Marie said.

I looked up to find her standing beside me, smiling sweetly.

SO MY CHAIN OF THOUGHT was interrupted there. We had supper. We put the kids to bed. Marie and I made love and the whole thing was forgotten.

Then, much later, long after midnight I'd say, I woke up to feel my wife slipping quietly out of bed. I began to stir.

"Ssh," she whispered. She kissed my forehead. "I love you. Go back to sleep."

I settled back on the pillow. Listened to her footfalls on the carpet as she left the room.

She was like that. She slept badly. She would get up in the small hours. Go to the bathroom. Check on the children. Sit on the bedroom window seat, looking out at the forest and the yard. If she still couldn't sleep, she'd go downstairs, drink a cup of herbal tea in the breezeway. It was just her pattern, she told me. Her biorhythm, as she called it.

But there was one time, a few years back, I'd found her crying. I'd come downstairs and seen the tears shining on her cheek in the breezeway moonlight. She'd been thinking about her life, she said. About her parents and how unhappy they'd been. And about how unhappy she herself had been—a runaway teenager working her way cross-country alone—until she'd met up with me. It was one of the rare times she ever spoke about that, in fact, about her life before our marriage. "Don't be all psychiatric with me," she'd usually say whenever I asked her about it. "I can't afford you."

So I learned to leave her alone. That was what she wanted. If she got up at night, I'd just wait for her, half asleep, alert in some part of my mind to her movements, sensing her whereabouts in the house until she came back to me.

But tonight for some reason I was wide awake the moment she was gone. She left the bedroom and I lay watchful and alone in the darkness. Almost at once, I found myself thinking about Mina again, about how Peter Blue reminded me of her. I would have to be especially careful about counter-transference in treating him, I told myself, especially as he was suicidal as she had been. It would be too easy for my unconscious to conflate him with my sister, to confuse my feelings about her with him so that I lost the objectivity I needed to help him.

While I was thinking about this, my wife returned from the children's rooms. She settled onto the window seat.

I watched her silhouette poised there against the treetops and the stars.

"You all right?" I asked her softly.

She glanced at me. I could just make out the light in her eyes. "I'm fine. Go back to sleep."

"What're you thinking about?"

"Oh . . . Just the children and all the things I have to do tomorrow."

"Eva was getting pretty fresh with you at dinner. Should I come down on her harder?"

"No. She's just practicing to be a teenager. She has to be ashamed of me for awhile. That's natural. All her friends' mothers are all sophisticated and went to college and everything."

I propped myself up on my elbow. I was afraid her feelings had been hurt. "She adores you, y'know," I said. "She lives in your love. We all live in your love. It's the air we breathe."

"Well, good. I'm glad. Now live in my love with your eyes closed and dream about my love and go to sleep," she told me.

"All right. I can tell when I'm not wanted."

I lay down again. Rolled onto my side, my back to her. But I didn't go to sleep, not right away. My thoughts returned to Peter Blue. I began thinking about his dream. The altar stone high in the whispering woods. The wooden cross and the light and the beautiful owl. I wondered what the owl symbolized to him. Classically, of course, the owl usually stands for wisdom. It was the bird of the Greek goddess of wisdom, Athena. Minerva, the Romans had called her.

I smiled to myself in the dark. Minerva. I had called Mina that sometimes. When I was a kid, it was my way of teasing her for all her obscure wisdom sayings. *I bow down to you, O Minerva.* Man, I really was going to have to watch out for counter-transference here. I was already seeing Mina in Peter's dreams . . .

Then I stopped smiling to myself. For the second time I felt that shiver, that superstitious thrill.

My God, I thought, staring into the dark. *I* know *that place. Don't I?*

And I did, it was true. That place in the woods. The place Peter had dreamed about. The hilltop, the altar stone, the wooden cross. Even the whispering noise. It was all real. I knew it. I'd been there.

A long time ago, I had been there with my sister.

F I V E

I DON'T KNOW WHY I WANTED to see the place again.

The coincidence—if that's what it was—the connections

between Peter and Mina, Minerva, the owl—well, they

were not really as coincidental as all that. Like most of these

things it had more to do with my thought process than

anything else. That Peter should've dreamed of a place I

was familiar with was not that strange in a town as small

as this. All the rest of it was just a matter of free association

on my part. That's what I told myself anyway.

And yet I wanted to see the place in the woods. The place

in Peter's dream. Just to make sure I was right, I guess. Just to make sure it was the same place I remembered. Or maybe that's not why. Maybe it was something deeper, something to do with my sister, with the anniversary of her death coming up. I don't know. I'm not sure. I just wanted to see it, that's all.

In any case, it wouldn't be much trouble to get there. It was not very far away from the Manor.

THE HIGHBURY FAMILY MENTAL HEALTH Clinic—the Manor—sits on forty-five acres in the posh north side of town. It's a sweet spot, green and graceful. Paved paths wind under maples, oaks and elms. The gabled rooftops of clapboard dormitories and treatment centers rise above the leaves. The place gets its nickname from the administration building, the building closest to the road. It's a grandiose neoclassical monster—sweeping steps, columned portico: a regular manor house. The rest of the campus is more modest than that. A very peaceful place, bordered by secluded mansions to the east, west and south.

To the north of the clinic is the Silver River Gorge Preserve. Five hundred and sixty acres of hardwood forest laced with walking trails. My own house was directly on the other side of it and on pleasant days when I didn't need the car I could hike to work and back right through the forest. That's what I did the next morning, a Wednesday.

I changed out of my jeans and sweatshirt in my office bathroom. Put on the spare suit I keep at work. I had just come out, was just buttoning my shirt, when the Manor's four other shrinks began to wander in one by one.

Gould came first. Just shuffled through the door without knocking. Thirty, bespectacled, shaggy of hair and beard. Patches on the elbows of his cord jacket. Coffee in one hand, bagel in the other.

"Greetings, my president."

The white-haired O'Hara followed, trucking behind his own belly. His Egg McMuffin dribbled grease through the corners of its bag. Next was Jane Hirschfeld, a prim stick of a woman. She had a bottle of juice. And finally there was Holden, bald as a billiard ball, athletic, hard. Coffee only, black.

"Hail to the chief," he said.

I was the president. That was my title. And it makes me sound very important, I'm sure. But the funny thing is it was intended as a more or less honorary position. The medical director and the chief financial officer were supposed to run the place. The president was just supposed to be a figurehead, a guy like me with a lot of local connections in high places. I'd taken the job ten years before when, as Mina predicted, I needed to find a way out of the city. My mother had died, my father retired and moved to Santa Fe by then. But the family was still widely known in Highbury and people seemed to think well of us. So the idea was, as president of a clinic my forebears had helped establish, I would serve mostly as a fundraiser and ambassador of good will—which would leave me plenty of time to do whatever research and see whatever patients interested me.

Unfortunately, a year or so after I came aboard, the clinic's world turned upside down. I won't bore you with the details. The revolution in health insurance shattered us. A quarter of our staff was wiped out, our level of care was compromised. The chief financial officer was practically carted off one day gibbering with exhaustion. Finally the clinic's board decided they had to bring in a new medical director. Enter Ray Oakem—or as some of the less mature among us had been heard to call him, the Wizard of Odd.

The Wizard was—well, he was odd, that's for sure. Picture a rooster with a goatee—a scrawny, strutting bearded guy, that was Ray. To give him his due, he'd been hired for his "expertise in strategies of short-term care"— to cut treatment costs, in other words. And he'd done it, he really had. He'd slapped the CFO back into shape, reorganized the Utilization Review staff which dealt with the insurers, and instituted an eleven-day course of therapy for substance abuse—the busiest part of the business. It didn't actually cure anyone, of course, but at least it kept the kids moving through the clinic at a rate the insurers were willing to pay.

In fact, the only thing you could really say against Ray was that he was an asshole. And that he was out of his freaking mind. Whenever he took time off from cutting costs and tried to contribute to the process of actually making miserable people feel better, he gave new meaning to the word *fiasco*. At one point he had actually tried to institute the sort of Boot Camp therapy that has had some success as a quick fix in certain prisons. I swear it to God. He said it would provide patients with "a short, sharp shock." Which turned out to be literally true as one of the poor bastards attempted to electrocute himself in a wall socket. Two others tried hanging before the threat of legal action brought Ray to his senses. Another time he tried to cure a girl later diagnosed as schizophrenic by having her sit in the dark with a blanket over her head. Gould and I had to physically eject Ray from the room before we could get her to stop screaming.

As a result of these and other moments of not-so-hilarious hijinks, the medical staff was left searching for a respected presence to defeat the evil Wizard and restore sanity to our treatment policies. I guess I happened to be standing around looking vaguely like a respected presence at the time. The clinic's doctors, social workers and nurses rallied around me. And while the board wouldn't fire Oakem because he was saving the place from bankruptcy, they did give me a certain amount of support when it came to protecting our patients from the Wizard's bright ideas.

And so I became a sort of unofficial co-director—and the chairman of this daily breakfast meeting of the four-person psychiatric staff. The meeting was purely informal stuff, just a get-together before rounds, but it did seem to restore morale after the Bad Times. Plus as a side benefit, it drove the excluded Oakem insane with bitterness and jealousy.

So anyway, in they came, Gould, O'Hara, Hirschfeld and Holden. They arrayed themselves around the room while I tucked in my shirt and began to tie my tie.

"After a hard night of fighting crime he changes out of his blue tights," O'Hara said, pulling out his Egg McMuffin.

"Do you have issues with my blue tights, Joseph?" I jiggled the tie's knot tight. "You can tell me, I'm a doctor."

But he was now noisily sucking the egg yolk out from between the muffin halves.

"Jesus, O'Hara, it's not a tit," Holden said.

"It's not?" O'Hara looked at it. "Damn it, I ordered the McTit."

Gould lifted his bagel. "Pardon me, folks, while I sublimate," he murmured. He sensuously tongued a dab of cream cheese out of the hole.

"I'm sorry you have to see this, Jane," I told Hirschfeld. "They're animals. Animals!"

She had a disarming smile, a surprising sense of humor. "Well, I never," she drawled, and she slowly slid the long neck of her juice bottle between her lips.

"Psychiatrists." I settled into my chair. "You're disgusting, the lot of you."

AFTER THEY'D ALL EATEN—OR whatever the hell they were doing—I joined Gould for his rounds. We walked together to Cade House, the mature youth unit.

It was a fine day. The morning air was cool. The green of the leaves was just fading, the light just turning slightly golden and autumnal. The campus was always at its most peaceful this time of year. The summer vacation was over. A lot of our patients were headed back to school. Gould and I walked slowly down the empty path, our hands in our pockets, our eyes roaming over the colors of the place. Below us, on the slope of a hill, the white-brick chimney of Cade House rose over a screen of maples.

"All quiet down at Cade?" I asked him.

"Oh yeah. You know—September. One of my eating disorders checked herself out last week. Figured she'd go home and vomit up some of that good old home cooking. Now I only got five in-house."

"My Cooper Bed's coming in Friday. So I can lay him on you?"

"The suicidal church burner, right? Sure. The more the merrier. It oughta liven up chapel at any rate. What kind of meds are you going with?"

"He refused Prozac at the hospital. I think I'll wait and see."

"Uh boy. Cal Bradley—last defender of the Talking Cure."

"That's me."

"And you'll be doing primary?"

I nodded absently. "Oh yeah, I'll take care of him."

We reached the unit, went inside. The Cade House inpatients had just come back from breakfast. They were gathered in the lounge. Gould paused with me a moment to peek in on them.

The lounge was dark—I mean, the wood of the walls was dark and the upholstered furniture and the faded covers of the books on the shelves. But a picture window stretched the length of the southern wall and the low sun came through it. A haze of smoke hung in the air lanced by beams of light. The kids—five teenagers: three girls, two boys— were draped over the various sofas and chairs. Drinking coffee, sucking on cigarettes.

Nora was perched on a chair arm, her smoking hand circling as she chatted to Angela on the couch. Nora was starving. An eating disorder. She was angular and bug-eyed, her T-shirt dangling from her bones. Angela, on the other hand, was stumpy and miserable. She wore long jeans and a long-sleeved sweatshirt. They hid the razor scars all up and down her. Brad was on the couch too. Sprawled rubbery in his khakis and tee. Laughing and nodding lazily. He'd turned violent on his parents while under the influence of various drugs. Austin, stretched on the shelf along the window, one long leg lifted, one elbow on his knee, had made two suicide attempts. And Shane—who was plopped sideways into an armchair with a book on her middle—she was a depressive. A tough case, borderline, getting meds and therapy and fighting them both every step of the way.

All but one were from broken homes like Peter. Brad was the exception but in his case the parents both worked in the city and were rarely home at all.

I stood with Gould on the threshold.

"What do you think?" I said quietly.

"Shouldn't be a problem. Send your boy on over," Gould said. "From what you've told me—hell—he ought to fit right in."

WHEN I STEPPED OUTSIDE AGAIN, I glanced down the hill. Cade House was the northernmost building on the campus. Beyond it was a mown field with a few benches on it. Then came the treeline and the trailhead into the Silver River Gorge Preserve.

That was where it was. The place that Peter had dreamed about. It was in the preserve, off toward the east, where the preserve bordered on private forest and watershed land. I was pretty sure I could find the spot again. I didn't think it would take me more than twenty minutes or so to get there. The urge to go, to see it, was powerful. It was very powerful, in fact.

Even after all this time, I really can't say why.

———

I COULDN'T GET OUT RIGHT away. I had a patient to see first, some paperwork, some phone calls. But I had almost an hour free for lunch. So a little after one o'clock I changed back into my walking clothes and headed down into the woods.

I didn't take my usual trail, the trail through the gorge, the one I would take home. This was the high trail instead, the one that skirted the gorge's edge. As I walked, the narrow chasm opened to my left. Imposing glacial boulders rose up on its far wall. Thick-trunked conifers shaded the depths of it from the sun. It looked dark and cool down there at the bottom where the Silver River ran.

Up here above, though, the green and yellow light fell pleasantly through the thatch of leaves. It shone on the white stands of birch and on the soft, unfocused blue of hemlocks and pines. Dead leaves whispered underfoot as I walked and traffic whispered out-of-sight on the nearby roads. The river whispered at the bottom of the gorge and its whisper grew louder as I neared Silver Falls.

That was where the trail ended—or appeared to end: right before the falls. There was a high, tree-topped rock formation here that seemed to block the way. For the uninitiated, this was it, this was the lookout point. You could stand here and watch the pretty single-tiered cascade drop into the shadows of the gorge. A fine sight. The river just hurled itself freefall from its high bed into the rocky pool below.

It was nowhere near full strength at this season but even so it sent up a powerful wash of noise.

I could hear this whispering, Peter had told me of his dream. *All around me. Very soft, but drowning out everything else. There was nothing else. Just this whispering, whispering, whispering everywhere.*

That's pretty much the way it was. The noise of the cascade's downpour wasn't deafening or anything, not here on the high ground. It just seemed somehow to erase everything else. Birdsong, insect buzz, the distant traffic noise—they all disappeared underneath it. There was nothing here but the steady plash of water. Whispering, whispering.

I turned away from the falls. Pushing through branches now, I moved off the trail. I worked my way around the rock formation. I was glad to see I had remembered it right. There was a hidden way to go on. It was a sort of ladder of roots and footholds leading up the side of the formation to a narrow path. Only the first few feet were difficult, then it was merely a matter of grinding my way up the short incline to the top.

And there it was. Right at the top of the formation, right above the falls, nestled among bushes, surrounded by birches and small clustered hemlocks. There was a little clearing, a little grove. Just as I remembered it. Just as Peter dreamed.

There was the "ancient altar" he'd spoken of, right in the center, a flat gray stone about knee high, about six feet long. The trees and low shrubs encircled it almost completely. But just at the edge of the clearing, just before the dizzying drop to the pool below, the growth was sparser. And there was the wooden cross. A birch really—its long leafless trunk—and the oddly straight, oddly naked branch

of a hemlock that pressed flush against it at the perpendicular.

I stood still a moment, breathless from the climb. Solitary with the trees enclosing me. With the sound of water
washing every other sound away. It was strange being there.
In the landscape of Peter's dream. And in the landscape of
my own memory too. Because Mina really had brought me
here one time. When I was eleven or so and she was eigh-
teen, about to leave for Barnard. She'd waved at the stone—
oh, with such world-weary adolescent sophistication. This
was where kids came to have sex, she told me. She herself,
she said, had lost her virginity here. Sex! Her virginity!
Well, I'd tried not to look thunderstruck, I remembered, but
I think my chin was somewhere down around my ankles.
"I thought I ought to show it to you before I leave," Mina
drawled. "You might need it in the unlikely event you
should ever get laid yourself."

A generous thought on her part anyway. My youth was
never anywhere near as exciting as hers. I never did come
back. And while hearing my sister talk about her sex life
had been shocking enough and exciting enough to remain
in my memory, the occasion, the details had sort of faded
away over time. I'd actually forgotten all about this place
until Peter's dream reminded me.

I let my eyes play over the scene now. I could see the
brown glass of shattered beer bottles among the roots of the
trees. Cigarette filters, torn condom packets. It looked like
today's teenagers still knew a good secluded love nest when
they saw one. That was the real connection between Mina
and Peter, I thought, nothing coincidental about it at all.

This was a place where Highbury teenagers came to make love. Just as Mina had been here with her first guy, so Peter had probably been here with his girlfriend. That's probably why the location had shown up in his dream.

I remembered how he'd described what happened. There had been a light behind the cross, he'd said. He stepped up to it, peered into it . . .

I turned now to the "wooden cross" myself. I smiled. There was a light behind it now too: the slanting rays of the afternoon sun. On impulse, I did what Peter had done. I stepped up to the birch and the hemlock. The water whispered all around me just as it had whispered to him. I peered as he had into the light behind the cross.

And down below, on the opposite side of the river, on a trail down there that led to the base of the falls, I saw my wife with another man.

PART

TWO

SIX

I HAVE A GOOD FACE TO hear confessions with. A sort of

emptiness was painted on it by the gods. My patients can

see in me anything they want. Their angry father, their

indifferent mother, their long-lost sympathetic friend. I'm

whomever they need to talk to, to deal with. That's the

beginning of transference, that's how the process works.

But it's not just in psychiatry. A cop in the interrogation

room will say, "Get it off your chest," and a felon will forget

everything he knows and unburden himself to a person who

wants nothing more than to slap him in jail. A wife will

tell her errant husband, "I just want you to be honest with me," and like an idiot he'll believe her. A reporter will tell a politician, "the public wants to hear your side ..." We need to tell our stories, that's all. What else connects us to each other but the tales we tell? So if in reality it would be wiser to keep our mouths shut then—what the hell?—we change reality. We transform it with our minds into whatever world we can share the truth in.

And that's how we really expose ourselves. Not in what we say but in the imagination we lay over the face of things. Because we can choose our words, strike our poses, but our delusions—no, those are wallpapered to our souls. Look at me writing this, for instance. Confessing this to you. I mean, you ought to be the perfect audience. You're not even really there, I'm just inventing you as I go along. I'm making you up wholesale. I ought to be able to imagine you any way I want. Laughing at my jokes, forgiving my trespasses, sympathizing with my sufferings. Admiring me no matter what. That Cal Bradley, you ought to be saying with an affectionate chuckle. What a guy he is. What a zany, stand-up helluva guy.

Instead when I look up from this page and picture you I see a snarky, smirking little bastard. Snuffling and sniggling at the cheap Hollywood irony of it all. The Psychiatrist Who Doesn't Even Know His Own Wife. Oh, ho ho ho.

Well, don't stop on my account. Smirk away, my imaginary friend. Believe me, I'm just getting started. You haven't even heard the half of it.

I STOOD IN THE GROVE of Peter Blue's dream. Stood there shocked rigid. I stared through the crossed branches. I looked down to the trail at the base of the waterfall. And I saw her—them—Marie and the man.

I'm no good at judging distances. It was a long way from the top of that rock formation down to where they were, seventy yards, a hundred, I have no idea. They hadn't been visible at all from the path I'd been on before, the formation blocked the view. Even from up here they were partially obscured by a network of low hanging branches. Later I would tell myself I wasn't sure—I couldn't be sure at that distance, with those obstructions—that it really was Marie at all. But I was sure at that moment. At that moment, as I stood there, I absolutely knew. I recognized the shape of her beyond a shadow of a doubt. Her hair, her orange windbreaker, her denim skirt. She was nearly turned away from me. I saw her in one-quarter profile only. But at that moment, I was sure.

I had a better look at the man. He was facing me. It was too far for me to see his features in detail, but I got a good overall sense of him. He was in his forties maybe. Small, edgy, sinewy, dark. His hair jet, slicked back, his smile gleaming. He was wearing jeans and a black T-shirt. The muscles of his arms were ropy, leathery, tanned dark brown. He was holding Marie by her two shoulders. He was speaking to her as he smiled.

"Marie?" I said. It was washed away by the whisper of the falls.

The dark man let one of her shoulders go. He laid his hand against her cheek, gently stroked her hair, her skin.

"*Marie?*" I shouted. But they couldn't hear me. Not

down there, not so near the base of the cascade. They couldn't have seen me either. They'd have had to look directly at me and even then I'd be hidden from them by the trees surrounding the grove.

I hesitated there another second—and another—spiked to the spot by the sight of them, by the sight of his hands so tender and intimate on her. Then I tore my gaze away, tore myself away. I charged back across the altar stone toward the little clearing's edge. I would go down the rock to the path, I was thinking. I would climb down the gorge to the river, slide down if I had to. I would wave my arms, catch their attention. Confront them. That was all the plan I had.

The branches crackled, scratching me as I pushed out through the screen of trees. I launched myself thoughtlessly down the side of the formation. Went down too quickly. The jutting rock face tore the flesh along my wrist. My sneaker-tip slipped off the edge of an indentation. I gasped, dangling for a second, my hand clinging to a tree-root, my feet scrabbling for purchase.

I dropped the last yard or so to the earth. The impact jarred my ankle, made my jaw clamp shut. Grunting with the pain, snarling with the effort, I limped around the formation, back to the trail, back to the lip of the gorge.

The whisper of the falls was replaced in my head now by my own panting breath. I steadied myself on a birch, started working my way down the steep slope. My sneakers sunk deep in slippery leaf-fall. I handed myself along from one birch to another to a pine. And then I fell—fell and slid in the leaves—another several feet down.

I snatched at a root, caught myself, pulled myself up. I looked and saw I was beyond the obstruction of the rock formation. I could see the spot again at the base of the cascade.

I stood, breathing harshly, holding to a low branch. Peering wildly through the trees and the water-spray.

But she was gone. Marie and the dark man both. They were both gone.

IT WAS NO USE TRYING to find them. There were three trails away from the river on that side. By the time I found a spot where I could cross they would be long gone on any one of them. After a while, I turned away. Slowly I managed to climb back to the upper trail.

I sat on a stone for a few minutes. Rested until the ache in my ankle eased, until my breath came back to me. I kept telling myself to think, that I must think. But I couldn't think. All I could do was remember Marie and the man with his hands on her—smiling with his hand intimate and tender on the side of her face.

I had to go home, to see her, confront her. I'd go back to the Manor first. Clean up, calm down. Cancel my afternoon. Use one of the clinic's cars to drive to the house. I got up—got up before I was really ready—still breathless, still in pain—and started hobbling back the way I'd come.

But as I walked through the woods, I began to consider. I began to ask myself: was I sure of what I'd seen? Was I even sure it was Marie? From so high up, so far away, through all those branches. And practically with her back to me too. And what about the man? I'd had a strong impression of him: handsome, dynamic, virile. Everything I'm not. Maybe it was just my insecurity that made me think a guy like that must be her lover. I mean, she was my wife of fourteen years. My devoted, simple, churchgoing wife. Maybe I was being ridiculous, the classic jealous husband.

Eyes down, unseeing, mouth open, breathing hard, I stumbled along the path back to the clinic. I kept thinking about his hands, the way he touched her. Caressed her. But maybe I was wrong about that too. Maybe it was different. Maybe he was—I don't know—imploring her. Or threatening her. That was possible, wasn't it? Maybe here I was fretting over being a cuckhold and meanwhile Marie was in danger of some kind. All right, all right, it couldn't've been that. It was such a gentle touch. And she wasn't struggling. She didn't even pull away. But maybe she knew him somehow. Maybe it was an old friend. Or her brother. She was estranged from her family—I'd never met them—but I knew she had a brother somewhere. Jake. Maybe Jake had turned up and was trying to reestablish relations . . .

By the time I neared the treeline I was scolding myself for having jumped to conclusions. Where was my trust for the woman I loved? My respect for her? I couldn't just go rushing back to the house. Burst in, confront her, interrogate her as if she were a criminal. What the hell kind of husband was I anyway?

I'd phone her, that's what. Casually. Just to make sure she was all right. After all, you know, maybe I really had witnessed her abduction by a rapist-murderer. I'd give her a call and say, "I saw you in the woods today." And she'd say, "Oh yes, I was taking a walk and I just happened to bump into my long-lost brother who was good enough to brush a bit of dust off my cheek and my hair with a touch so very gentle, tender, sensuous . . ."

Sick at heart, I heaved myself out of the dappled forest and into the full daylight of the Manor's north meadow. Wearily, I made my way back to my office to dress my wounds.

IT WAS ANOTHER FORTY-FIVE MINUTES or so before I called her. She wasn't at home. I reached her on her cell phone. I could hear Tot squealing in the background when she answered.

"Where are you?" I said.

"Tot is having a playdate," said Marie. "Oh, Tot, sweetheart, don't . . ." I heard something crash. "Darling, can I call you back?"

"I'll talk to you this evening," I said.

I didn't get to tell her that I had seen her in the woods.

IT'S HARD TO DESCRIBE WHAT my state of mind was the rest of that afternoon. If you've ever found a lump on your body or an ugly-looking mole—or just suffered through a bout of hypochondria—it was something like that. I would manage to reassure myself, to focus my mind on something else, and then it would come back to me—the way he touched her—and I would be in a cold sweat again. Could she be in love with someone else? Could I have lost her without knowing it?

I had another patient in the afternoon. A meeting with

Public Relations. A conference with Oakem and the CFO. It was an endless wait before I could break away and go home. And then it was no better. Because the children were all around. J. R. wanted to tell me about a shot he'd got off in basketball practice. Eva had some long story about her friends in the school choir. Tot wanted to show me her crayon drawings. They followed every footstep I took. I couldn't get a moment alone with Marie.

I found myself watching her. I did. I was sitting on the floor with Tot and I actually found myself stealing glances at Marie as she set the table. I was searching her face, you see, for signs of—something—deception, betrayal, secrecy. But she was the same as always. Laughing with Eva, patient with her, sweet. It couldn't have all been falsehood, I told myself. And I mean, hell, she wasn't even wearing her denim skirt. She was in khaki slacks and a long-sleeved plaid blouse—a completely different outfit than the woman in the woods. I'd made a mistake that's all. I'd thought I'd seen her when I hadn't. I was just going to forget the whole thing.

I felt better. Sitting there on the floor, I studied Tot's drawings solemnly. "Oh, that's great, sweetheart," I said. And then I remembered. The way he touched her. And there it was again, the doubt, clammy and miserable.

I was ashamed of myself. I was ashamed of what I was thinking.

But I couldn't stop it. I couldn't make it stop.

THE LONG, LONG EVENING ENDED, finally ended. I gave Tot a bath then put her to bed. Read to J. R. a while. Gave

Eva a kiss. Marie lingered a little to clean up in the kitchen. I went upstairs to wait for her.

Ours was the only bedroom on the third story. A private place at the back of the house with windows on the forest and the sky. There were two armchairs, one for each of us, one on each side of the bed. Sometimes at the end of the day we would sit up here together for half an hour or so. We wouldn't talk much. I would read some psychiatric journal or other and Marie—who was an excellent seamstress—would work on clothes. Or she would page through those celebrity magazines she loved. I couldn't stand those magazines but she loved them and she would pore over them and shake her head and make a *tsk* sound to herself, which I found incredibly endearing. Anyway there were the armchairs and the nightstands and a dresser and the bed. The bed was not very large but that was all right because we always slept in each other's arms.

I sat in my armchair by the bed and waited to ask Marie about the man in the woods.

I had a book open on my knee but I was staring at the door when she came in. She was carrying a bottle of wine and two glasses. She was smiling a little.

"Are you busy?" she said. "Or can I get you drunk and take advantage of you?"

I tried to return the smile. I laid the book aside on the nightstand. I found myself searching her face again as she came toward me. She put the wine and glasses on the nightstand by the book. She bent and kissed me warmly on the forehead.

"Is everything all right with you tonight?" she said. "You seemed all far away or something."

"No, I'm fine," I said.

She kissed me again, on the lips this time. "Well, you pour the wine and I'll get undressed and then I'll make everything very nice."

She moved to her closet on the far wall. I didn't pour the wine. I sat with my hands together, twisting the fingers of one hand with the other. She opened the closet door. I could see her reflected on the full-length mirror inside.

"I saw you . . ." I cleared my throat. "I saw you out in the woods today. Out by the waterfall."

She was unbuttoning her blouse. She glanced at me, still smiling. Her eyes were untroubled, clear. "What? You saw me out in the woods? I didn't go into the woods today."

I cleared my throat again. My throat felt very thick. "Uh . . . You, uh, weren't out in the woods, out by Silver Falls? This afternoon, around one o'clock or so? One-thirty?"

"No, jeez, I had lunch with the fair committee today. Jenny Douglas has been making us all crazy. Then I had to rush to get Tot from her playdate." She wrinkled her nose at me. "I can't be lazy like you, you know. Wandering off into the woods anytime I want."

"I could've sworn it was you," I said—I said it to myself as much as her. Because the truth was, by then I couldn't have sworn. The truth was it seemed almost certain to me now that I must've made a mistake. I mean, I pride myself on my insight into people. That's my job, that's what I do. Plus I knew Marie—I thought I knew her—better than anyone. She couldn't just look at me and lie like that. She wouldn't.

So relief began to flood through me. In fact, I was embarrassed at how strong it was. God, had I really been that worried? Had I really suspected her of cheating on me?

Marie, at the mirror, watched me. She was standing with her fingers on her blouse, the top open, the lace of her bra visible, appealing. Her eyes narrowed at me with suspicion.

"Just what was she doing out there?"

"What?" I was so lost in my own thoughts I was taken off-guard. "Who?"

"*Who*. Never mind, *Who*. This woman you saw. This woman you thought was me. If you thought she was me why didn't you call her, say hello or something?"

"Well, she was too far away. I was up at the top of the falls and she was, um, down . . ." I snagged the bottle on the nightstand, pulled the cork out. "I'll, uh, pour the wine," I said.

Out of the corner of my eye, I saw Marie prowling toward me with slow steps. "She was with a man, wasn't she?"

"Um, what?"

"Don't 'um, what' me. Cal. Look at me." I looked at her sheepishly. She came toward me, her smile just a twitch at the corner of her lips now. "Is that what you've been moping around about all night? You thought you saw me in the woods with another man?"

"Well, no . . . I mean, there was a man . . ."

"And were they kissing?"

"No, of course not . . ."

"Oh, you liar. They were, weren't they? Calvin Bradley! How could you think something like that?"

"Well, I didn't . . . I mean, I didn't really think any-thing."

"Oh, don't tell me that. I know you. You did." She took the wine bottle out of my hand, set it on the stand. She hung over me, a prosecutor, her hands on the back of my chair, her arms on either side of my head. "You thought you saw me kissing another man and you've been worrying about it all night."

"I have not."

"You have so. You goof." She turned and settled into my lap. "You were jealous." She tilted her head against mine, pressed her brow against mine. "Weren't you?"

"Jealous?" I said.

"Uh huh."

"Well, let me see. It's kind of hard to remember."

Marie laughed. "Oh, my stupid."

"I was devastated," I told her. "I was, like, Olynthus."

She kissed me. "Mm." Whispered, "Who's Olynthus?"

"It was a city in ancient Greece. Philip of Macedon razed it to the ground. I was like that."

"Don't try to sound smart when you've been so dumb." She moved around to kiss my cheek, my neck.

"I wasn't dumb."

"You weren't dumb?"

"I was kind of dumb."

"You poor sweetheart." The breath of her whisper was warm in my ear. "Could you ever, ever, ever really think that I would do anything to hurt you? Ever?" She pulled back, looked down at me. "When you're my guy, my baby? My whole life? Could you?"

I reached a finger up to trace her face. "Okay, I guess that was pretty dumb."

"Before you, everything was just awful for me, you know that," she said. "And then you made everything so wonderful and happy. And you're so good to me and I love you so much. Not to mention the fact that I happen to worship you like a god."

"I worship you too. That's just the thing. That was the core of the problem right there. Oh hell."

I drew her to me, held her tightly. Pressed my head between her breasts. Drew deep draughts of the scent of her and let her heartbeat surround me.

After a moment, she wriggled against my lap. "Feels like I better get out of these clothes in a hurry before something gets ripped."

"Ripped can be nice," I murmured into her body. "Ripped can be fun."

"Never mind. I like these slacks. Unhand me, you beast."

I let her pull away, but only slowly, my arms reluctant to release her. With a long breath I sat back in my chair. My gaze traveled over her. She bit her lip seductively. She watched my eyes as she slowly stripped off her blouse.

My breath caught in my throat when I saw the bruise on one of her shoulders.

It was nothing, barely visible at all. A small faint patch of purple she could've gotten—anyone could've gotten— anywhere. But it was right where it would've been if a man had held her. If he had held her by the shoulders a little too hard and pressed his thumb into her flesh.

I couldn't help myself—I said, "What'd you do to yourself there?"

Reaching for the button of her slacks, she glanced at the spot unconcerned. "What? That? I don't know. I must've banged it or something."

"It looks like someone grabbed you."

"Oh, that's right," she said with a laugh. "I almost forgot. My boyfriend in the woods. He's so rough."

"Very funny."

"Well, then don't be such a dope. Your job right now is to sit back and relax."

I sat back. She unbuttoned her slacks. She wriggled out of them slowly, swirling her hips. And when she came to me again, when she was naked and the heat of her was in my hands, I pressed my lips against her neck and whispered, "I couldn't live without you, Marie."

"I couldn't live without you either."

"I just want to do this—what we're doing right now—all the time, okay?"

"I just want to be perfect for you," she whispered as she began to undress me. "That's the whole point of everything I do."

Maybe if I had loved her less there would have been no murder.

SEVEN

HOW COULD I HAVE BEEN SO stupid? I kept asking myself

that over and over. How could I have ever convinced myself

that that was my wife I'd seen in the woods? My wife! How

could I have believed it even for a second? If nothing else,

the sheer coincidence—that Peter's dream could've led me

to discover my wife's infidelity—the implausibility of it—

that alone—should've made me realize it was nonsense.

I'd been irrational. Almost delusional. It wasn't like me. I

tried to work it out in my mind. It must've been about

something else, I thought. It must've been about my sister.

The upcoming anniversary of her death. That was the obvious choice. Peter's dream had reminded me of that and then I'd thought I'd seen what I'd seen . . . It was clear: Mina's suicide must've been eating at my unconscious.

I analyzed it this way. Mina had been driven to despair at least in part because of her self-destructive relationships with men. And here I was at exactly the age at which she died and the most healthy and satisfying aspect of my life was my own sexual relationship, my marriage to Marie. I must've had terrible buried feelings of guilt that I had succeeded so well where she had failed so terribly; that I had lived, in short, where she had died. And when Peter—suicidal Peter Blue—told me a dream that reminded me of the spot where Mina's ruinous sex life began, I felt compelled to go there, to rub my nose in memories of my sister's sorrow. Then when a couple of lovers had happened to wander past, it was perfect. I seized on the opportunity to punish myself, to convince myself for a little while at least that I didn't need to feel guilty because my marriage was not as successful as I had thought.

It was all about my sister, about my guilt. That made sense. That made sense of everything.

It was an altogether reasonable explanation.

ON FRIDAY, AS ORDERED BY the court, Peter Blue checked himself into the Manor. Gould did the intake interview. Then a social worker, Karen Chu, took Peter over to Cade House, got him settled in and introduced him to the other teenagers. I didn't speak with Peter myself until our first scheduled session toward the end of that afternoon.

Karen brought him over to me at about 4:30. I had planned it that way: It was a pleasant hour in my office at that time of year. Outside the large window behind my desk the sun was settling behind the treetops. Its beams, reaching through the leaves, hung yellow in the office air, glowed red on the faded bindings of the books on the shelves. The picture frames and knickknacks glistened. The edges of the room grew faintly hazy. It gave the place a comfortable, homey atmosphere. A good atmosphere for our first session. It would make up for that other meeting in the secure ward at Gloucester State.

I had one corner of the room reserved specifically for therapy. There was an upholstered armchair there for the patient, a high-backed leather swivel chair for me. When Peter came in I led him over there. Stood straight, waiting silent, almost formal, by my chair while Peter's long body subsided gracefully across from me. Then I sat down as well.

It was obvious to me right off that his mood had lifted since the last time I'd seen him. His sensitive features were relaxed. The corners of his mouth lifted. His pale eyes were bright, fairly flaring, as he turned his head this way and that to survey the room. He looked almost child-like to me. He seemed to take everything in with a sense of wonder, as if he had wandered into someplace magical.

"This is great," he said mildly. "I mean this whole place. The clinic. It's a great place. I love it here."

"Good."

"Thank you so much for getting me in. My lawyer told me what you did. Really. You've saved my life for a while."

"More than a while I hope."

He laughed briefly. "Well, no one has more than a

while. That little while. But thank you. It's so great to be where there are trees again. Where I can walk outside." A shiver took him suddenly. He rubbed his strong hands together quickly as if he'd grown cold. "I'm a little nervous about this part though."

"About talking to me?"

"About being *analyzed*. Brr. What a terrible fate—y'know? I can't think of a more terrible fate. I have this image of my headstone: 'Here lies Peter Blue. *Analyzed* in the nineteenth year of his life.' "

"Why is that so terrible?"

"Oh . . ." A smile floated over his lips. He drew a breath. "Just because you ruin things when you stick meanings on them. I just like to think about—things the way they are, you know."

"No, I'm not sure I understand. What things?"

"Oh, you know. Just whatever. Whatever I'm thinking about. The forest. The sky. The way the earth smells—those things don't have hidden meanings. God is just in the realness of them. Reality is how God sings."

Oof, I thought. *Our old friend God again.* I tried not to roll my eyes. "I hardly think our conversations will endanger the nature of reality," I said.

"No," said Peter Blue, still smiling. "No. But you know. You'll tell me this thing is a symbol for that thing. You'll tell me this means something else, means that. You'll *analyze* it." He actually shuddered. Whispered: *"Analyze!"*

"God, you're right, it does sound awful," I said.

The laughter burst out of him. His face lit up with pleasure. "Doesn't it though?"

"Okay. Well, how about this?" I said. "How about if I don't tell you anything? How about you tell me what things mean to you?"

"But that's just it." He made a graceful gesture. And his voice was mild and mellifluous as he patiently tried to get this through my thick skull: "Things don't mean anything to me. They just are what they are. They're just— God's way of singing."

I nodded once benignly. God's way of singing. Got it. Swell.

Conversations like this are not unusual at the beginning of a therapeutic relationship. The patient is afraid the doctor will invade his mind, expose his secrets, gain power over him. So he launches a sort of pre-emptive strike against what he presumes will be the doctor's methods. If analysis is invalid then the analyst is no threat, that's the idea. What Peter was really saying—the psychiatric translation of it, if you will—was that he was anxious about what his therapy might reveal. A very specific anxiety in this case, I thought. In fact, I felt certain I knew exactly what was worrying him.

So I said, "What about dreams, Peter? Are dreams just God singing?"

He shrugged. "Sure. Everything. Why do you ask?"

"Well, this particular type of *analysis* you're talking about—finding symbols, putting meanings on things— that's a method that would primarily apply to the interpretation of dreams, isn't it? It sounds like you're concerned we might uncover some hidden meaning in the dream you told me about?"

Peter gazed at me blankly. "Dream? What...? Oh. The owl one." He gave a fond smile, remembering. "Yeah, that was beautiful. But no, I wasn't thinking about that at all."

"Weren't you?" I said.

"Nope. Maybe it was you."

I didn't answer. I admit I felt a little less certain all of a sudden. I felt a cool dampness at the back of my neck. *Was* it me? Was I wrong?

Peter made a face. "Ooh, you're not going to tell me the dream meant something, are you? That would be too awful. It was so perfect just the way it was. It was, like, I couldn't go out into the woods so God brought the woods to me."

I nodded vaguely, stalling for time. I should have left it alone then—I knew I should've. I should have moved on to other things. But I couldn't stop myself—I said, "What else? Do you have other associations with the dream? Does it make you think of anything?"

Peter snorted. "No. Why? What does it make *you* think of?"

The damp at the back of my neck resolved itself into a bead of sweat. I cleared my throat. "What about the place in the dream?" I persisted.

"The place?"

"The location, yes. The spot where you saw the owl."

"What about it?" said Peter, baffled.

"Does it remind you of anything? Have you ever been there?"

He considered. "Not that I know of. Have you?"

"Well, I'm not the point here," I said quickly. "It's not my dream." The drop of sweat ran down behind my collar, down between my shoulder blades leaving a long, cold trail. I pressed on. "What about the owl? Why do you think you had a dream about an owl?"

"Oh, because it was just so beautiful," he said happily. He shook his head, his eyes slipping closed. "I can still see it. It was just—incredible."

We sat in silence. It was strange. I felt suddenly all alone in the room. As if by closing his eyes Peter had some-how left the premises. As if his self, the reality of him, had been transported elsewhere and I'd been left behind with this hollow image of him in the chair.

And then he opened his eyes—and just as suddenly it hit me with considerable force: his eyes, the expression in his eyes, lofty, sad and funny all at once—it wasn't just me, it really was my sister's expression, it was her expression to the life. For a startled second, I almost felt her there with me. I almost heard her speaking. *Maybe you are wrong, baby. Not just about the dream—maybe you're wrong about a lot of things...*

Peter broke the moment. He gave a comical groan. Bowed his head, shook it in mock misery, pinching the bridge of his nose between two fingers.

"What," I said, taken aback. "What is it?"

He groaned again and laughed and raised his head. "I can't believe it. I just thought of something. Damn it. There was an owl my father and I used to take care of together. God! Damn it! I'll bet that's just what you're looking for, isn't it!"

It was. I confess it: it was exactly what I was looking for. But I smiled only slightly. I kept my eyes impassive.

"Analyzed!" cried Peter Blue.

I managed to suppress my sigh of relief.

PETER'S FATHER, RAYNOR BLUE, HAD worked as the caretaker for the Audubon Society over in Westbury. It was a popular local spot. They offered guided hikes and nature programs. I took my kids there from time to time.

There was a cabin on the grounds where they housed and displayed birds—three or four birds who were injured or just unfit for the wild in some way. When Peter was a little boy it had been part of his father's job to feed them. And one of them at the time had been a male snowy owl. Wintering in the south one year, the owl had been struck by a passing car as he coursed low over the road between two stubble fields. His broken wing had never healed properly and he became a ward of the Audubon. Visiting children had dubbed the owl Chip after the potato chips with the owl on the bag.

Glistening white with a five foot wingspan, Chip was an awesome creature to behold. But he was affectionate too in his proud way—or little Peter felt he was anyway. Raynor would bring his five-year-old son to the cabin in the early mornings and let him lay out the dead mice for the bird's breakfast. Then after mealtime Chip would sit on Raynor's gloved hand and allow Peter to preen the feathers at the back of his neck where he couldn't reach. Sometimes the bird would turn his head full around, 180 degrees, and glare warmly at the boy with his raptor-yellow eyes. Peter still remembered the sense of pal-hood he felt in those moments, as if the owl's ferocious look were a kind of rough joke between them. *I guess I can't eat you, kid, so I might as well love you instead.*

"After my dad left . . ." Peter said—he spoke in a distant tone, a tone that suggested this was a minor thing, almost nothing, his dad leaving. "After my dad left, I could still go see Chip every day. Our house, the caretaker's house, was right on the grounds and the Audubon people let us stay there while we looked for another place to live. So I could walk right over and see him. But I wasn't allowed to feed him anymore. I could only look at him through the glass because my dad wasn't there to take him out for me. And then a few weeks later anyway, Chip died. No one knew how old he was. You can't tell with owls. He just died."

He lapsed into silence. "Do you remember your father leaving?" I asked him.

The question seemed to surprise him. He had to think it over. "I guess I do. It was sort of a non-event though. I mean, one day he just didn't come home from work. My mother just shrugged when I asked about it. She yelled at me. Told me to leave her alone. There wasn't any big horrible shock about it or anything. It just sort of dawned on me day by day that he wasn't going to come back. I guess by the time I really understood it, I'd already accepted it."

I nodded. Peter Blue stared into the afternoon air, stared at nothing.

"Boy, what I do remember: I remember when Chip

died. I was really, really broken up about that." He continued in that same musing tone. "I remember I went off in the woods behind the house . . . All by myself. I just sat on the ground out there under these tall pines. Cried. I cried so hard it hurt—it really hurt—like some huge snake was in my stomach thrashing around, trying to break out. I just sat there and just rocked and rocked and cried and cried and cried." He drew in a long breath. Shook his head. "I sure did love that big old bird."

E I G H T

THE NEXT AFTERNOON, SATURDAY, I CHAUFFEURED

my son home from his basketball game and found Police

Chief Orrin Hunnicut waiting for me in the front drive.

Marie stood chatting with him at the edge of the lawn. Tot

was leaning against her leg, shyly tangling and untangling

herself in her mother's skirt. The big man dwarfed them.

His height, the massive girth, the shoulders. Just the *sub-*

stance of the guy, the coarse, bristling fleshiness of him. He

made delicate Marie and delicate Tot look all the more tiny

and delicate still.

As I pulled my minivan past the chief's SUV, I saw Hunnicut take Marie's hand, swallow it in his two gigantic paws, press it warmly. I knew he must be thanking her yet again for the time she spent sitting by his wife's deathbed. I caught a glimpse of his face, his enormous face, with his lips trembling and his eyes going blurry with sentiment. Embarrassed, I took my time parking the van.

J. R. hauled his gear straight into the house through the door in the garage. I strolled out toward the chief and Marie. It was a beautiful day, I remember. The reds and yellows of the first changing leaves were achingly sharp against the blue sky. The air was cold and dry with the smell of the leaves woven into it. A good day to be at home, to be with the family. I already wished the chief had not come.

As I approached them, Hunnicut knelt down to address Tot. It was like watching some kind of construction machinery maneuver into position. "Darling," I heard him say. "I hope you know what a fine lady you have for a mother. I hope you thank God for it." Marie and I exchanged a look as I approached. Hunnicut was clearly in Full Mawkish mode. And poor Tot—I half expected her to run screaming into the house at the sight of that huge maudlin rock-face looming over her.

She refrained, thank heavens. I joined the group. Hunnicut rumbled to his feet, up and up above me, crewcut against the sky. His handshake was strangely loose and flaccid. I'd noticed this before. It was as if he were some kind of bear or something who hadn't quite cracked what the whole handshake business was about.

He said, "Doctor." I said, "Chief." I invited him inside but he growled, "I don't wanna interrupt your family's Saturday afternoon. If you could just spare me half an hour, I thought maybe we could take a little drive together."

I hesitated. I'd promised Tot some play time—I was looking forward to it. But Hunnicut leaned close, spoke low to me in a voice like snoring.

"It's about this boy Peter Blue," he said.

SO OFF WE TRUNDLED IN the police department four-by-four. Up the long driveway with Marie and Tot waving good-bye to us from the lawn.

"Our women," Chief Hunnicut said, glancing back at them in the rearview mirror. "The Good Lord sure knew what He was doing the day He made them, didn't He?"

He did actually say that—you couldn't make stuff like that up. And he seemed irked when I didn't answer, when I didn't join with him in solemn appreciation of God's Amazing Gender Idea. We sat in uncomfortable silence as the SUV bounced out onto the road.

We drove along the forest lanes around my house. The trees crowded the roadside. A yellow leaf fluttered down to the pavement now and then. Soon we came out onto upper State Street. We went past the Common, past the churches. Past the elementary school and the high school. The school football game was just over. The sidewalks were busy with parents and kids returning to their cars. Hunnicut knew every other one of them it seemed. They smiled at him, waved hello. He waved back, grinned at them, a raw, red, meaty grin. He made noises of pleasure in his throat from time to time.

"You're a popular man," I said.

"They're good people," he answered. "Good."

We rolled on into West Highbury, his own neighborhood for most of his life. He and his wife had raised their two children here. The houses were smaller, one story some of them, with no more than a strip of grass separating one family's chimney from another's satellite dish. Women swept their porches beneath American flags. Kids circled tricycles in the driveways. Big-bellied men raked the leaves off their front yards. They waved to the chief too, most of them, and he waved back. "Heh heh heh," he chuckled amiably.

He was smiling out his side window at a little girl when he said to me, "If the state attorney or the judge finds out I came to you about this, there'll be a goddamn shitstorm, if you'll pardon my French. A goddamn shitstorm."

"All right, I understand that," I said. "And you have to understand that my dealings with Peter Blue are completely confidential. I can't give you a single piece of information about him. Not one."

"Oh, sure, sure, sure. That's fine. I know what I need to know. I just want to get my two cents in here, that's all." He threw a casual salute to a woman unloading groceries from her car trunk. "See, to me, a man beats up on a girl, burns a church, steals a gun, pulls that firearm on an officer of the law—well, call me a hard old bastard if you want to, but it seems to me he's racked himself up a little debt to society. He ought to be made to pay that debt—not go off to some rest home somewhere to be pampered for a few weeks and then let out to do it all over again. Can you see where I'm coming from?"

"Sure. Of course I can. But what's this got to do with me?"

"Well, from where I'm sitting, plenty. The judge gave Blue to you for thirty days. After that, he's gonna ask you what you think. Your answer—well, that's pretty much gonna be the deciding factor in whether Blue gets off scot free or does the jail time he deserves."

"Well, you're probably right about that. But I can only call it as I see it," I said.

The chief nodded largely. "I appreciate that. I do. I just wanna make sure you see it as clearly as possible."

We left the houses behind and turned onto a long, drab lane. A few sad shacks stood in unmown grass. Then even these were gone and we were riding beside a colorless landscape: a cemetery, a littered field, an electrical plant. The SUV jounced over the broken macadam. The coils and towers and cables of the plant grew up thick and tangled like the forest in a martian fairy tale.

"I figured I could at least talk to you," Hunnicut said, "because—well, I figure a woman like Mrs. Bradley wouldn't marry someone unless he had a lot to recommend him."

"Well, thanks. I tell myself that too sometimes but I think the truth is: I just got lucky."

That actually made him laugh—or snarl in a laughter-like manner. "Well, I doubt that," he said. "I do. I doubt it."

He spun the steering wheel. With a bump and a swirl

of dust the SUV left the pavement. We thudded over a dirt path winding through high grass. The grass clicked and whispered against the sides of the car. I couldn't see through it to where we were going.

Then, another jolt, and the grass parted. The chief's SUV came to a halt.

"Here," he said. "Take a look at this." I followed his gaze.

We were at the edge of an old limestone quarry. It was a strange, secluded place. The sky—even the cloudless sky—seemed to hang low and heavy over the land here. Pressed beneath it, great slabs of white stone lay like ruins in the dust. In the midst of these the earth gave way into a broad pit. The walls of the pit were crumbling and loamy. At the bottom, more slabs and boulders jutted out of stagnant pools of oily green rainwater. It was like coming on a prehistoric site, a remnant of some long-abandoned thing.

But it was not abandoned. There were people here. Twenty or twenty-five of them, I'd say. Teenagers and young adults. Slouching among the rocks. Lounging against the cars and motorcycles and trucks they'd parked in the grass not far away. There were sinewy boys in muscle shirts or windbreakers. Pale girls nearly pouring out of their tank tops, straining the seams of their jeans. They smoked—dope and cigarettes. They tilted back bottles of beer. Some couples pressed hip to hip, grinding against each other.

And then they stopped. All of them. The minute the chief's SUV pulled into sight. They stopped whatever they

were doing and glared at us, sullen and malign. One kid—
with a gesture of grand arrogance—bogarted his joint into
the pit-water. Another scratched his cheek with a raised
middle finger. A third squeezed his girlfriend's breast so
that she jumped and then wriggled against him, snig-
gering.

"Ever seen this place?" the chief asked portentously.

"I guess. I must've driven past it. I've never really
come out here like this. I've always heard it was kind of a
hangout though."

"Just gets worse and worse every year," he told me.
"You and me, Doc, we grew up on different sides of this
town. Me, I've known this place since I was a kid and let
me tell you: It just gets worse and worse. The older ones
corrupt the younger ones coming in. Shit, with all the divorces and the mothers off working—the pornography in
any movie you go to and all those games, those video games,
with people getting blown away right and left—the
younger ones are just as bad as the older ones soon as they
get here. Hardly any wonder they wind up stealing. Break-
ing into people's homes. Hurting people. We had a rape
right in those woods, right over there not too long ago. Lady
hiker. One of these punks from the quarry got all jumped
up on cocaine and took after her. Now you got kids burning
churches, pointing guns at police officers. What do you
think's gonna happen if we don't do anything about it? They
lose all respect for me, all respect for authority. Hell, it'd
be no surprise if one day one of them gets his hand on some
kind of assault weapon, walks into a school or a McDonald's
somewhere, just opens fire."

I stared at him, speechless.

"All those folks you saw waving to me," he went on. "The west side, the north side, doesn't matter, rich, poor. They ain't waving and smiling like that cause they think I'm handsome Dan, let me tell you. If I'm a popular man around this town, it's because people know that—while they're at church or at the PTA or the little league game or whatever or just safe in their homes—they know I'm out here keeping the animals in their cages. I'm keeping things from falling apart so that everything doesn't turn into crap like this."

"Uh huh," I finally managed to say. But I was thinking: *Wha-at?* I mean, what in the freaking world was the man talking about? I turned to look at the quarry again. It was a teen hangout, that's all. Most towns have one somewhere. And sure, the kids here looked tough. Undereducated, underemployed. There were probably even some burglars among them. Some vandals, drug users. Some who got pregnant too young. But the place hardly looked like a sneak preview of the apocalypse or anything. And as for Highbury overall, yeah, we had divorces and overworked parents and trashy movies just like everyone. But this was a strong, old-fashioned family community. The juvenile crime rate was down here, way down. It had been falling for ages. That rape he'd mentioned—that was three or four years ago. And far from taking out Mickey D's with an AK, no one had fired a gun in anger here for God knows how long.

So I mean, what was he talking about? Keeping the animals in their cages. Coaxing a rabid raccoon out of a garbage can was more the sort of thing the town's police force dealt with. The longer I sat there—staring at Hunnicut, then the quarry, then Hunnicut again—the more I began to wonder if the chief was talking about reality at all. Maybe he was talking about something else. About the death of his wife maybe, about his grief over that. Maybe it was *his* world, his interior world, that was crumbling around him. Maybe he was projecting that apocalypse onto the relatively placid, prosperous town in which we actually lived.

"What does this have to do with Peter Blue?" I finally asked him.

Now it was Hunnicut's turn to stare. The flint eyes sunk deep in his fisty flesh flashed into mine. "He's one of these punks, that's what. He spends all his spare time here."

"Peter?" I blurted out, startled. "He does?"

"Yes, sir." The chief was clearly pleased at my surprise. "There, you see. That's what I mean. There's something, living in the world you live in, you might not know. But I know. I'm out here. That's what I do while you're raising your family and going to work at your clinic and so forth. That's why someone like Blue can go up to the judge, go up to you, and fool you. Wrap you round his finger. Make you think he's just a poor, little abused boy put upon by the world. Just needs a little understanding, that's all. But he can't fool me. You want to see who Peter Blue really is, you look out there. Right there. There's some of his buddies now."

I followed his gesture. Out to the far side of the pit where some cars were parked among the stones. I saw a small cluster of men off by themselves. Older than most of the others. And an unsavory crew by the look of them. There was a mountainous biker with a yellowing beard. Two filmy-eyed drunkards jawing by a pickup. A hungry twenty-year-old jumpy as a crack bandit, watching us narrowly, ready to run.

I have to admit it: I really was surprised. It was hard to imagine Peter—dreamy Peter—hanging around thugs like that. "Are you sure you have the right guy?" I was about to say.

But before I could speak, a movement caught my eye. Someone among the stones over there, the farthest stones, deep in the high grass, almost halfway toward the edge of the woods. He was hidden behind a rock, leaning against it. But he curled around it to take a look at us and that's when I saw him. A hard, mean-featured face. The black hair slicked back above a lined forehead. Lean, lined cheeks, leathery and tanned and tough. The cigarette pinched between his thumb and finger came to his pursed lips. Tendrils of smoke drifted up around him. He took his look, a long look at us, leisurely, contemptuous. Then he curled away behind the rock again.

"That man," I said softly, my lips hardly moving. "Over there. Do you know him? That one behind the rock? Do you know who he is?"

The chief peered through the windshield. "I didn't get much of a look at him. Why do you ask?"

"No reason," I said. "I just thought I recognized him, that's all."

I continued watching another moment. The man did

not show himself again. I'd seen him for only a second really, hardly even that.

But it didn't matter. I recognized him well enough. He was the same man I'd seen out in the forest, out by the watefall. I was certain of it. He was the same man.

N I N E

"STRANGE THING," SAID GOULD. "YOUR COOPER Bed.

This Peter Blue."

He was using the side of his finger to smooth the cream

cheese on the circumference of his bagel. He was tilted back

in his chair—my chair—his feet on my desk. And I was in

the chair across from him, my feet up too, soles at an angle

to his soles.

This was the breakfast meeting at my office the following

Thursday. O'Hara, in the other chair, was bent over his own

belly busily searching his brown bag for crumbs of his egg-on-a-roll. Hirschfeld was on the sofa, kicking a spindly leg crossed over a knobby knee, tilting back her juice. Holden was posted ramrod straight at the window, hands knuckle-deep in his pockets, the back of his pale hairless head toward us. He had the habit of surveying the out-of-doors with grim suspicion as if he always expected the armies of the night to come over the far hill and charge.

I was distracted. Lost in my coffee. Still thinking about the man at the quarry, the man I had seen in the woods. Had he really been one of Peter's friends? Would Peter know why he had been in the forest—and with whom? I couldn't just come right out and ask, of course. It would be completely unethical. In order for a patient to expose his deepest emotions to a therapist he has to feel a tremendous depth of trust. I was already beginning to win that trust from Peter. He was already telling me in sessions about the loss of his father, his mother's drunkeness. We were making good progress. Every word I said to him at this point had to reinforce his faith in me and guide his understanding of himself. I couldn't risk our relationship by questioning him about matters of purely personal concern to me.

But all the same it bothered me. The whole weird business. Peter's dream. The man at the waterfall. The woman he was with—the woman I had mistaken for my wife . . . It was like a little fist clutching inside of me, a little clutching fist of doubt. It couldn't be possible that Marie had lied to me but . . . But if I recognized the man at the quarry so easily, how could I have been mistaken about seeing her?

That's what I was thinking when Gould spoke. "Strange thing. Your Cooper Bed. This Peter Blue."

I blinked out of my coffee, looked up at him. Having groomed his bagel, he was tearing into it. Chewing hard. Elaborately combing the excess cream cheese out of his beard. His spectacles caught the light and winked as he waited for me to answer.

"What about him?" I said. "Isn't he fitting in at Cade all right?"

"Oh yeah, yeah. No problems there."

"The other kids accept him."

"Well, actually, that's kind of what's strange."

"What do you mean?"

"Well, for instance, I saw him having dinner with Nora Treacy last night."

"Nora . . ." I tried to place her.

"My E.D.," Gould said, chewing. "Anorexic."

"Oh yeah." I remembered the starving girl in the lounge with the T-shirt dangling from her bony frame. "So they had dinner together. What's so strange about that?"

Gould gave a little laugh, made a little gesture, spread his hands, as if the answer were too obvious for words.

Holden, still at the window, glanced back at him over his shoulder. "You mean they were *eating* dinner?" he asked.

"Pork chops," said Gould with a mystified shrug. Another bite of bagel. He spoke around the mouthful. "Most days with her it's dramas, negotiations. 'I don't belong here. I can't eat this, I'm a vegan. I can't eat that, it makes me ill. My mother's coming to take me home any minute. Fatcheta-fatcheta-fatcheta.' The usual usual. Most days one of us has gotta do half an hour of finagling just to get her baseline calories into her."

"She ate pork chops?" Jane Hirshfeld said slowly from the couch.

Gould—enjoying the interest of his audience now—popped the last of the bagel in his mouth, pulled the crumbs from his beard, dusted them from his hands. "Mmph," he said, chewing. "And she just did it, like that. Came into the cafeteria with your boy Peter. Talking, laughing, like they're old friends. Goes on the lunch line, just sort of casually orders the same thing he's having. You know, chop, vegetable, mashed potatoes. I'm having lunch, right? I'm watching this. They sit down together. The social worker—Karen Chu—I see her heading over there. I wave her back, you know, cause I'm watching. And at first, the two of them, Peter and Nora, they're just talking, talking. And I see Nora's doing the hand thing—you know, teenaged girls, they connect, they get excited, everything's with the hands." He did an hilariously accurate impression of it, lifting both hands, rigid, fingers spread—as if he were being electrocuted. And crying out falsetto: " 'Oh! That is just so incredibly, totally *true!*' You know, she's doing that. And then when *he* starts talking—Peter—*she* starts picking at her food. Kind of absentmindedly like. She's picking up a string bean with her fingers. Munching on it, dipping it in the mashed potatoes. I just wish I could've heard what your Blue kid was saying, cause she's listening and nodding and laughing and pretty soon, at the same time, like she's not even thinking about it, she picks up her knife and fork and starts cutting into the chop. And I'm watching this. And she just starts eating the chop, the potatoes, while he's talking. Listening, nodding, just eating away. I mean, at one point,

I turned around to look at Karen and she's, like, fucking pole-axed!" He did his impression of Karen Chu, jaw to her chest, eyes bugging. "I mean, poor Karen, she's put so much sweat into this girl. I been teasing her we can't just have Karen Chu, we need Susan Swallow in there too. You know? Chu and Swallow? And the two of us, we're watching this, right? And Nora just—she just cleaned her plate."

Even O'Hara at this point raised his nose from his lunch bag. "You sure she didn't just throw it right up afterwards?"

Gould raised both his hands. "They were all in the lounge for about an hour afterwards. I kept an eye on her. She never even went to the head."

There was a beat of silence, then another. I looked at Holden. Holden made a face, impressed. I looked at O'Hara. He made the same face, cocked his head. I made the same face. Looked at Hirschfeld. Hirschfeld ran her tongue beneath her upper lip, tapped her chin thoughtfully with her juice bottle.

"Obviously it's just the behavioral training finally taking effect," she murmured.

"Sure, nudged along by a little sexual attraction," I said. "She likes Peter, she wants to please him, look nice for him."

Holden nodded at the window pane.

"Right," said O'Hara. "That's obviously it."

"Probably," said Gould. "But if not, Cal, you better straighten this kid out in a hurry so we can go ahead and hire him on staff."

———

THE WEATHER HAD HELD ALL week. It had been cool and crystal clear. I walked to work and back across the woods whenever I could, knowing the days would soon be too short for it. No matter how well you know the trails it's very difficult to find your way through the forest by night.

But I was delayed at the clinic that day by a deeply ridiculous meeting with Director Oakem. It was one of those times when he tried to get on my good side by being a Regular Guy. I hated that. He kept trying to talk to me about baseball and automobiles and God knows what. I wanted to grab him by the shirtfront and say, *Stop. Stop being a Regular Guy. You can't. You're too bizarre. Face up to it and let's move on.* Unfortunately I couldn't come up with a more tactful way to put that. So in the interest of peace I kept my mouth shut and was forced to hang around his office for forty minutes pretending we were pals.

By the time I wangled my way out of there, it was getting late. The sky above open ground was still light enough—the sun was still visible low between the buildings—but I knew it was going to be dusk soon down in the woods. I hesitated. Thought about driving home in one of the clinic cars. But I needed the exercise. It was the only exercise I ever got. So I changed quickly into my walking clothes and hurried off.

This was the trail that led down into the gorge. And sure enough, as I descended along it, I could see the color draining from the leaves, draining from everything. The air began to thicken with shadows. The shadows began to fold over me.

For a long time, I could still make out the trail before me well enough, I could still find my way. It was only when

I looked up into the distance that I began to feel a little nervous. The farther reaches of the forest were beginning to blend together, were becoming a tangled mass of coiling silhouettes. And that mass was creeping in on every side of me. Soon it would be full dark.

I walked faster. I wanted to get across the gorge as quickly as I could. I knew there'd be more light once I climbed up to higher ground. I figured if I hurried I could just get within sight of my house before the last of that light failed.

I reached the gorge bottom. Crossed the stream, picking my way carefully through the twilight. The air was nearly ink blue here. The black boulders, the black trees, the black twists of vines felt very close around me. The black leaves on the black branches seemed to bear down on me from above.

I was glad when I felt the trail start upward under my feet. I had to strain my eyes now to see it, even right there in front of me. Nightsounds were rising, growing louder on every side. The frogs croaking by the water, the leaves whispering in the wind, the branches swaying, creaking like ghost-house doors and then suddenly . . .

Suddenly I heard a footstep. I stopped short, swung around fast. Listened. Listened. There was nothing now. But I was sure I'd heard it. A footstep in the leaves behind me.

I stared into the darkness, stood still and stared. I felt my breath going in and out of me quickly. The frogs croaked. The river burbled. Ordinary forest sounds. Maybe it was just an animal I'd heard. Yes, that must've been it. I was about to turn and move on.

Then a twig snapped loudly. My eyes darted to the noise. I tasted something coppery at the back of my throat. There was a man standing among the trees, watching me.

I looked right past him at first. He was just another shape among the shapes of the forest. Then he registered on my mind. My eyes went back and found him. My pulse thumped faster inside my head.

He was standing off-trail among a tangle of low branches. Standing very still—it was unnerving—frightening—how still he stood. Judging by the position of his arms, he had his thumbs hooked in his belt. Relaxed enough but very still, very still. Just standing there. Just watching me.

I couldn't make out his features at all. But my thoughts went instantly to the man at the quarry. Maybe it was just my imagination but this shadow seemed like him somehow. I could picture him though I couldn't see him: his hard, leathery, contemptuous face.

I called out. "Hello?" My voice sounded weak and foolish to me.

He said nothing.

"What do you want?" I called more strongly.

He answered this time. He snorted. A harsh, unmistakable sound of derision. I could almost hear him sneer. Then, very slowly, he said:

"I want you fucking dead."

I was afraid.

I told you from the start that I'm no hero. I was a preacher's kid—I'm a thinking man—I've never been in a fistfight in my life. Oh, I have the same daydreams of violent adventure as any man. I dream of dodging bullets and bad guys and rescuing damsels in distress. No matter what I might say philosophically to the ladies at some cocktail party or other, in my heart of hearts I know as all men know that physical courage is the bare minimum standard of masculinity. But this is a confession. I'm committed to telling the ugly truth. And I have to tell you that right then at that moment I was so fucking terrified that my abject failure to live up to the minimum standard of masculinity was not much of a concern at all.

I tried to force the quaver out of my voice, tried to speak with some authority. "Do you know me?"

"Yeah, I know you, you piece of shit. You're a piece of shit."

He said this softly, slowly. His voice was just another of the nightsounds in the blue dark. The dark grew thicker.

"All right. Why don't you just tell me what you want," I said.

He gave a short easy laugh. "Yeah, how about if I just rip your fucking head off? How's that?"

And still he never moved. He was so motionless that as the night got darker and darker he began to disappear into it and I thought that soon—soon he would be invisible to me; he would come leaping out at me from nowhere. The dark closed in and I could feel that terrible moment coming closer and closer. I could feel him waiting for it, biding his time. I was so weak with fear my legs would barely hold me.

But I saw a stick lying on the ground. At some point I just became aware of it. It was stout and a yard long. It jutted from the low brush by the trailside. Near panic now, I swooped for it, seized it. *Shit*, I thought at once. It was rotten. Flimsy and light.

All the same I brandished it at him. I growled at him as ferociously as I could. "Just stay back, just stay the hell away!"

That made him laugh again, a low snarl of a laugh deep in his throat. And without another warning, he sprang.

His hands jerked up with unbelievable speed. His arms went out to me. He gave a short, throaty, animal roar.

I staggered back. The rotten stick in my hand waved wildly and snapped in half. All the strength went out of my legs and arms. In another second I'm sure I would've bolted and run—run uselessly until he dragged me down.

But then I realized he hadn't moved. He had already drawn back his arms, resettled himself into his relaxed position. He had just been trying to scare me, that's all. And now he was laughing at me—laughing because I had been so scared.

"Fuck," he said thickly after another moment. "Fucking shit."

He turned his back on me. He moved away. He was gone into the darkness. I could hear his footsteps sounding softer and softer on the leaves.

T E N

I AM COMMITTED TO THE UGLY truth. Still I hate to tell—

I hate to remember—how I made my way home that night.

How scared I was as I climbed the path out of the gorge.

Running sometimes. Sometimes stumbling over roots and

stones. Small frightened noises came out of me as I scanned

the dark woods on every side. I was half convinced my

attacker would circle back and pounce on me out of the

night. I kept playing the scene of it in my imagination,

terrifying myself all the more.

Finally I saw the lights of my house up ahead through the

treeline. My fear eased a little—and the moment my fear eased I began to feel ashamed. What a coward, what a wimp I was! Thank God no one had seen me.

Breathing hard, hanging my head, I slowed to a walk as I moved across the lawn to my house.

THEN I WAS IN THE bright lights of the kitchen. There was the smell of a warm roast cooking. Tot was wrapped around my leg. Eva hugged me. Marie gave me a kiss.

"Yuck, you're all sweaty," Eva said.

"I had to hurry home to beat the dark," I told her. I had prepared my excuses before I came in. I spoke naturally. No one could've heard how shaken I was. "I'll run upstairs and change."

I called the police from the bedroom. I talked with an Officer Stone. He was very good, professional and sympathetic. I explained that I hadn't really seen the man who'd confronted me, that I couldn't really describe him. There was no reason to send an officer over—it would only frighten my family. I had been threatened by violent patients in the past, I said, and the police had always been kind enough to send a patrol car by my house for a few nights. Officer Stone promised he would have that taken care of.

After I hung up, I sat on the bed for a few moments. I was not only ashamed now. I was angry too. More than that. I was seething with rage. *That bastard!* I kept thinking. *That bastard!* These were natural feelings, of course, after an incident like this. I felt I should be able to process them in a rational and therapeutic manner.

Then, when that didn't work, I got up, went to the closet, and took down my gun.

It was a lightweight .22 caliber revolver made by Smith & Wesson. That was actually everything I knew about it. I'm no gun fancier. I don't even like the things. But three years ago, a former patient of mine had eloped from a hospital and broken into my house. Fortunately no one was home when it happened. The culprit, a fifteen-year-old boy, gave himself up to the police the next day. The police then came by and returned what he'd stolen from us: two pairs of Eva's underpants. White underpants with little pink and purple flowers on them. Eva was only eight years old at the time.

About a month after that, we'd gone on vacation to Vermont. In Vermont, it turned out, you could walk into a store off the street and buy guns without a permit. I remember making some excuse and sneaking out of our lakeside cabin one day. Slinking into a shop called Green Mountain Guns 'n Ammo. Like a teenager buying pornography. The shop's proprietor was just like a pornographer, in fact. A blandly evil fat man in a regulation plaid shirt, he had winked and crooked a finger at me, drawn me to the far corner of the display case to show me the really good stuff.

"Now the eight-round cylinder'll give you all the firepower you need," he murmured intimately, "but with the aluminum frame it'll come in at under ten ounces. The drawback there, of course," he added with a little man-to-man smirk, "is that your recoil might be a little too powerful for the wife." *Your* recoil. *The* wife. I remember that specifically. Anyway, all I knew was I wanted to plunk down my four hundred plus dollars and sidle the hell out of there. Which I did. And then smuggled the weapon home among my luggage while visions of being pulled over by Connecticut's state police danced in my perspiring head.

Of course when *the* wife found out about *my* gun we had the only serious argument of our marriage. As a result, I had to keep the thing in its locked box on the top shelf of my closet. I'd only dared peek at it twice in all these years—both times when the rest of the family were out.

But I took the box down now, by jingo. Set it on the dresser. Worked the combination lock. Opened the lid. There was the revolver. Its body gleaming silver, its grip blunt black. Its eight bullets laid out in eight bullet-shaped niches in a row beneath it. It looked pleasantly deadly—a very comforting sight. The only jarring note was its name— *AirLite*—etched in delicate letters just behind the cylinder. At a moment like this I would've preferred a moniker with a bit more muscle to it, something like *ButchKill* or *DeathGod*, say. But that was a minor point.

I stood there above the weapon, strangely fascinated. Soon, as I gazed down at it, I found myself inspired to heartwarming fantasies of homicide. I saw a little mind-movie in which I was confronted again by the foul-mouthed shadow in the woods. Only this time I was armed. Yeah. I had taken my revolver in to be cleaned, see, and I just happened to be carrying it home in my backpack. And when the thug threatened me in the dark bottom of the gorge, when he said, *How about if I just rip your fucking head off?* why, I simply pulled out my gleaming .22 caliber and *Blammo! How about that? Shitface! Asshole! How about a little*

taste of the AirLite DeathGod? *You fucking savage fuckhead!*
Blammo! Blammo!

"Cal? Cal, what are you doing? Put that awful thing
away."

The wife. My wife. She had come in behind me.

I turned slowly to glare at her over my shoulder. My
heart was on fire. *Blammo!*

"Cal, are you all right?" she said. "Oh, sweetheart,
what's the matter?"

A long-held breath flowed out of me. I summoned my
senses back into the moment. I clapped the box shut and
locked it. Shoved the stupid thing back deep on the closet's
top shelf.

"Sweetheart?" said my wife. She touched my shoulder.
I couldn't look at her.

"Did the kids notice I was upset?" I asked.

"No! No. You were just like always." I nodded, grateful
for that at least. "What's wrong?"

My head hung, I humped wearily to the bed. Lowered
myself onto the edge of it. Staring at the floor. "Someone
attacked me in the forest."

"Attacked you? Oh my God! Are you hurt? What happened?"

I lifted my eyes to her face. I felt a head-rush of confusion. She was so real and familiar and so pretty, hovering
over me all concerned, her blue eyes liquid, all her smile
lines turning down. It seemed as if she existed in this world,
this true and solid world and that then there was this other
world in my head, this vague and fantastic place where the
man in the woods was the man from the quarry and the

man from the quarry was the man at the falls and the man at the falls had been with Marie—my Marie—and it was all centered around, all connected to her somehow...

I shut my eyes, shook my head to clear it. "It was nothing. He just cursed at me, threatened me. It was too dark to even see him."

"Oh, you poor thing, you must've been terrified." She sat next to me. She took hold of my arm where it lay limp on my leg. I could feel her breath on the side of my face. "We have to call the police right away."

"I already did. They'll patrol the house for a few nights..."

"Well, do you know who it was? Was it a patient? It must've been one of your old patients."

"I already told you," I said with a flash of irritation. "It was dark. I couldn't see him." And then more gently I said, "He may have just been some homeless guy. I'm not even sure he knew who I was."

"Oh, you poor sweetheart. To meet him in the dark, in the woods like that? You must've been so scared."

"I don't know," I muttered. "I picked up a stick. This stupid, rotten stick. To defend myself. It broke in my hand." I didn't tell her how he had roared at me and I had jumped back and almost run away. I couldn't bear to tell her about that. "I felt like such an idiot."

"That was so brave though," she said.

"Brave!" I snorted—as the man in the woods had snorted, with the same contempt. "I wasn't brave at all. I was completely terrified. I was scared out of my wits."

"Well, of course you were scared out of your wits. I

mean, he could've had a knife or a gun or—or anything! And you stood up to him like that?"

"I didn't stand up to him."

"You did." She rested her head against me so I could smell her and feel her hair against my cheek. So I could press my cheek against her soft hair. "Aren't you the one who's always telling J. R. that courage isn't about not being scared, it's about what you do when you are scared?"

"I don't know. Do I say that? God, I'm wise, aren't I? I wish I were *my* father."

Marie laughed. She took my hand, interlaced her fingers with mine. "Well, everyone gets scared," she said. "But I've never seen you run away from anything. That's why you've always been my hero."

I closed my eyes, resting against her soft hair. I squeezed her hand gently. "Stupid stick," I said.

"THE TRUTH IS: I'VE BEEN lonely all my life," said Peter Blue. "After my father left . . . When I was little, the other kids—the other boys—they never had much to do with me. They thought I was weird I guess. I guess I was really. Off in the woods communing with God. I never played sports or anything." He laughed. "Communing with God was the only thing I had any talent for." There was a silence and he studied the office rug. The afternoon sun was pooling pale and gentle there at his feet. Now he was telling me things he had never told anyone. "To be a man is a surprisingly complicated thing it turns out," he went on softly. "You would think you could just do it but . . . I don't know.

I think about it a lot. I guess I don't feel very—*manly*. I never really have. And I've always felt—bad about that. *Really* bad. I still feel bad about it. But then, you know, when I think about it? I'm not even sure what it is. To be a man. I mean, what is it? Everyone tells you what it's not— that it's not swaggering around or punching people—that's what they say anyway—but . . . I think maybe if my father had stayed—maybe I could just look at him and say, 'That's what it's like. That's what it means. That's what a man is.' But without that . . . it's just such an abstraction to me. It's like, I wrack my brains—what is it, what is it? And then other guys, they just seem to know. Without even thinking. Sometimes I look at some guy—even if he's some kind of absolute asshole, you know—I look at him and I envy him, I sit there and envy him because he just seems to know how to be a man."

I nodded thoughtfully. As if I were listening to him. But I was not listening. I was thinking: *Blammo!* I was thinking about that bastard in the woods. When I pictured him now, he had the face of the other man, the man at the quarry. I heard him say, *How about if I rip your fucking head off?* and he had the mean, lined, leathery features of the quarry man—the same cold, vicious, defiant eyes—the same sinewy muscles and the black hair slicked back. With grim satisfaction, I saw the bolt of fear flash through him as I leveled my .22 . . .

"What?" said Peter Blue. He stopped mid-sentence with a mystified half smile. "What are you thinking? Why are you making that expression?"

Caught out in my secret mind, I quickly assumed a look of lofty wisdom. "I'm listening," I lied. "Just go on."

Peter went on. "The trouble is, the only people who ever talk about manhood are people who don't know. Because part of being a man is not having to talk about it. Women—I mean, you can't trust women on this at all. They lie, for one thing. They'll tell you they think a man should be gentle or considerate or some stuff. But all they really want is a man who's a real man. They'd rather have him manly and kind if they can get it—at least, I guess they would—but they'll take him manly and cruel if they have to. Or they'll take him kind and wish he were manly and spend their lives dreaming about that. But if you ask them what that is—to be manly, to be a man—they start babbling and lying about it—because they don't really know! Because it's an abstraction that some men understand in their hearts but women don't because they're women. I mean, that's the whole point. If you even have to talk about it, you're no better than a woman is."

With his legs crossed, his fingers drumming on his knee, he glanced off nervously into the room's darkening corners. His smooth features contracted for a second as if with pain. He swept the hair back off his forehead. He shuddered.

I kept nodding, meanwhile, as if I understood. But I was thinking. I was thinking about how Peter knew this guy, this hoodlum from the quarry. If it was the same man, and if Chief Hunnicut was right, then Peter knew him, they were even friends. It seemed hard to believe: a friendship between such a dreamer and such a thug. But if it was true, then maybe Peter knew why the man had accosted me in the woods. And then surely I had the right to question Peter about that. Didn't I? If it wasn't just about my wife having a secret meeting. If it involved my safety, my family's safety. Surely it would be ethical to question him then.

Well, of course, no, it would not be ethical. It would be a terrible breach. The kid was sitting there with his soul exposed to me. Depending on me to focus on him, let him free associate, help him find his way to his own insights. Trusting me with the deepest part of himself. This would be the worst possible time to interrupt his flow of thought with thoughts of my own for my own reasons.

Peter was looking at me again. He smiled—forced a smile—but the pain was still in his eyes. The gray eyes full of sadness and humor were now also glistening with his pain. "You know, it's like Jenny," he said. "Jenny is—she's the only real girlfriend I ever had. I'm talking about—you know—as far as having sex and everything like that." He swallowed—went on hesitantly. "And, at first, you know, it was . . . I had a hard time. Getting it going. The . . . I'm talking about the sex. I worried about it a lot and I had a hard time—you know—doing it. But then Jenny—she was always telling me it was all right. She said she liked the way I was and it was all right. And then after a while, I kind of just relaxed with her and then . . . well, it was good. The sex was good together. We had a really good time for a while . . ." He gazed at me through his pain a long second. He tried to laugh but it sounded false. "I thought it was good anyway. But women—they do lie. They really do. They can fake the whole deal any time they want to, can't they? I mean, she said she was happy but it sure seemed awfully easy for her to just leave me like that. When the college accepted her, I mean, that was it, she was gone. It didn't even seem to bother her, not really. She was glad, in fact. She kept saying how she was the first one in her family to go to college. She was excited about it. And soon she'll have a boyfriend who's one of these guys who just know, who don't have to ask how to be a man, who don't worry about that. And she won't have to reassure him all the time and secretly wish for someone else. And she'll be happy—happier without me."

He stopped there. And for a second, I was so involved in my own thoughts that I could only stare at him, barely comprehending. But at some level, in some part of my mind, I guess I must have been listening to him the whole time. Because suddenly the logic of what he'd been saying fell into place like tumblers falling and a portion of his story unlocked and opened to me.

I felt a current of excitement run through me. I sat forward in my chair. Because it was not just his story that suddenly made sense—it was part of my story too.

"You felt that Jenny's leaving you to go to college somehow reconfirmed your sense that you weren't a real man," I said.

Peter averted his eyes again, shrugged.

"Is that why you got angry?" I asked him. "Is that why you knocked her down?"

"I didn't knock her down. I told you it was an accident."

"Yes, you told me that. But we both know it wasn't really an accident, Peter. You were angry at her. Then she put her hand on you and her sympathy made you even more angry. So you busted her one—you busted her one and she fell. Isn't that what really happened?" I kept my voice quiet but the current of excitement coursed through me and grew. Peter wouldn't look at me. "Let's put this out on the table," I said. "Here you are, you're a sensitive guy. You've never been with a girl before. You needed to feel comfortable with her before you could relax enough to make love. Okay. Nothing wrong with that. Given your temperament and inexperience, I'd say that's pretty normal. But for you, it felt humiliating. It confirmed your sense of inadequacy: you weren't a he-man right off the bat. But Jenny was understanding, you started to trust her and eventually you were able to consummate the relationship. And there you were feeling much better about yourself. And suddenly she's— quote—leaving you—unquote—she's going off to college. And you're hurt and you're scared and you start to wonder: was it all a lie? Maybe she's been faking it all this time. Maybe she's just been looking for an excuse to go off and get herself a *real* man."

Peter moaned aloud. He brought a hand to his forehead, covered his eyes. "Oh God, I'm so sorry. It was unforgivable."

"So you wanted to prove to her you *were* a real man . . ."

"Oh Jesus."

"So you hit her."

"Yes. Yes. Oh Jesus, Jesus. It was unforgivable."

"You bitch-slapped her, didn't you?"

"God damn me to Hell. I don't know what . . . I guess I thought . . ."

"You thought . . . what? What did you think?"

"I don't know, I don't know."

"Yes, you do, Peter."

"No."

"You thought that's what a real man would do? Didn't you?"

"Oh God. God damn me." Miserable, he shook his head. I sat motionless, leaning forward in my chair. I hesitated, unsure whether I should go on. My blood was racing and everything had become confused, his story and mine had become confused together. How could I be sure which was which? How could I be sure what was right for me to do?

"Who told you," I asked him, "that it was manly to hit a woman?"

He massaged his forehead, still covering his eyes. "What do you mean? I don't know. No one. No one. It was just me. I was such an idiot."

"Come on, Peter," I said. The blood pounded hard in my neck. "It wasn't just you. That's not like you at all. Someone had to tell you that. Someone you looked up to, someone you respected, who had influence over you."

Slowly, Peter's hand came down. He narrowed his eyes, looked at me hard. "I ... How ...?"

"You wanted to know how to be a man, a real man," I said. "Your girlfriend was slipping away from you and you didn't know how to stop it. Your dad was gone so he couldn't help you. But you knew someone else, a real tough guy, one of these guys you were talking about who just know what manhood is without having to ask. Like you said, maybe he was an asshole but he was a man so you admired him, you envied him, you listened to what he said . . ."

Peter's lips parted. "How do you know this?"

"He told you: You can't let a woman just walk out on you. Right? Once she's in college she'll think she's too good for you. Don't let her push you around like that. Teach her some respect. Show her the back of your hand. Isn't that what he said? He egged you on, didn't he?"

"How do you know this? How do you know these things?"

"Who was he, Peter?" I couldn't stop myself now. I couldn't find the border between his story and mine. "Who said those things to you?"

Peter shook his head, staring at me, staring. "How do you know?"

"Who was he?" I asked him.

His mouth opened as if he would speak and then closed as if he would not. And then he said, "He said he would kill me if I told you."

I was about to speak again but the words died on my lips. I sat back in my chair. I felt faintly nauseous. "Kill you? He said he would kill you?"

Peter nodded. But then he said, "Although I guess . . . I guess if I told you—you couldn't tell anyone, right?"

Distracted, I didn't answer.

"Isn't that right?" he said. "You couldn't tell anyone."

"What?" I said. "Oh. Yes. Yes, that's right."

"So if I told you, there'd be no way that he could find out."

"It would be totally confidential," I said.

A long moment passed. A long breath came shuddering out of him. Then he told me.

HIS NAME WAS LESTER MARSHALL and he was the lowest kind of scum. He'd appeared in town several months ago. Started working at the dump, part-time, off the books. That's where Peter met him.

Peter could see at once that Marshall had a way about him. People spoke to him with respect. Or maybe it was caution. Or maybe it was fear. The boss at the dump, Jason Roberts, never barked orders at Marshall or yelled at him the way he yelled at Peter. And when Marshall started to pal around with Peter, started to kid him and spar with him in a joking way—then the boss stopped yelling at Peter too.

After a while, Marshall didn't come to the dump anymore. Peter found he was sorry about that. He missed the man. He'd never known anyone like him. Then one day Peter was walking in the woods and there Marshall was. They started talking. Then they went to the quarry and talked some more.

Peter went to the quarry a lot after that. Marshall had great stories to tell. Even the toughest studs out there liked to listen to him. He'd been in bar fights, car chases, even shootouts all over the West and the Midwest. He'd even done some time in prison in Missouri. For armed robbery, he said. Peter couldn't help it. He found himself entranced with the guy. And Marshall liked that. He liked being the Big Dude. He liked to dole out advice: how to hit a man once so he'd go down and stay down, how to treat a woman so she knew who was in charge. Peter had never really had any man-to-man talks with anyone before.

Of course Peter was an intelligent kid. He could see what Marshall was. A criminal, a bully, brutal, remorseless. But he fooled himself. He told himself that he wasn't taking Marshall's advice seriously. He was just studying Marshall, just enjoying his exotic tales. He told himself he was too superior to the thug to really care about him. He told himself that—but in fact he did care about him. He was enthralled. Deep down, he didn't feel superior to Marshall in the least. Deep down, he envied him: his arrogance, his aura of danger, his knowledge of the world. He even admired the violence in him which they both mistook for masculinity. Here was someone who didn't have to ask what it meant to be a man. No sir. He just knew.

Peter didn't realize how completely he'd fallen under Marshall's spell until that night he argued with Jenny.

"And it was like Lester just flashed into my mind and I suddenly just wanted—to show her," Peter said. "To show her I was . . . And then suddenly I'd hit her. Suddenly she was on the floor. It was *horrible*. I wanted to kill myself. That's why I stole the gun. I wanted to kill myself. And then that fat bastard Hunnicut . . ." His laugh sounded like the echo in a tomb.

"So I guess we can safely say I pretty well screwed up the whole manhood thing all around, huh?"

With that he fell silent, his chin to his chest. His arms hung limp on the arms of the chair. The pool of sunlight at his feet was spreading and fading. The time for our session was over.

I sat across from him in the leather chair. Just as weary, just as wrung out, limp. Still a little nauseous too. I didn't know whether I had done the right thing or not. Our stories had become too confused, too mixed up together. And now there it was between us—there *he* was—this thug, this Lester Marshall—almost like a solid presence in the thickening shade of the room—almost as he had been in the forest when he stood so still he mingled with the darker and darker shadows around him—standing there—watching me—watching both of us now.

"And he said . . ." I began. I had to clear my throat. "This Marshall character. He said he would kill you if you told me this?"

Peter's chin lifted and fell almost imperceptibly. "If I told anyone. He came to my house after I got out of jail. He asked me if I'd mentioned him to you or the police. I told him no. He said I better not."

"Did he say why?"

He made a face at the floor. He was exhausted now. It was time to let him go. "He acted all mysterious about it," he said. "Lester liked to do that, act mysterious. He thought it made him seem important or something."

"Well, do you think he's a fugitive? Do you think he's hiding from the police?"

"I don't know. Probably. He's that kind of person. I never saw him do anything bad though. He just hung out at the quarry mostly. Drank, smoked dope. He said he had just come here looking for his girlfriend."

I nodded. "His girlfriend." But now again—again, that little shiver went through me. That cold little twinge of synchronicity, coincidence and the mysterious. A sickening dread; a weird sickening certainty. Even before Peter said quietly:

"Yeah, his girlfriend. Someone named Marie."

E L E V E N

ABOUT FOURTEEN YEARS AGO, JUST BEFORE I got mar-

ried, I took a walk with my sister. Mina had come up to

Highbury for the wedding week and one afternoon we

slipped away together to escape the panic and preparations.

My sister was always at her best in Connecticut. She cut

down on the booze consumption around our parents. She

got away from her latest horrible boyfriend—she always

left him in the city whoever he was. And she ditched that

dismal artistic black wardrobe of hers. She was too damn

pale for it. It made her look like a mime. Instead she'd go

up to her old room, dig some button-down blouses and creased khakis out of her dresser. Tie a cardigan over her shoulders. Generally assume the full dignity of the New England aristocrat she was. And it was as if suddenly she made more sense somehow. The strong, handsome features, the willowy figure, the sardonic drawl—you felt they were finally being displayed in their natural setting. I used to think: if she ever came home for good the townspeople would probably elect her queen.

There was this country lane we loved. Sunset Road. We strolled along it by an open meadow. It was late June and the rolling vista of unmown grass was snowy white with Queen Anne's Lace. Cows milled on a hummock in the middle distance. A silo rose on the hill beyond. The sky made a backdrop of pale blue with small clouds drifting lazily at the horizon-line. It was beautiful; and it was poignant—nostalgic—being there with her.

She had a switch in her hand, I remember. She was brushing the weeds at the roadside with it as we strolled. "So—this is it," she said. "Off you go."

"Into the wild blue yonder. Sure looks that way."

"Nervous?"

"Yeah, about the ceremony a little. Not about the girl."

"No." Mina paused to contemplate the view. "No, she's perfect for you. Really. Perfect." It'd been more than a year since that day I'd gone to her apartment to tell her about Marie. Any fears I'd had about my family accepting my choice—well, they were long gone. Marie was so patient with my mother, so solicitous of my father—she always knew where his glasses were, brought him soup when he watched TV at night—they both adored her. "You got this one just right, boy-o," Mina went on. "You're going to be disgustingly happy."

"I'd like to think that's sibling envy and hostility I hear."

"No. Hell, no. Not at all. Are you kidding? One of us has to live the jolly version of life. This way, at least, I can visit it from time to time, see what it looks like." I smiled. "And just so you don't blow it for me, let me give you one piece of unsolicited sisterly advice."

"Sure. You're holding the switch."

"Don't think the woman to death, baby, okay?"

"Oh, gimme a break, Minerva. What's that mean?"

There were times—a lot of times—when Mina would turn those eyes on me, those dynamite green eyes, and I would feel, not exactly like a child again, but like an innocent, like her baby brother. Even though my life was all in order and hers was a shambles. We stood at the side of the road face to face, at the edge of the meadow. She held her stick like a teacher's ferule, down at her thighs in her two hands. "She's appallingly devoted to you, you know that, right?"

"Yeah. Well, I'm appallingly devoted to her too."

"Okay but . . . Well, you know what I mean. It's not the same. There's not a man on earth who can love someone like that. There aren't that many women. You're a lucky son of a bitch. I mean, if I were a feminist I'd be forced to kill her."

"I thought you were a feminist."

"Well, don't remind me. I mean, at this point, I'm half

in love with her myself." I laughed. But Mina went on, looking at me intently. "The woman would walk through Hell to bring you a cup of coffee."

I felt my cheeks get warm. "I know."

"Well, just drink that coffee, Cal. That's what I'm trying to tell you. Just drink the goddamn coffee and shut the fuck up. Okay?"

And saying that, she walked on, whipping at the weeds.

NOW, YOU'RE PROBABLY ASKING YOURSELF: what did she mean by that? And I can tell you: I haven't the foggiest fucking idea. But like so many of Minerva's mystic utterances it came back to me. It came back to me as I was driving home from the Manor that evening, that evening after Peter Blue told me about Lester Marshall and his girlfriend. Marie.

I was driving home because I was afraid to walk through the woods again. I was driving and I was still afraid, more afraid. My heart was in my stomach. The suburban lawns and houses were shaded over with dusk. My headlights picked out a narrow corridor of pavement between the silhouetted trees. I was staring down that corridor and thinking: *It can't be my Marie. That's ridiculous. She wouldn't just lie to me. I know her.* And then I remembered my sister, that walk along Sunset Road. *Drink the coffee and shut up.*

She wasn't supposed to be my wife. I was never any good with women. And then suddenly there was this girl— so pretty—this vision of a girl—and she was in love with me. She was in bed with me. And I mean, the sex! Even now, after fifteen years of it—I would never have imagined: she made every neuron in my body dance a hilarious buck-and-wing. And she gazed at my dull old face as if I were some kind of movie star. And she brought me my coffee in bed in the morning. *She would walk through Hell...*

So maybe that was the question: had she? I mean, had she walked through Hell? I never asked her. I drank the goddamned coffee and I shut the fuck up. I never pressed her to talk about her abusive family, her runaway past. I never begged her to tell me why she couldn't sleep at night. Why she cried at night sometimes. I never said to her: *I'm your husband. Tell me! Please.* She said she didn't like to talk about it and I let it go. Because I wanted her to be happy. Or because I was so happy. I'm not sure which. I just drank the coffee and shut the fuck up.

And so when I said *I know her*, I had to ask myself: *Do I? Do I really know her?*

And surely—the answer came back to me as I drove—surely I would have known her better, I would have seen her far more clearly, if I had only loved her less.

"DO YOU KNOW A MAN named Lester Marshall?"

She was in the kitchen when I asked her. Washing dinner dishes. Tot was in bed. The older kids were doing homework in their rooms. Marie and I were alone and the running water masked our voices. I had brought two plates in to her from the table. I stood holding them out to her as she rinsed a glass, as she set it in the washer.

"Don't do that," she said. "Go relax if you haven't got any work to do."

"Do you know a man named Lester Marshall?"

I was in suspense as I watched her. I watched her closely. Watched her as I would watch a patient, alert to every gesture and expression. There was nothing. She took the dirty plates from me, paused with them in her hands. "Lester Marshall . . ." She stood considering. A pale ringlet of hair hung loose down one soft cheek. "I don't think so. Is he a parent at one of the schools? Or at church or something?"

"No, nothing like that. He's just a guy—said he spent some time in Missouri, knew someone in town named Marie . . ."

She rolled her eyes. "Oh! Missouri! I don't know if I'd remember *that* long ago. Did he say he'd met me somewhere?"

She did turn away now but only to hold the dishes under the faucet. I was the one who averted my eyes. Embarrassed, I stared at her red hands as the water ran over them. "He was a convict in Missouri," I said softly. "He was in prison there."

"What?" She laughed. "Well, then I guess we were in different parts of Missouri, weren't we?"

"I don't know. Sweetheart. I don't know what part of Missouri you were in. You never tell me anything about that part of your life—you know?"

"Well, I wasn't in prison, goofy! For goodness' sake." She laughed again, glancing at me. "Cal, why are you looking at me like that? What are you thinking?"

I can't begin to tell you how much I wanted to end

this conversation. All I had to do was believe her and everything would be fine, everything would go on as it always
had. And how could I not believe her? Just look at her. That
gentle face. Staring at me in blank confusion. The water
from the faucet hissed a long moment.

"This was the guy . . . I think this was the guy who,
uh, confronted me, accosted me on the trail the other
day . . ." I said finally.

"Oh, have they caught him?"

"No. No. But . . ." I had to force the words out. It made
my stomach turn. "The thing is, he's . . . apparently, he's the
same man I thought I saw with you. Out by the waterfall."

"With me?" She said it as if she didn't even remember
our earlier conversation. "What . . . ? Oh that! But I told you
that wasn't me."

"I know."

"You're not still jealous, are you? What do you think—
I was lying?"

"No, of course not. No." But what else did I think?
"It's just when I heard he knew someone named Marie . . ."

"Well, Cal, it's not the most uncommon name . . ."

"I know, I know."

"Oh, sweetie, stop, okay? I know that man in the woods
upset you, but you're being silly about this. You know I
don't lie to you."

"I know, I just . . . I had to ask." I forced myself to meet
her eyes, her searching eyes. "I mean, you wouldn't . . . You
would tell me, wouldn't you?"

"If I were running around with some convict in the
woods? You'd be the first to know, okay? I mean, gee, Cal."

"All right. I just meant if there was something—anything that was bothering you. You would tell me, right? So I could help you. So we could deal with it together."

She bent to set the rinsed dishes in the washing machine. Her hair fell forward and her face was hidden. I looked down at her and I thought there was something... Just for a moment, some hesitation in her posture, in the slope of her shoulders... I clenched inside, bracing myself for what she might say.

But I must've imagined it. She swooped up, swinging back her hair. The look she gave me was the old look, warm and familiar and exciting. "Of course I would. You goose. You know I would." She leaned over from the sink and kissed my lips. "But right now, the only thing bothering me is you. So go read your paper or something so I can finish up in here."

ON FRIDAY, I STOOD ON the crest of a hill, the low rolling hill on the grounds of the Manor. I was just above Cade House, the mature youth unit, set in its grove of maples. I was looking down past it at the field that ran to the forest's edge. It was lunchtime. Another one of these crystal days, these first autumn days. The green and yellow and red woods pressed against the blue, blue sky.

And there, on the lawn, near the border, near the base of the trees, Cade's six in-patients were beginning a picnic. I could hear their voices. I could hear their laughter on the faintly chilly air. I could see Peter at the center of them. He was smiling his most beautiful smile.

He was holding what I guess was a lunch box, some

kind of lunch box. I couldn't make it out from where I was. It looked very small but he kept pulling sandwiches out of it. Sandwiches and then bags of chips. It was as if he were performing a magic act. The sandwiches kept coming out of the little box long after you thought it had to be empty. He kept placing the food into the others' reaching hands.

"Are you seeing this?" said Gould. He had spotted me from a distance and strolled up beside me. "This is what I've been talking about."

I knew what he meant but for some reason I didn't want to admit it. I said, "What? What am I supposed to be seeing?"

Gould stripped off his wire specs, polished the lenses on the hem of his corduroy jacket. "Your Cooper Bed. Peter. What is he, some kind of faith healer? Look at the effect he has on them. Look at Nora. She's been eating normally almost since he got here. Shane—I mean, she's a depressive; Austin was suicidal. Look at them. Laughing, happy. Brad; Angela. All of them."

"Well, they're having a picnic, Larry." Gould made a face at me: that wasn't going to cut it with him. "And anyway," I went on, "if there is some change I doubt it has all that much to do with Peter specifically. It's probably just some kind of confluence of the treatments kicking in and a—a group dynamic he's contributing to."

"Right. Right. A confluence. Group dynamic. Sure. I'll buy that. It's just not what they say."

"Who, the kids? Why? What do they say? Is he telling them anything? He's not counseling them is he or preaching to them or anything?"

Gould made several noises that seemed to be the beginnings of words he couldn't finish. Then he wound his glasses back over his ears and shrugged. "Well, if he is, they're not telling. The ones I asked, they just say they feel better around him. He's—a cool guy, quote unquote."

We stood together, watching the kids. Then after a while, Gould wandered off, shaking his head at the ground. I went on standing there, went on watching the group on the lawn below. Their laughter and the chatter of their voices drifting up to me. I felt very far away from them and alone.

Things don't mean anything to me. Isn't that what Peter had said? The gospel according to Peter Blue? *Things just are what they are. They're just God's way of singing.* It was nonsense of course. The kind of impossible, google-eyed theology only a teenager could love. And yet I wished . . . I stood watching the teenagers laughing and talking and eating and I wished for just one minute I could feel that way. So I could stop. Stop thinking, stop trying to pick things apart. The connections. The coincidences. The synchronicity. The look in Peter's eyes and the look in my sister's. His dream and the place where Mina first made love. That place and the man beneath the waterfall. The man at the quarry. Peter. Marie. I just kept trying to make sense of it, to figure out what it all meant. And it just kept going around and around in my mind and it was twisting me up inside, wringing me like a rag and I couldn't make it stop because . . .

Because in my heart of hearts I thought Marie was lying. I'm not sure why I thought so but I did. I thought she was lying to me with that same sweet face I knew, with that same gentle voice as always. And if that was true . . . If that was true then I was living a different life than I thought I was. An entirely different life with a different woman in a different world. I was alone in a different world.

It's funny. Sometimes now I remember that day and it makes me wistful, nostalgic. I see myself in my mind as if I were looking at someone else. There I am on the hillside with my hands in my pockets. Brooding darkly over the picnic going on below. Peter is down on the lawn, down by the treeline with the other kids. Pulling sandwiches from his little box until it seems the thing must have no bottom. The fine weather, the sound of laughter—there's just something charming about the scene to me now. I can remember how alone I felt. I remember I felt twisted up inside and afraid. But I don't feel those things anymore. I just see myself on the hillside and the kids picnicking below. And it makes me wistful. It makes me wish I could go back to that day. Back to me there and to Peter and to Marie.

Because, in retrospect, it was the last peaceful day for any of us.

THE NEXT MORNING I TOOK my daughter to the playground. Looking back, I suppose the bastard must have followed us there. I can't say for sure. I didn't see him when we first arrived. I didn't see him at all until it was too late.

The playground was in back of one of the elementary schools. Madison Elementary on Flowers Street. You had to park in the lot and then cross the broad driveway to get to the schoolyard. So as I helped Tot out of the car seat in the back of the Volvo, I scanned the area carefully to make sure there were no other cars around. There were none, I'm sure of it. I remember specifically. I even let Tot run off alone across the driveway to the grass.

She loved to come here with me, especially on days like this when there were no other kids around and we were alone together. For the next forty-five minutes or so she blew through that place like a hurricane. Shrieking, giggling. With me staggering after her, trying to keep up. I chased her slithering through the big plastic pipes, pushed her on the swings as she squealed. I held her dangling from the monkey bars and caught her at the bottom of the big winding slide. "Daddy, Daddy, Daddy!" she kept shouting as she ran from one place to the next. Her blue eyes were shining, her big cheeks were practically scarlet. Her yellow ringlets trailed behind her as she ran. Finally—finally—she paused to rest. Alighted on the solitary bench near the sandbox. I stumbled after her, collapsed beside her.

"I hope you know CPR," I said.

"Look at the clouds, Daddy," said Tot.

Sitting over her, breathless, I brought her snack from its paper bag. She emptied the box of grape juice with a few long pulls at its straw then hoisted a giant Toll House cookie in both her little hands. Quiet at last, she chewed on the cookie and contemplated the sailing clouds.

For a while I'd almost forgotten everything else. Running through the playground after Tot. I'd almost put Marie and Lester Marshall and the whole business out of my mind. But now I sat over my daughter, looked down at her.

Watched her munching away, gazing up at the sky like that. I reached out and touched her hair. It was so soft, wispy, a breath against my fingertip. She looked so placid sitting there, so content.

Oh, I knew I was being morbid. But I dealt with the children of divorce every day. The children of miserable marriages. It was my goddamn office they ended up weeping in. And if Marie was lying to me, if she was having an affair ...

Tot pointed a chubby finger. "That cloud looks like a sea horse," she said.

Marshall must have been her ex-lover, I thought. What else would bring him all this way? He must be some old lover from Missouri who had come back, who had come to find her. And, sure, maybe he was a thug, an ex-con, but maybe she found him exciting too. Maybe it was a thrill to be with someone like that again after fifteen years with a man like me, a drab, low-key, boring ...

"Take a bite of my cookie, Daddy."

She held it up and I bent down to nibble at a corner. "Mmm," I said. And I thought: *That's ridiculous.* I couldn't have been that wrong about her all these years. Could I? Couldn't there be some other explanation? I mean, okay, maybe the guy was an ex-lover or an old friend or something. But maybe when he came back Marie was afraid of him. He was dangerous, a convict. Violent. Maybe Marie was being brave—even heroic in a misguided way. Maybe she was trying to protect me from this guy. Or maybe he'd threatened her somehow and she thought she had to handle it alone or ...

Tot popped the last of the cookie into her mouth. There were crumbs on her chin. Her lips were ringed with chocolate. I dabbed at her with a paper napkin and I thought:

Blackmail. It sounded ridiculous. Just the word. It sounded melodramatic, like something out of a movie. But what if he was blackmailing her and so she couldn't tell me because . . .

"Can we go home and ride my trike?" said Tot.

"We sure can," I murmured.

"Yay!" she said.

And before I could stop her, she darted off the bench, darted across the yard, darted for the edge of the curb, right for the driveway.

I heard an engine wheeze and roar.

"Tot, wait!" I shouted.

I looked up the driveway. I saw the car at once. An old rust-scarred battleship of a machine—a Chevrolet, I think, I never learned for sure. It must've come in while we were playing. It was planted at the far end of the drive, pointed down toward the exit. Pointed toward Tot.

I was already on my feet, already running after her. But it was no good. Tot got to the curb an arm's length ahead of me. I reached for her, felt the light touch of her hair on my fingertips again. Then she was gone.

"Tot!"

The moment she stepped into the driveway, there was a loud screech of tires. The Chevy leapt from its place and sprang at her.

Tot froze. She stood dead still, staring open-mouthed at the onrushing car. Even I didn't understand, didn't *believe* what was happening. I thought the driver would swerve, would try to stop. But he was aiming for her. He was shooting the Chevy at my daughter like a bullet.

I see that moment now, that endless moment. The car streaking down the drive. My daughter paralyzed in front of it, waiting for the impact. My mind was so much with her it was as if I were inside her body, looking through her eyes, helplessly watching the car get larger and larger. I was so much with her I was hardly aware of myself. I was hardly aware that I had left my feet, that I had launched myself at her through the air.

A still second. A tableau. Tot standing there. Me flying toward her. The car. Then suddenly it all sped up. Everything converged at once. I had her. For one second, I had my hands on her. And the staring headlights of the car, its grinning grill were huge, bearing down on us.

Then it was all in a tangle, rolling over and over, and then—the concussion—a horribly painless blow to the side of my forehead. White stars exploded in front of me, went out. I heard the Chevy's tires screech again. I felt more than saw the big car rushing past me, careening into the street, rocketing away. I felt a wave of muddy blackness go washing over me.

"No," I said. I willed myself to stay conscious. I rose to my knees and collapsed back to the asphalt. I rose to my knees again.

"Tot!"

My voice was thick and far away. The clouds rolled over me out of focus. My arms, my hands were empty. I held them out of in front of me. She was gone.

"Tot!"

I'd had her. I'd had her for a second. I'd rolled with
her, tried to roll with her out of the Chevy's way. I had
smacked my head against the curb as I came down. I'd lost
her . . .

"Oh God! God help me please! Tot!"

Still on my knees, I turned to the left, to the right.
There she was. Lying there. Lying on her back on the asphalt behind me. Her mouth was open, her eyes were blank
and staring. Her face was gray as ashes. She did not breathe.

And then she did. She heaved in one enormous wheez-
ing gulp of air. Held it a second—a second more. Her
cheeks went purple. She sat up. And then the breath came
rushing out of her in a ragged, deafening howl of terror
and pain.

I laughed crazily as I stumbled toward her. That
howl—that single howl—went on and on and on. I can still
hear it. Her fear, her suffering. So beautiful. So fucking
beautiful. She was alive.

THREE

TWELVE

I SAT IN A CHAIR BY the window. My daughter lay sleeping in my arms. The blinds were drawn. The room was dim and shadowy. The door was closed—only a low murmur reached us from the hospital halls.

Tot slept deeply. Her mouth hung open. Her thumb hung limp in her cheek, pulling her lips askew. Her head was warm against me. Her pink sweatshirt rose and fell steadily.

I stared down at her. Her clothes were dirty from her fall. Her hands were scuffed and red. Where the knee of her pink pants was torn, a small bandage was visible. It was decorated with blue teddy bears.

From time to time I had to shake myself, like a dog flicking off water, to clear away the images of the way it might have been.

AFTER A WHILE, THERE WAS a muffled knock. The door cracked open. Police Chief Orrin Hunnicut peeked around the edge—just peeked timidly. Then I lifted my chin in welcome and the whole mountainous substance of the man came rumbling in.

He towered above us, Tot and me. He hovered heavily, in the attitude of a mourner. The block of a head was hanging down, the mighty shoulders were folded, the meaty hands were clasped before him respectfully. He contemplated my sleeping daughter a long time, just like that. Then he lifted his eyes—his small, hard eyes—to me. The room was dark but not so dark I couldn't see what he was thinking. An attack on a child—on Marie Bradley's child especially—touched every key in him of sentiment and righteousness and cruelty. Whoever had done this thing was going to pay. Pay hard. In some lonesome cell, in a dark field off the highway, Hunnicut would take a hot pleasure in delivering justice personally.

For a silent second he thought this thought to me. And I thought: *Do it, Orrin. Yes.*

When he actually spoke, though, he spoke softly, thundered low so as not to wake my daughter. "Doc says she's gonna be okay." I nodded. Hunnicut gestured at the gauze on my forehead. "She says you oughta have some more scans and whatnot for that though."

"I'll be all right," I said.

He smiled a little. "She says you're a stubborn head-shrinker who thinks he's a real doctor."

"Yeah. Well..."

"I know what you mean. Hell, she's hardly older than this one here. Chit of a girl, they throw a white coat on her, she thinks she knows something..."

Tot snorted, shifted in my arms. The big man fell silent to let her settle into sleep again. She sucked her thumb a few times, then was still. Hunnicut frowned down at her. Extended one sausagy finger and brushed a ringlet from her brow.

"You get a look at this guy, Doc?"

I took a long breath. I'd been trying to figure out what I would say when he asked me that. I hadn't figured out anything. My head was too rattled by the concussion, my mind felt like sludge. There was too much to think about. Peter Blue—he'd given me Lester Marshall's name under the condition of strict confidentiality. And Marie—Christ, I might send Hunnicut off on a trail that led straight to her. But then there was that image of what might have happened if the car had struck my little girl and oh, I wanted the bastard. I wanted him caught. I didn't know why he was after me. Was he afraid Peter had told me something? Was he in love with my wife? I didn't know. But I knew he was the one. I knew it. And I wanted to be sure beyond any doubt he would never come near my family again. I thought... I'm not sure what I thought. I had some vague notion I could give Hunnicut only the information I wanted to and no more. Through the fog in my head I could hear myself saying:

"I think it was a man named Lester Marshall. I couldn't swear to it in court but..."

"Can you describe him?"

"Forty or so. Black hair. Lean, muscular. I understand he spent some time in prison in Missouri. That day you took me to the quarry—I saw him there."

"I remember that," Hunnicut said. "You think he's the same fellow who came after you in the Silver River Preserve?"

"Yes."

Hunnicut nodded. We were both silent again and our eyes met again. I had a feeling it was he who was reading my thoughts this time.

"Any idea why this Marshall character would try to hurt you or your family?"

If my mind had been clearer maybe I could've come up with something. I couldn't. I muttered, "I'm not sure. I don't know. Maybe he's an old patient of mine or something...I don't know."

The chief didn't pretend to believe me. He went on studying me a long time. Finally he lifted his chin. We understood each other. "Okay, Doc," he said. "Okay."

Then Tot started in my arms as the door flew open and Marie came rushing in.

THE ROOM WE WERE IN was some kind of waiting lounge. I'd been allowed to use it as a professional courtesy. There was a round table, some plastic chairs, a soda machine. The armchair I was sitting in. The armchair was right across from the door. Hunnicut had to step back to get out of Marie's way.

She didn't stop to look at him or look at me. She swept across the room. Took Tot from my arms. Clutched the child against herself hard. Tot woke up and whimpered. "Mommy?" she said and she began to cry. Marie swung gently back and forth, holding her, rocking her. She was dry-eyed, blank-eyed. Staring blank-eyed at nothing. She whispered distantly. "Sh, sh, sh." Over and over. Her face expressionless. Her stare empty. "Sh. Sh. Sh," again and again from another world, from some planet of far-off feeling.

It didn't seem right to watch. I turned away. Hunnicut was tactfully examining his shoetips. But now he raised his head to look at me again. Judging by the murder in his eyes, I'd say there was not much difference then between his heart and mine.

"Get him," I said.

He said, "Oh, I will."

And with a slight bow toward Marie, he thumped to the door and left.

I sat there. Marie cradled Tot against her, swung her gently this way and that. Tot whimpered quietly against her shoulder. Marie stared past her into space. After a while, a long while, something, some awareness, seemed to come back to her. She seemed to notice me sitting there for the first time. She glanced down at me as she swayed.

"God bless you, Cal," she said softly.

"No, no." I shuddered again like a wet dog. "I let her get away from me."

"No," Marie insisted. "You saved her. God bless you." Her voice finally broke. Her lips pressed together. Her eyes filled. She cradled the child against her.

I buried my face wearily in my two hands.

I WAITED FOR HER IN the bedroom that night. Waited to talk to her out of the children's earshot. I'd brought a bottle of single malt with me. I had a hell of a post-concussion headache and my nerves felt like a bunch of wind-up toys set loose in a box. So I had a drink while I waited. Then I had another drink. I've never been much of a drinker—my mother and sister were discouraging examples. By the time I was halfway through my third shot I was sunk deadweight in my armchair, foggy-witted, fighting sleep.

Marie dragged herself in then. Weary, drawn and pale. She stood by the closet, undressing, her face slack with exhaustion.

"The kids seem pretty upset," I said.

Slowly, stiffly, she removed her blouse. "Oh, Eva's just making the usual opera out of it," she murmured. "J. R.— you know, he keeps it all inside him. He says he'd beat the driver up if he saw him." She smiled a little to herself. "Meanwhile Tot talked it all over with her doll and fell right to sleep. She'll probably forget the whole thing by morning." She turned the smile on me. "They all think you're a hero though."

That only touched my anger off again. I didn't feel like a hero. "I'm glad we didn't tell them the—the *motherfucker* did it on purpose. It'd only worry them. The motherfucker."

Marie studied me. I rarely cursed in front of her. "Have you been sitting up here drinking?"

"I have a headache."

She gave a tired laugh. "You have. You're drunk."

"I'm self-medicating."

"Oh-ho, right. Is that what you call it?" She glanced at the whiskey bottle, still nearly full. "Well, you're a cheap date anyway."

"Marie," I said, "we have to talk."

"Oh, not tonight anymore, Cal," she said. "Tomorrow, okay?"

She shrugged out of her bra. I watched her. I rubbed my fingers against the whiskey glass in my hand. I knew it was urgent that she talk to me. I told myself it was urgent anyway. But it didn't feel urgent somehow. All those things I'd been thinking about in the playground—they were all gone from my mind. The shock and the concussion had knocked them right out of me. I didn't remember any of it. So though I told myself I had to talk to her I didn't really care just then. I just wanted to touch her, to be inside her with everything still around us, to make this day end.

She drew off her jeans and her panties. She pulled a flannel nightgown over her head, let it flutter down over her nakedness. I rubbed my fingers against the cool glass.

"Marie ..." I struggled to sit forward in my chair. "Marie—if there's anything you know about this ..."

"About what? Oh, God, you mean that man still. Oh, Cal, of course there's not."

"But I just want you to ..."

"Cal, please. *Please*, sweetheart. In the morning.

Okay?" Her hand went trembling to her lips. Her eyes filled. "Oh my God," she said.

I set the glass aside. I had to fight my way out of the chair but I went to her, put my arms around her. I held her face against my chest. I felt my shirt grow wet with her tears.

"I keep seeing what might have happened," she cried.

"I know. So do I."

"Oh God, if we'd lost her . . ."

I held her hard. "They're gonna catch this guy," I said. "The chief'll probably have him by morning."

After a few moments, crying more softly, she laughed into my wet shirt. "Doesn't *anything* take your mind off sex?" she said.

"I'm sure there's something. I just can't think of it."

She sniffled. Rubbed her cheek against me. "Mm. Well come to bed then and hold me and make love to me. It'll be better than all that liquor anyway and you'll sleep."

WE DIDN'T TALK THAT NIGHT and we didn't talk in the morning either. In the morning, there were the children to think about again. Eva had some sort of fit over what she was going to wear. She went stomping around the house yelling, "You can't blame me for being upset!" J. R., meanwhile, followed me everywhere I went. He sat on my bed while I tied my tie. He asked me questions: how I'd reached Tot in time, how my head felt, what the police would do to the driver when they caught him. Tot stayed close to her mother. Sitting at the dining table while Marie made breakfast. Singing to herself and drawing a picture of a fisherman to show to the Sunday School teacher. It took an all-out effort from me and Marie both to round them all up and herd them into the minivan in time to get to church.

Then church. I dreaded going that morning. I'd changed the bandage on my head, made it as small and inconspicuous as I could. But of course word of the "accident" had gotten out and we were besieged with sympathy. People kept coming up to us and telling us how lucky we were, how grateful we must be. And once we were in our pew I could feel them stealing glances at us. Trying to catch a glimpse of our exalted expressions of thanksgiving. As if we were supposed to tell God what a brick he'd been for not murdering our child. She was three fucking years old and He'd decided not to grind her into the macadam. I mean, hallelujah, what a guy.

Well, if that's what they were looking for, they could forget it. Whatever I was feeling during that particular service, it wasn't religious uplift, that's for sure. I didn't even get my usual nostalgic pleasure at the tradition and respectability of it all. I went through the motions. I stood when we were asked to stand, I knelt when we were told to kneel. I sang—I think "Abide with Me" was on the boards again that day. It all just seemed silly more than anything. I just found myself looking around at my neighbors and wondering: How many generations of my kind are going to waste the best part of Sunday morning with this sort of magical horseshit? It was as if I'd never seen them all quite so clearly before. Standing and kneeling and singing. With the light filtering down on them through the stained-glass saints. And the columns rising up among them into the rafters. Pamela Harrington in her blue dress and pearls and Franklin Worth in his Wall Street suit and Ginny Finch with her dull husband Lester and yea, even Monty Collingswood with his rich wife Jane. All of them—just bubbles in this meaningless fizz, sailing for a single second to the surface where *pop!* they would be gone, as in gone. Air beseeching the empty air. Nothing praying to nothing. Hey, what can I tell you? Thoughts come to a fellow in church, you know, and those were mine.

I turned to Marie. I was irritated and bored. I wanted to ask her if we could skip coffee hour after this and just go the hell home. And before I could get the words out, I bit them back. Guess why. What do you think? That's it: she was deep in prayer.

It wasn't even the scheduled time for it. We'd just taken our seats. Father Douglas had just climbed into the pulpit, was just beginning to drone through the announcements. Bible Study group, the Autumn potluck, the Feed the Homeless project...But Marie wasn't listening. Her chin was lifted. The line of her gaze skimmed across the top of the priest's head. She was looking at the maplewood Christ crucified on the wall behind him. Her blue eyes were bright. Her lips were moving silently. And when I looked down I saw her hands on her skirt, clasping each other, twisting and rubbing, wringing themselves red. Even in my cynical state of mind, it touched me. It was sweet. It was sexy: how she gave herself over to things; how completely she believed. After a second or two, her lips stopped moving but she went on gazing up at Jesus eagerly, nodding slightly—*as if He were actually answering back,* I thought. And then . . .

Well then, to be honest, any of our well-wishing neighbors in the market for an exalted expression of thanksgiving would've gotten their money's worth and more. As I sat there watching her, Marie's face grew bright. Brighter and brighter. Her chest rose and fell rapidly as her breath quickened. She smiled a secret smile. It was like a pang in me: how adorable she was. By the time the recessional began, she looked as transcendent as a shepherd on a Christmas card. She practically floated to her feet as the choir filed out. Her gaze remained locked on the crucified Christ. Her bright eyes glistened through a film of dew. Her hands were still clasped together, held at her waist, but they were placid now, each resting in the other at perfect peace. Her breath grew slow again. I heard her heave a deep sigh of contentment.

Well, I thought, *I guess there's no getting out of coffee hour now.*

It turned out I was wrong on that point though. And maybe I should've been more careful what I wished for. As we stepped into the aisle to follow the choir to the door, Hal Michaels, the Sexton, edged through the crowd to me.

"There was a call at the office for you," he murmured. "It's your clinic. They want you there right away. It's an emergency."

THE MINUTE I PULLED INTO the Manor parking lot, I felt my gut clench. There was Chief Hunnicut's SUV parked in front of the administration building. Just slung there at the base of the stone steps with another cop car right beside it. I jerked my minivan into the nearest slot. Was hurrying toward the building when April West, a social worker, came out through the front doors to intercept me.

We met on the stairs. "They're at Cade House," she called down to me. "Mr. Oakem took them over. Dr. Hirschfield said I should tell you to hurry. I don't know what it's about."

Well, I knew what it was about. I was pretty sure I did anyway. And by the time I got to Cade I was so pissed off I wouldn't stop for anyone. I charged past the lounge. I caught a glimpse of the kids in there, the inpatients. Nora, Brad, Shane and the others huddled sullenly under a cloud of cigarette smoke. Up ahead, by the entrance to the residence hallway, was Jane Hirschfeld. Pacing back and forth, her bony body electric with repressed fury. And beyond her, just within the hall, was Oakem, the Wizard of Odd himself. Looking more like a rooster than ever. Striking a defiant pose and stroking his goatee.

Hirschfield broke off pacing, came forward to meet me. "Cal, this is absolutely outrageous . . ."

But I just touched her shoulder and steamed right by her. Then Oakem was in front of me, almost blocking my way. Over his head I could see Peter Blue's door. There was a uniformed police officer standing guard beside it. When I saw that, the anger bubbled up into my throat, nearly choking me.

"You were in church and couldn't be reached," Oakem was saying in his high voice. "The chief got in touch with me and I . . ."

"What the hell's wrong with you?" I said. If he hadn't swung out of my way I would've walked right over him. I stormed down the hall.

I reached the cop. He was a sandy-haired boy in his early twenties. He raised his hand to stop me.

"I'm sorry, sir . . ." he began in his best official monotone.

"It's all right, son," I said gently—and so took him by surprise that I was able to brush past him and open Peter's door.

The scene within the room was quietly horrible. Chief Hunnicut standing, looming, glowering there in his immensity. Peter Blue sunk deep into his desk chair, cringing, hunched and lantern-eyed.

There was barely room for me. The place was just a cubicle. A mirrored dresser to my left. To my right, the desk nestled under a loft bed. The second I crossed the threshold, Hunnicut was pressed close to me, towering over me, glaring down. I could smell him, the dark, soapy smell. And Peter—Peter with his hands hanging between his legs and his head hanging—his knee was brushing my pants leg. I could feel him trembling.

The door was still open. The young cop and Hirschfeld and Oakem—they were all watching. I knew it and the chief knew it too. He seemed to grow even more solid, more immovable as he stood there over me. If I hadn't been nearly crazy with rage I don't know where I'd have found the courage to confront him.

"You have no right to come in here like this," I said hoarsely.

Hunnicut colored. He growled, "Well, pardon me, sir, but that's pure bullshit. I'm conducting an official police investiga . . ."

"Then you have no moral right. This man is my patient."

"I respected that." He shifted around. The barrel of his belly swung within inches of my chest. "You didn't give me his name and I didn't ask any questions. But my independent inquiries have revealed that he was a close associate of this Lester Marshall you mentioned . . ."

"So you waited till you knew I'd be out of touch and barged in here . . ."

"It's your own damned daughter who was nearly run over!" he shouted. Even in my anger I jumped. The chief worked his neckless head back and forth like a bull about to charge. "Now this Marshall character—this man you think might have been responsible—isn't making himself easy to find . . ."

Peter Blue cried out suddenly, "I don't know where he is! I told you!"

It was awful, an awful sound. That cry of his: strained and weak and frightened. I knew he must've despised himself for it.

And Hunnicut despised him too. He shifted his hard little eyes toward the boy and sneered.

"There's the answer to your question," I said quietly through my teeth. "He doesn't know. Now get out of here, Chief. Leave him alone."

Well, Hunnicut didn't like that, not one bit. He reared up. He inflated. Even his jowls went red. For a moment I thought he would physically eject me from the room. And he could've done it too—easily. I was plenty worried he would. But, to my enormous relief, he decided to let it go. God knows why. Maybe he played out the political chess game in his head and figured my contacts were bigger than his contacts. Or maybe he realized he'd gotten what he came for: a fresh chance to bully and intimidate this boy who had not only transgressed against God and man, hastened the fall of America and civilization but also just stuck in his craw somehow. Anyway, I don't know what he was thinking. All I know is that his huge frame relaxed. He shook his head. Snorted. Muttered, "Minute the little prick pulled a gun on me, I shoulda shot him where he stood."

Then, barely waiting for me to jump aside, he ploughed out the door.

I HAVE TO ADMIT I felt a moment of primitive gratification at the big man's retreat. The look on the younger cop's face was gratifying all by itself. He was standing in the hall just staring, just astounded. His behemoth of a boss had been faced down by a pudgy little egghead! It was a long second before he could pull himself together enough to scurry after Hunnicut down the hall.

Our fearless director had already used his wizard-like powers to vanish without a trace. The slime. But Doctor Hirschfeld was still there. She stepped into the doorway, smiling.

"Well, I for one am sexually aroused," she said.

I laughed. "Go reassure the kids."

"Jawohl, mine president."

I shut the door. I turned to Peter Blue. My triumph went sour in me on the spot.

Oh shit, I thought, *I've lost him.* It sure did look that way. I'd worked so hard these last weeks to gain his trust. We'd come so far together, so close to understanding why he'd done what he'd done. And now there he was. Hunched forward in his misery, head hung, hands dangling, forearms on his knees. And when he raised his face to me, his cheeks were tearstained. His eyes were swimming, lost. The words from my own report came back to me: "Peter tends to form intense attachments to people and then reject them with equal intensity when he fears they've betrayed or abandoned him."

"You told?" he said. He swiped at the tears with one hand. "You told him about Lester?"

I sighed. I settled down onto his desk. "Yes."

"You *promised* you wouldn't tell."

"I know. I fucked up."

"You fucked up!" he declared, pointing his finger at me. And then, hurt, he spread his hands. "How could you do that?"

"Someone attacked my daughter. She's three years old. Someone tried to run her down with a car. I thought it might be Marshall."

"Lester?"

"I was so afraid and angry, I was so desperate for him to get caught before he tried again, I gave Hunnicut the name. Just the name, that's all. I didn't mention you. It never occurred to me he would come barging in here like that. I'm sorry. I was too crazed; didn't think it through. I should've discussed it with you first."

He nodded—grimly, but it was something at least. A start maybe. If he was going to forgive me, if he was going to trust me again, it was going to take some time. Right now, I was glad to see the bulk of his anger was focused on Hunnicut. "I *told* that bastard I didn't know where Lester was!" he said, as much to himself as me. "I kept telling him!" He shook his head at the floor. "He talks to me like I'm dirt. He makes me feel like I'm dirt."

"That's what he means to do," I said.

He sniffled, stifling his running nose with the heel of his palm. "Why does he hate me so much?"

"Oh, it's not just you. The guy's angry at everything. His wife died recently. He needs something solid to hold onto. The church, his authority, I don't know. You attacked those things and he wants to see you pay."

"I'm not going to prison. That's for damn sure. I know what they do to you in prison. I'll kill myself, I swear it. You tell him that. I will. I will not go there. I know what they do."

It was a moment before I could answer. I managed to maintain a decent psychiatric deadpan but in all honesty I was hard pressed not to slap my forehead. How had I missed that one? How had I managed not to think of it sooner? He was terrified of prison because he was afraid of homosexual rape! Of course. The ultimate outrage to his masculinity. Every single thing Peter had done had been a misguided attempt to assert his manhood. He'd slugged his girlfriend trying to be a tough guy like Lester Marshall. He'd set fire to the church to stand up against the parental authority of Father Fairfax. Maybe it was an attack on his other father figure too—the God he'd invented to replace the father who'd run away. But the point is he was trying to be a man. And then Chief Hunnicut showed up on the scene and delivered the ultimate punishment. The big cop had slapped Peter "like a woman" and taken his gun away. And as if that weren't bad enough, he'd thrown him in jail. In danger, as he thought, of rape. So of course he had tried to hang himself. A last panicky attempt to salvage his gonads. Christ, it was Psychology 101.

The understanding set off a cascade of ideas in me but I had no time to deal with them then. I made sure to keep my voice neutral. "Look, obviously I can't promise you anything," I said. "But I can tell you right now I'm going to make every effort with the judge to keep you out of jail. Hunnicut's not the only power in town. My word's as good in court as his. Better, if it comes to that. So don't let him come stomping in here and terrify you."

"Well, he does terrify me."

"Well, he terrifies me too but you know what I mean."

That got a small smile out of him. His tears had stopped falling now. He sat up, plopping back in his chair.

"I'm sorry Lester attacked your daughter," he said after a moment. "Was it because of me?"

"I don't know. I'm not even sure it was really him. To tell you the truth, at this point, the thing that worries me most is that he might try to come in here and hurt you. The way Hunnicut screwed this up the word might get out, he might think you ratted him out."

Peter slowly shook his head, frowning past me at the opposite wall. "I don't care what Lester does anymore. It doesn't matter."

"Yeah, well, all the same, I don't want to live with the guilt, thanks. I'm gonna put an extra aide up here to watch your back until Hunnicut finds this bastard and hauls him in."

He didn't seem to hear me. He went on frowning at the wall.

I pushed away from the desk. "Listen," I said, "I'm sorry this happened. I am. But don't panic, okay? It's going to be all right."

"Okay," he said dully.

"We'll talk some more tomorrow."

Peter nodded slightly. "Okay."

But by tomorrow, he was gone.

THE REST OF THAT SUNDAY passed in a weird, abstracted sort of calm. My family and I stuck close to the house. The children played croquet in the grass. I raked the leaves. Marie worked in her small vegetable garden.

J. R. and Eva were on their best behavior. They didn't agree on much but they both loved Tot. They showered her with attention all afternoon, included her in everything. The three of them chased around among the wickets, whacking the balls, laughing, shouting.

As for Marie, that luminous, transcendent expression that had come over her face in church—it stayed with her through the day. She was singing as she knelt in the brown earth down by the forest. I could hear the *chuck* of her spade and her thin, high voice. Sometimes I would see her raise her face to the sky. Brush back her hair to show herself to the pale sun. She was singing the hymns we had sung in the morning. She was smiling as she sang.

And me, I was in a strange, edgy state. As I worked my piles of yellow leaves slowly to the treeline, I kept my ear cocked, waiting for the phone in the house to ring. I wanted to hear that Lester Marshall was in custody. And I was afraid to hear it too. I was worried. About everything. I was worried that Hunnicut was so angry at me he would let the matter slide. I was worried that Marshall might attack Peter if he wasn't caught. Or Tot again, or me. And I was worried about what would happen if he was caught. Would he say something—could he say anything—that might incriminate Marie?

But still, since the shock of the attack, since the concussion, my thoughts were not as clear as they'd been in the playground. All my worries seemed to sort of float together into a general haze of dread. I just wished the damn phone would ring so the suspense at least would be over.

In the evening, the kids played board games in Eva's room. I sat in the breezeway trying to read. Marie started work on dinner. I could hear her singing still.

The sun went down into the forest drawing the light after it across the lawn. Crickets began chirping in the twilight. It was getting cold. The breezeway walls were mostly glass, panel after panel of sliding windows. One of the windows was open but I was too lazy to get up and close it. I had a suspense novel open on my lap. I stared down at it. But my mind kept going back to Lester Marshall.

I had only had that one clear look at him. That's all. Out at the quarry. Curling around the rock. Giving me the baleful stare. His sinewy body in his black T-shirt. His lined, narrow face, tanned like leather. His slicked-back jet-black hair. I remembered the way he lifted that cigarette to his lips—like some villain on TV, with that kind of slow, studied, aggressive malevolence. The smoke curling up around his eyes. For a moment I felt his presence so powerfully I scanned the room to make sure I was alone.

After a while, I heard Marie's singing grow louder, then she came in. She was carrying a tray: a teapot and teacup, a bowl of apple slices.

"Dinner'll be a while. I thought you might like something."

"That's nice of you."

I watched her as she set the tray down on the table by my chair. I watched her face in profile. Tranquility like a halo round her. Those bright, bright eyes. Again I felt the sweetness of her spasm through me like pain.

She straightened and smiled down at me. She had changed from her gardening clothes into a skirt and a pink blouse. She looked fresh and pretty. Her expression was so serene it almost made me feel my anxiety was foolish.

"Aren't you cold in here, sweetheart?" she said. "God, it's freezing. Oh, well, no wonder. You have the window open, silly."

She went to the open window, slid it shut.

"It is getting to be fall now, you know," she said. "You have to close these at night. I bet you were just too lazy." She locked the window. Brushed the stray hair from her eyes. Stood with her back to me, watching the twilight in the trees. "It's even starting to look like it might rain tonight."

"I wish Hunnicut would hurry up and catch this guy," I blurted out. "I feel nervous sending Tot to school tomorrow."

She faced me. She was smiling now as if I'd said something cute and foolish. "Oh no, sweetheart. Tot is going to be absolutely fine at school tomorrow. Everything's going to be fine." She came back across the breezeway to me. "Really, Cal. I mean it. I don't want you to worry anymore. You've been so worried lately about everything. Thinking I was off in the woods with that man who cursed at you—and now thinking he's the one who attacked Tot."

"What do you mean?" I said surprised. "You think I'm wrong?"

"I'm just saying you've been worried and upset."

"Well, I mean, something's not right, Marie. I mean, it's pretty obvious something's not right."

She was standing over me. She touched the hair on my temple. Her hand smelled of apples. "Do you remember when we bought the Volvo?" she said.

"The Volvo? Yeah. Sure. Two years ago."

"And you scraped the side of it on the garage."

"Yeah, like the second day. So?"

"And then right after that you ran over that thing, that crosswalk sign and dragged it up State Street. Remember? The whole steering got funny."

I didn't say anything. I did remember. I was beginning to remember.

"And you told me—I don't remember what word you

used. It was some kind of scientific word. But you told me you were getting into accidents because we bought the car on the anniversary of the day Mina killed herself."

"Jesus," I whispered.

"Remember you told me that? You said you felt guilty about Mina and you were trying to break the car without knowing it. You explained the whole thing to me."

"Jesus, is it today?"

"And then remember last year when you kept dropping things? You broke my nice serving dish."

"I forgot all about it. It is today, isn't it."

"That was right around this time of year too."

"Jesus Christ," I whispered again. "Jesus Christ."

She kept stroking my hair with her fingers. "Whatever happened at the school yesterday I'm sure Chief Hunnicut will find out all about it. Okay? So don't be upset anymore. Mina wouldn't want you to be upset."

"But . . ." So many things ran through my mind at once I felt them more than thought them. The couple in the woods—was it not Marie and Marshall? The man who'd accosted me—was he just some random nut? Could the car in the playground have been just an accident—some kid driving too fast? "I mean, what do you think?" I said. "Do you think I . . . ?" My voice trailed away.

"Mina loved you so much, Cal," Marie said, stroking my hair. "She loved you so much. She would want you to be happy. And I want you to be happy so much. I love you so much and you've made me so happy, me and the children." She leaned down and kissed me. A whisper of a kiss, warm lips soft on mine then gone. "Don't worry so much anymore. We all love you, every one of us. Everything is going to be absolutely fine."

When she left, I sat alone in a pool of lamplight. The dusk outside deepened into dark.

FIVE-FORTY A.M. AND THE phone rang. I sat up in bed out of a half sleep and thought at once *They've got him.* But when I fumbled the handset to my ear I heard not Chief Hunnicut but the voice of Barbara Crouch, the Manor's night supervisor.

"I thought you should know right away," she said. "Your Cooper Bed's eloped."

"Peter? Peter Blue?"

"Yeah, that's the one. He's escaped."

THIRTEEN

I WAS PACING BY MY OFFICE window when the others

arrived. Gould and Hirschfeld and the Cade House social

worker, Karen Chu.

"We've gotta notify the police," said Gould as soon as the

door was shut. "I mean, the kid's here on some kind of

court arrangement, isn't he?"

"We can't set that animal Hunnicut on him," Hirschfeld

said. "Christ, he'll go after him with dogs and rifles."

"And I'm concerned about what'll happen to Peter if they

put him back in jail," said Karen. She was a blocky little

Asian woman, her black hair chopped short at the jawline. Very earnest; compassionate but humorless. "He's expressed a lot of anxiety about that to me."

"Yeah, that's putting it mildly," I said. "He's sworn to kill himself in jail. And if Hunnicut even finds out about this, he'll go straight to the judge, demand to have Peter taken out of here and locked up."

"It's not like we have a choice here, Cal. I mean, God forbid he should do something, hurt someone . . ." said Gould.

"Oh, he's not going to hurt anyone," Hirschfeld said. "He'll probably just come wandering back after a couple of hours."

"Maybe . . ."

I turned away from them, gazed out the window. It had rained overnight. The sky was still cloudy. The sun had risen but the darkness over the trees and rooftops was only slowly giving way. I sighed heavily, peering into it. My fault, I thought. My goddamn fault. And if anyone found out about this Peter would go back to jail for sure. And die for sure.

I needed some kind of heroic idea here. One of those brainstorms where you snap your fingers and say, "I've got it!" Nothing; there was nothing.

"Damn it," I said. I turned back to them. "If we could find him . . . You know? I mean, if we could get to him fast, bring him back ourselves before anyone else found out . . ."

Hirschfeld lit up. "Well, we can do that. How many places could he be?"

"His mother's, his girlfriend's . . ." Karen said. "It's worth calling, at least . . ."

"Whoa, whoa, whoa." Gould raised both hands. "Far be it from me to play the voice of reason here. But are you guys out of your fucking minds? This kid committed arson. On a church! And assault and stuff. He's here by arrangement with the court. I mean, I'm no lawyer but isn't he, like, a fugitive now?"

"Oh for Christ's sake," said Hirschfeld.

"No, I mean it," Gould said. "I mean, you guys are talking about a cover-up. We hide this from the cops— forget about any legal trouble we get into—what about the public? You know this town. The people with money anyway. To them, this is a girl-beating church-burning cop-killer roaming their streets. They find out we covered for him, we'll never raise another fund as long as we live. Not to mention the fact that Cal'll be fired and we'll have to live under the rule of Commander Stupid. Not to mention the fact we'll all probably be in jail anyway."

He stopped, his hands crossed on his chest. He looked at me. Karen Chu looked at me. So did Jane Hirschfeld.

"What do we do, Cal?" Jane said.

They waited for my answer. I glanced at each in turn, then each again, and they all kept looking at me. The truth was I already knew Gould was right. I couldn't risk the entire clinic for one boy. We had to call the police.

I was about to say as much when it came to me. Just like that. Not exactly heroic maybe but a nice little empathic leap. All of a sudden, I just realized where Peter was.

I didn't snap my fingers but I came pretty damn close. I said, "Stay here. Let me see if I can get him back before the roof falls in."

———

WELL, I FIGURED IT WAS worth a chance. One chance. If Peter was where I thought he was, I would bring him back and we'd concoct some story to cover his absence. If not, I'd call the cops—what else could I do?

I left the others to hold the fort and headed into the woods.

Peter had dreamed about the spot overlooking the waterfall. When I'd asked him if he'd ever been there, he said no. I let it pass at the time. My mind was on other things. But it was ridiculous. Of course he'd been there. And if he was willing to lie about it, it must've been important to him, precious to him, something he wanted to protect. I was pretty sure I understood why that was. In fact as I tramped along breathlessly beneath the trees, as I remembered my last conversation with the boy, I began to understand more and more about him altogether and how he had ended up at the Manor.

I trudged along the edge of the gorge, the damp leaves swishing beneath my feet. In the heavy gloom of the dawn forest, the boulders and evergreens on the gorge wall loured black and menacing. Mist and shadows lay over the river below. Barely visible beneath them, the river whispered.

I was sick with anxiety now, more anxious with every step. Back in the office, when it suddenly occurred to me that Peter was out here, it felt like an inspiration. But as I got closer and closer to the lookout point, I began to suspect it was really just a wild guess. And if I was wrong, if I couldn't find Peter and bring him back, well, my chance to help him was pretty well finished. Maybe he was pretty well finished himself.

The way began to grow lighter. The sun was burning through a broken field of clouds. The sky through the birch leaves above me began to show gray with fissures of pale blue. I could hear early traffic now whisking along the nearby roads. Farther away, beyond the preserve, came the boom of a hunting rifle and then another; the deer season had opened. Below me, the river's whisper rose into the louder sough of the falls. I was nearing the end of the trail.

I arrived at the base of the rock formation. The mist was billowing out of the gorge here, shifting to and fro around my legs. Through it, I could make out the broad band of Silver Falls where it tumbled lusterless from its height. I started away in the opposite direction, off the trail into the underbrush.

It was dank and uncomfortable in there. The dripping branches made my hands wet, dampened my jacket. *Man, I run a full-service clinic if ever there was one*, I thought. On top of this, the suspense just grew worse and worse as I neared my goal. It was gnawing at me. I reached the rugged path to the overlook and started up.

By this time I'd given up hope. I felt sure I'd been wrong, that Peter was not here, that all was lost. I humped it up the steep path dutifully but I was already planning what I'd say to Hunnicut when I called him. I crested the rock, confronted the bushes and low trees that screened the clearing. Sure enough, Peter was nowhere in sight.

Still I pushed through the trees, through into the grove

that overlooked the falls. And there I pulled up short, amazed. So help me, at that very moment, a single beam of sunlight pierced through the clouds, through the branches, and pinned Peter Blue where he stood. It picked him from the drab surroundings and lit him golden. And what a sight. What a sight he was.

I stood thunderstruck and stared. I had never seen anyone in such a state, no sane person anyway. He was transported; ecstatic. Standing on the broad altar stone, standing completely taut, completely frozen. The wooden cross—that leafless hemlock branch perpendicular to the birch—was right behind him. His back was bent like a bow, his arms flung wide, his face flung upward to the sky. His eyes were open just a little, his lips just a little parted. He seemed less to breathe than to throb with a pulse that coursed through his whole body. I could almost hear him beating like a heart, like the forest's heart. That was the image that came to me. As if he had become himself the life and center of the place. *I can stand in the woods any time I want,* he'd told me the first time we met, *and God will flow into my veins all through me and He and I are totally connected.* Well, there it was. Sure enough, there it was. As I shook my wondering and relieved and dumbfounded head clear of that first sight of him, I found myself thinking of church, of the people in church yesterday, kneeling and standing and singing—even Marie with her fraught prayers. Man oh man, they just weren't in it with this kid, no way. This was the raw stuff, direct radio contact. For a second there, with the sun hitting him like that and all, I could almost—almost—have convinced myself that there was something more to it than what I knew and believed, that the eerie thrill he sent through me of connection and coincidence, that weird intuition that his secrets were linked to my secrets and his dreams had somehow mingled with my life was really but a faint whisper of this—this grander intercourse I was witnessing now, this full communion with the hidden sense of everything.

Then he came out of it. I could feel it in my own nerves, the tension releasing. The pulse beating inside him slowed, smoothed out, became steady breathing. His arms seemed to grow heavier and heavier and drop in incremental stages to his sides. His frame relaxed, came forward, slumped. His head hung, not sadly but wearily, the shaggy black hair falling over his brow. And the beam of sun—or so I remember it at least—broadened as the morning sky cleared and the light became more general around us.

I was almost directly in front of him—below him a little because he was up on the flat stone—but he showed no sign he saw me. And then all at once he said softly, "How did you know where I was?"

"I'm a great fucking psychiatrist, that's how," I burst out in my relief and irritation. "Who just saved your sorry ass from the chief of police, by the way. He would've hauled you in for this, y'know."

He nodded slowly, breathed out, breathed in. "I'm sorry. I'm sorry. I panicked. The way Hunnicut just came in like that. The way he spoke to me. I just felt—alone. I was scared. I didn't know who I could trust."

"You can trust me," I said.

He lowered his eyes to me. It was wonderful. All the

fear was gone. All the wit and sadness in them had been restored as if by magic. And he smiled—that beautiful, that thousand-watt smile.

"I know I can," he said. "And it's all right now."

It was a weight off me—I hadn't realized how great a weight until that moment he forgave me and it was gone. I nodded gratefully. "All right," I said.

"I had a nightmare, y'know," he told me quietly. It was his old way of talking, dreamy and distant, as if he were discussing someone else. "That's what set me off. I had a nightmare and I woke up in a sweat and I just got up and got dressed and started running. Can I tell you about it?"

With my emotions heightened as they were, the mention of another of his dreams sent a shiver through me. As if the first had really led me to some revelation and this next might lead me on to more. It was ridiculous. I brushed the feeling aside, brushed the muddy rainwater off my jacket sleeves. Moved farther into the clearing. "Sure," I said. "Why not? Go ahead."

He turned a mournful gaze on the sunlit trees. "I dreamed I was kneeling by a pool of water," he said. "And I was looking down at the reflection of my face? And I noticed something strange: my reflection started coming up toward me. It was still in the water but it seemed to be coming closer and closer to me as if it were rising in some way from the bottom of the pool up to the surface. It was scary. In the dream, I mean, I found it very frightening. But I couldn't stop watching it. My reflection just kept rising closer and closer. And then it started to change. It was terrible." He shivered where he stood. "I kept wanting to run away or turn away or close my eyes—just not see it, just do anything not to see it—but I couldn't. I just had to kneel there staring down into the pool. And my reflection kept rising up closer and closer to me and now—now I could see it was all—rotten. My face was all...rotten and decayed with pieces crumbling away and the skin all horrible and bloated and the eyes just...all cracked and glassy, staring back at me." He made a noise. Waved his hand before his face as if to dispel the image. He stood with his eyes closed a long, silent moment. Then he murmured, "I suppose you think it means something."

"Nah."

He burst out laughing. I was glad to see it. I laughed too.

After a while I gestured at the stone he was standing on. "This is where you and Jennifer used to come to make love, isn't it?"

He cocked his head at me affectionately. "You sure do figure things out, I have to hand it to you."

"Well, thank you," I said. "Thank you for handing it to me. Now let's get back to the Manor before the cops come and cart us both away."

I THINK IT WOULD BE fair to describe our return as triumphant. We had hardly stepped out of the woods when the doors of Cade House opened and its youngsters streamed down across the grass to welcome us. To welcome Peter anyway; they ignored me. But Gould came out right behind them and then Karen Chu and they approached me smiling. We three adults stood apart. Gould shook my hand.

"You're a great man," he said.

"Yes," said Karen earnestly. "Well done."

"If anyone asks, our story is he went for a walk in the dark and got lost."

"Will Hunnicut buy that?" Karen asked.

"To hell with him," I said, turning to her, "it's all his fault to begin with. Our job now is just to reassure Peter he'll be safe here and make sure he feels..."

"Look at this," Gould said softly. He touched my shoulder to get my attention. "Just—I mean, it's striking. Look."

They were on the grass a little below us, a little closer to the trees: the five young in-patients of Cade House and Peter. And it certainly was striking, the way they surrounded him. Nora and Angela, Brad and Austin and Shane. They were all milling round him, close, very close. Brushing up on every side of him, practically circling him, touching him, stroking him with their fingertips as if to assure themselves he was really there. They gazed at him, studied him with puppy dog eyes. They murmured to him and their murmurs came to us like a low chant: *Are you all right, we were so worried about you, is everything okay?* As for Peter... He was tall, remember, his sensitive face was visible above the little pack. We could see him smiling down at them, his beautiful smile, responding to their touches and their murmurings with gentle murmurs of his own.

I watched—all three of us watched. I couldn't help but think of Peter as he was in the grove, as he was when I'd come upon him not twenty minutes before. His body bow-taut in the beam of sunlight, flung back, arms open, all of him recklessly open to whatever song it was the wild woods sang to him. I alone had seen this, I alone. And yet I couldn't help but feel there was some connection between that ecstasy of his and this almost awestruck reception they were giving him. As if, I mean, they had been there too, had witnessed it too and this greeting was their form of celebration. It was—I don't know what to call it—eerie, I guess is still the word. Disturbing. Just the passion of their affection for him. I was disturbed by it.

I looked away, unnerved. "All right, I'm out of here," I muttered to no one in particular. "Some of us have work to do."

ANOTHER CHAIN OF THOUGHT—AND this one led me to the heart of things.

I had a session with Peter scheduled for four that afternoon. Sometime around 3:30 or so I was at my desk, at my computer, online. I was trying to distract myself with research on a paper I was doing about the misuse of anti-depressants. It didn't work. My mind began to wander. Some scintillating study or other was on the monitor but I'd lost the thread of it long ago. I sat with my arms crossed on my chest, gazing blankly into space.

I was thinking of Peter. That moment in the clearing again. The look on his face, the golden light. I couldn't get it out of my mind. And it reminded me after a while of the specifics of that first dream of his. The grove, the light, the owl. And so I thought these over again—not in the super-stitious, half-mystical way that had unnerved me in the forest—but in the good, analytical fashion that had led me to him in the forest in the first place.

Because I understood now that the owl represented Peter's father in part. But not just his father. He wasn't able to face his rage at his father for abandoning him so he had instead transformed the man into this all-loving God he went around communing with. The owl was that father-God too. And by extension, the father-owl-God represented Peter's virility—which had been confirmed in fine old non-mystical fashion by his forbearing girlfriend Jennifer. That nexus of meanings is what had clued me in to the signifi-cance of the altarstone. The owl appeared in that specific place in his dream because that's where he'd finally man-aged to lose his virginity—just as my sister had lost hers there . . .

And then the chain of thought came together very fast. Thinking of my sister brought my mind back to the con-versation I had had with Marie in the breezeway after the car nearly hit Tot. And then I was thinking of the car again—the Chevy—racing toward my daughter. And with a chill I thought of how just moments before it happened we had been sitting so happily on the playground bench together . . .

And then suddenly I thought: *blackmail.*

I remembered. I remembered what I'd been thinking about the moment before Tot had run away. Blackmail. I'd been thinking that maybe Lester Marshall was blackmailing my wife.

The minute the idea came back to me, I had a sick, sour feeling: I realized it would be easy to find out the truth. There was only one way Marie could've paid off a blackmailer without my knowing about it. Most of our money was in the hands of an accounting firm that had served my family literally for generations. Even I didn't really follow what all the various trusts and funds were doing. And to put it bluntly, Marie was nowhere near sophisticated enough to pillage any of them without word getting back to me through the firm. But there was one account, the household account, that was completely in her control. And what with one thing and another, it had accumulated more than sixty thousand dollars in it over the last several years.

I was already online. I just rolled my chair closer to the desk. Took hold of the computer mouse and clicked the bookmark for my bank. I tapped in my password and waited while a column of account numbers came up on the screen. Then I trailed the cursor down to the household account. I did it quickly, carelessly, without really thinking about it. But when the account was highlighted on-screen, I hesitated. I caught my breath. I was about to cross a line. I understood that. I wasn't sure whether it was worse to stop or to go on. To know or not to know.

I clicked on the account number. The transaction history appeared.

The money was gone.

Almost sixty-five thousand dollars had been paid out in cash over the last two months. I stared at the numbers. My mind raced to explain them away. It couldn't be done. It just couldn't. Lester Marshall had been coming to Marie in secret. He'd been blackmailing her, She'd been paying him off. It was all true.

I felt a cold sweat break out on my forehead. *The lies she told me!* I thought. *The lies!* It was she I'd seen in the woods all along. She and Marshall. And every time I'd asked her about it, she'd lied. Lied! She was lying still. Maybe she thought she was protecting me. Maybe when Marshall came at me in the forest, when he'd aimed his car at Tot, he'd been sending her a message: keep your mouth shut or else. Maybe she'd done what she thought she had to do to protect us all. But still. Still! To lie like that. So well! So sweetly! And the way she teased and kidded and caressed me into believing her. She used my devotion to get around my doubts. She made love to me to distract me. And last night—Christ! Last night she had used *psychology* on me! My simple, uneducated girl! She had outsmarted me! I guess there was a kind of heroism in it—I guess. I guess you could see it that way. But just then I could only sit there, ill and shaken, and think about how she'd lied.

And then, of course—then, inevitably, came the next question: what else had she lied about? All these years, I mean. Just what did Lester Marshall know about her, after all? What was he blackmailing her with? This thug, this ex-con punk, this foul-mouthed piece of garbage—what did he know about my wife that I didn't know? Why she couldn't sleep? Why she wandered through the house at night? Why she cried sometimes for no reason? Why she wouldn't speak about her past? Jesus Christ!

My hand was trembling when I raised it to wipe the sweat off my brow.

Then there was a quick knock at the door and Peter Blue came in.

"I SUP-POSE," HE SAID—DRAWING out the word ironically, "I sup-pose we have to talk about what happened. My great escape."

He was sitting upright in the paisley armchair, turned three-quarters to me. His tone was easy and droll enough. But the aura of peace that had surrounded him after his trip into the forest had faded wholly away. The fingers of his two hands twisted together nervously above his lap. And there was something frantic in his gray eyes; frantic, quick and watchful. I wasn't surprised by this at all. I'd been expecting it. He knew as well as I did: the hour of confession was coming, had come. His reflection—to borrow the imagery of his nightmare—was rising to the surface of the water.

I smiled at him gently. I made an encouraging gesture with my hand. *The lies she told me!* I cried out in my mind. I shut the cry off.

Peter, meanwhile, stalled for time. "Talk and talk," he said with a sigh. "You know, if I've got to analyze every experience I have there won't be any time to live them. Even if there is, it'd be too much trouble."

He waited to see if I'd laugh. I didn't. I fought down my nausea. *The lies!* I fought down that constant cry. I had to focus on him. It was the only way I could get through this. I forced myself to focus.

Peter glanced into a corner, fidgeting. Finally, he went

on. "I don't even really know what else to tell you. It was like I said. Chief Hunnicut bullied me and threatened to arrest me and I was angry at you for telling him about Lester and I had that nightmare and . . . I panicked. That's all." He sounded as if he were reciting it. "I went into the woods because that's where I feel closest to God. He comes to me there and I feel this . . . This spirit of perfect love comes into me and everything is—is perfect love. And I feel better. I'm not angry at anyone anymore." He gave a little shrug. "I know you don't understand that. I know you want me to say what it all *means*, right? But I already told you: from my point of view, it doesn't mean anything. Nothing means anything. It just is. It's perfect and beautiful."

"Reality is how God sings," I said.

"That's right. Yes. That's right."

"I understand," I said. The nausea had spread through me now, all through me so that I couldn't really call it nausea anymore at all. It was just a general sickness with things, a general sadness. I shifted uncomfortably, crossed my legs. Worked hard to keep my face impassive. "But it does seem to me that certain verses of the song of reality are being left out."

"Why?" said Peter quickly. "What do you mean?"

"Well, I mean, we can't just hear the parts of God's song we want to hear, can we? We have to listen to it all."

The frantic spark in his eyes flared up more frantic still. He sniffed, made a curt dismissive gesture.

"What did you think?" I said to him softly out of my own sorrow. "Did you think that if you closed your eyes and kept silent it would go away? Did you think that it would only become real when you saw it, when you named it? Is that what you ..." I had to swallow before I could get out the rest of it. "Is that what you thought?"

His nervous hand jerked to his temple as if yanked by a string. He pressed his fingers there, grimacing. "You know, I wish I hadn't done this, come here. It was stupid. I don't even believe in this whole business."

I watched him—not without feeling. Oh, I felt for him plenty but I could see too how inevitable this was. The truth would come out and he would face it. It had to be that way. For him. For both of us. I knew it would hurt. I knew as well as anyone. And just then I couldn't have even sworn that it was a good thing overall: to look into the face of so much pain. But it was unavoidable. In the end what else can you do? In the end there's only the truth or blindness, the truth or madness, the truth or death. It's not much of a choice, believe me.

Peter was quiet. And I kept quiet for a long time. Then I said, "Why did you really run away?"

"Because—I told you!—that bastard Hunnicut... You're the one who told him ..." He waved me off. "I'm tired of talking about this." He wouldn't look at me. He frowned into the rug. Silence again for a half a minute, a minute, more. Then he burst out, "I mean, it's not like I don't know what you're going to say. I mean, it's pretty obvious how your mind works at this point. That's what makes it so boring." I nodded. He gave a mirthless laugh. Went on in a sort of sing-song, "Chief Hunnicut makes me feel like a weakling, like a wimp and he keeps threatening to send me to jail and I'm afraid of being raped and then

I have this ridiculous dream where my reflection is all rotten and I panic and run away . . . Do you think I've never read a book? You're going to say I'm running away from my—my secret homosexual impulses or some sort of bullshit."

I couldn't help myself. I actually chuckled. "Oh come on, Peter."

"Well, isn't it? Isn't that what you're going to say?"

"That's what you *wish* I'd say."

"What do you mean?"

"Well, we're famous for it, aren't we—psychiatrists? For confusing psychology with history. Telling one girl she's fantasizing about her father when the guy is actually molesting her. Convincing the next girl she's been molested when she's actually just nuts. Is that what you're going for? You want me to sit here and bang my head against the Veil of Perception for fifty minutes? Well, sorry, friend. It's a real bad day for me to be doing that, okay? So why don't you just tell me what happened?"

He shook his head and went on shaking it, a little tremor of denial, his hands fidgeting and fluttering in his lap. The expression on his face never changed, never changed. He went on sitting there, erect and very still but for his shaking head, his fluttering hands. He went on looking at me and the frantic fire in his eyes burned slowly out until they were dark and hollow. And still he went on, looking at me, shaking his head, went on, went on.

Then his body quaked once and he sobbed.

And very gently I said, "Come on, Peter. Let's talk about what Lester Marshall did to you."

THE SON-OF-A-BITCH. THE LOW-LIFE, CONVICT son-of-a-bitch. He hadn't raped Peter, not exactly, not legally anyway. But morally it was rape enough for me. He'd smoked out the desperation of Peter's need for a mentor, a father figure, a guide into manhood, whatever you want to call it. He'd probably understood that desperation better than Peter had himself. And one night when they were at the quarry and had had too many beers, I guess it occurred to Marshall how amusing it would be to take advantage of the boy, to assert his power over him in the good old time-tested prison manner. So out in the forest beyond the rocks he explained to Peter about jailhouse rites of passage. And then he cajoled and bullied and threatened and taunted the younger man into performing an act of oral sex on him. I doubt there was much pleasure in it for Marshall. It was just part of his convict language of power and submission. It was hardly an act of desire for him at all. But of course for Peter it was a nuclear bomb. It laid waste the cities of his heart. Poor kid was just finding himself at nineteen years old, just forming a first relationship with a girl, just growing up really. And his worst fear was that he wasn't a real man, whatever that means. So what was casual nastiness to his ex-con buddy felt to him like the sky falling. His interior world was overrun with chaos. He couldn't be sure who he was. Had he wanted it to happen? Had he enjoyed it? Did he have some kind of feelings for Marshall? He began to start with fear at every shadow in his own mind. There was only one thing that reassured him: Jennifer, his sexual relationship with

Jennifer. And when she announced she was going to college, Peter Blue felt the last prop of his masculine self-image had been taken away.

Lester Marshall, of course, thought the whole business was hilarious. He had himself a good old time twisting the knife. Jennifer was leaving because Peter wasn't man enough to hold onto her, he said. Why hell, if he'd been any kind of a man at all he wouldn't have been so eager to drop to his knees out there in the woods, would he? Man-Bitch.

"The bastard," Peter said, spit flying from his lips. "The hateful bastard!"

The lies, I thought quietly. I watched him as he sobbed into his two hands. "You're going to be able to live with this, Peter," I told him after a few moments. "It's only an experience, it's not your identity. I think we'll be able to move beyond it without burning down any more churches."

He laughed once forlornly. But wiping his face with one hand he said, "I told you: I didn't set fire to the church. I set fire to the music."

"Right," I said. "The music. You did tell me that."

I glanced at the clock on the shelf behind him. His hour was up. And I was desperate to get away. But I waited while he found the Kleenex on the lamp stand, while he blew his nose.

"Just the songs, the hymns—they were so awful there on the page," he went on. "They were so beautiful when Annie—Mrs. Fairfax—when she sang them in the choir. When she sang them in the choir it was like spirit, pure spirit, flowing through her ..."

"Yes. I remember. You told me."

"I just wanted to let them out. That was the thought in my head. Let them ..." Haggard, he trailed off, staring into the middle distance. "Out of the notes, out of the paper. The dead page. I wanted ..." His hands rose absently to his chest, to the center of his chest. "... let them out ..." he murmured dreamily to himself. And, as he spoke, he drew his two hands apart in a peculiarly familiar motion. It took me a moment to identify it: It was as if he were stripping off a shirt or a jacket. Only it was his body, I think. I think he must've wanted to take his body off like that. To free himself, I mean, as he'd freed the music, from the dead page of his own flesh.

FOURTEEN

IT WAS NEARLY SEVEN BY THE time I got home. I knew

right away that something was wrong. As I turned the Volvo

into the driveway the headlights swept across the house and

I caught a quick glimpse of three worried faces pressed to

the picture window in the living room. Eva, J. R. and Tot

were kneeling on the sofa, looking out for me, looking anx-

ious, even afraid.

I had spent the fifteen-minute ride from the Manor re-

hearsing scenarios in my mind. Half a dozen ways I could

confront Marie about the money, half a dozen ways she

might respond. All of them stank, of course. All of them featured me struggling to maintain my famous deadpan while I somehow came to terms with her lies, my self-delusion. By the time the Volvo's tires crunched on the home gravel, I was so steeped in fantasy and dread that the sight of my frightened children brought me back to the real world with a jolt. I parked the car quickly and hurried up the front walk.

The kids were already at the door, already had the door open. They waited for me, big-eyed and quivery. As the eldest, Eva played spokesman, her voice unsteady.

"Mommy's sick," she said, "she's throwing up."

Then all three of them burst into tears.

I headed for the stairs. The crying children trailed after me.

"She wouldn't let us call you," Eva sobbed. "We wanted to. She said we couldn't. She yelled at us."

"She didn't yell at you, Eva," I said.

"She did, Dad," J. R. snuffled grimly.

"She yelled at you?" Well, that explained the waterworks. I couldn't recall Marie ever yelling at any of us.

"She said, 'For God's sake, not now!' And she didn't even make dinner, not even for Tot," said Eva.

"Jesus," I muttered.

"I told you you should call Dad," said J. R.

Tot wailed miserably, trying to clutch at my moving legs. I stopped, stooped, picked her up.

"It's okay," I said. "Gee, you guys, she probably just has the flu or something."

"She never gets sick," said Eva. "And she *never* yells."

"Well..." I said. I handed Tot to her. "Why don't you give your sister some cereal or something. I'll find out what's what. It'll be okay."

Three pairs of eyes followed me as I quickly climbed the stairs.

Marie lay curled atop the bedspread, fully dressed. The lights were off. I saw her only dimly, the shape of her and the dark of her slacks, the dark of her blouse against the white bed. I hurried to her, sat beside her, gently placed my hand on her brow. It was slick with sweat but there was no fever.

"Cal?" she murmured.

I could smell the sickness on her breath. The tang of vomit wafted from the bathroom.

"Keep your eyes shut," I said. "I'm going to turn the light on."

I switched on the bedside lamp.

Her face was gray, her skin seemed paper thin. Her hair was plastered damp to her temples. She lay motionless as I stroked her.

"Must've eaten something..." she managed to say. "Just let me sleep for half an hour, Cal... then I'll get up and make dinner. 'Kay?"

"Ssh. Never mind about dinner. What did you eat?"

"Shrimp. I had a shrimp salad for lunch."

"You have diarrhea?"

"Nuh." Her voice faded sleepily. "Just threw ... up ..."

"Was your vision blurry at all? You have any trouble swallowing? Any trouble breathing? Anything like that? Here, roll onto your back for me."

With a whispered whine, she rolled onto her back. I palpated her right side, her middle. "Any pain here?"

She shook her head at me weakly. "Don't be . . . a doctor, sweetheart. 'Kay? I just ate . . . bad shrimp. I feel better since I threw up, really. I just need to sleep . . . a little, that's . . ."

Her voice dimmed to nothing. Another moment and her lips parted, her breathing steadied. She was asleep, just like that. I sat above her, still stroking her hair, still watching her face. She seemed very fragile just then. And I ached for her. It occurred to me for the first time how alone she must've felt in all these lies of hers. Like Peter Blue talking to me that afternoon—like me writing this now to you—only confession could set her free.

After a while, I remembered the children. I got up and went to the closet. Fetched down an old knitted quilt she'd made. Covered her where she lay. I switched off the bedside lamp again and left her in the dark to sleep. I went downstairs.

I told the kids their mother would be all right—and that was it for them, the crisis was over. Oh, they had to eat my scrambled eggs for dinner and throw away their own paper plates and even clean off the table themselves but by God they soldiered through it as bravely as Londoners singing pub songs in the underground during the Blitz. Eva seized the chance to play the bossy Mom and J. R. teased her for it more or less affectionately. And Tot sent them both into hysterics with her scholarly dissertation on the art of throwing up. Bit by bit, the excitement of the evening drained away and they were left exhausted.

Tot went to sleep right after dinner but it was ten by the time the older two could be persuaded. Then, finally worn out, they dragged themselves to bed as well.

So I was sitting alone when the phone call came.

THE AWFUL END OF THAT awful, awful day. I was sitting in my armchair with the room mostly dark. One light on in the dining room somewhere, everything else in shadow. I stared at the floor. My hand worked nervously over my mouth and chin. My mind went from one thing to another. The money. Blackmail. Marie. The children. I thought about the children. How they'd been giggling at dinner. How they'd been laughing in the grass among the croquet wickets. "All souped-up and energized on love and kisses." *My God*, I thought suddenly, *how wonderful she's made them!* And not just them. Me too. How wonderful she had made me too. What a useless, self-satisfied, niggling intellect I would've been without her. She was the life in me. She was my life. *I want to be perfect for you, Cal. That's the whole point of everything I do.* And, I mean, why? Why had she wanted that? Why for me? *Just drink her goddamn coffee*, Mina said, *and shut the fuck up.*

Which is when the phone rang and shattered my thoughts like glass.

I thought to look at my watch. Ten forty-five. What now? It was unlikely to be good news at that hour. The phone was on a table by me. I picked it up.

"Chief Hunnicut, Doc. Hope I'm not calling too late."

For a second, I felt a little twist of fear. Had he found

out about Peter's escape? But no, he sounded friendly, happy. As if our confrontation at the Manor had never happened. And I realized: it was Marshall. He must've found Lester Marshall. My mind raced. I didn't know whether to be relieved or terrified. "No, no," I stuttered, "Not at all, I'm awake. What's up?"

"Thought your wife and your family might sleep a little better knowing our friend Mr. Marshall won't be bothering you again."

I could hardly get the words out. "You found him?"

"Well, fact is a lady hiker found him. Out in Silver River Preserve. You know that swimming hole right under the waterfall?"

"Yes," I said. "Yes, I know it."

"Well, she was standing there looking into the water and old Lester just came bobbing right up to the surface."

"Bobbing . . ." For a second, I saw the scene: the hiker kneeling by the waterside, gazing at her reflection, her reflection seeming to rise to the surface until, to her horror, it transformed into the bloated, rotting face . . . *Peter's dream. The images in Peter's dream.* But it was a mad thought. I forced it violently from my mind.

"Scared the shit out of her," Hunnicut laughed. "Pardon my French."

"Wait. Wait. Are you telling me Marshall is dead?"

"Hell yes, he's dead, he's goddamn dead!" said Hunnicut with another laugh. "Somebody deposited a bullet in the center of his forehead. That's gonna kill you all right."

He went on chuckling. I couldn't take it in. "You mean someone shot him? Someone—shot him?"

"That's the story," said the chief. "Seems like our boy Lester just went out and got himself good and murdered."

PART

FOUR

FIFTEEN

MARIE WAS ALREADY FIXING BREAKFAST BY the time I

came downstairs the next morning. The children were al-

ready orbiting around her.

"There you are," she said with a laugh. "You fell asleep in

your clothes last night."

"Yeah, I did," I said. "Are you all right? Are you feeling

better?"

She was still a little pale but there was no other trace of

the sickness in her. Not that I could see from where I was

anyway. I was standing in the dining room a few feet

from the kitchen threshold. She was at the counter in there, reaching for some cereal in the cupboard. Tot was tugging at her slacks. Eva was buzzing back and forth around her, opening and closing cupboard doors for no reason I could make out. J. R. had just wandered back inside with the *Times* and was taking it to pieces in search of the sports section.

"Can I have Corn Chex? Can I have Corn Chex? Can I have Corn Chex?" Tot said.

"Yes, darling, ssh," said Marie. "I'm talking to Daddy. I'm fine," she went on to me. "It really was nothing. It was that Morelli's. I'll never have lunch there again, that's for sure. I'm sorry I worried everyone. But you all seemed to do fine without me."

She smiled at me. Maybe in her eyes, I thought. Maybe there was still a hint of sickness in her eyes. I couldn't be sure.

I stood where I was, fully dressed, in jacket and tie. Holding my day-pack down by my side. I watched her smile and tried to smile back.

After shooting Lester Marshall between the eyes, Hunnicut said, the murderer filled Marshall's pockets with rocks. Marshall had been lying there with a large section of the back of his head blown off by the bullet's exit. Hunnicut had gone into great detail about that. He'd relished that. Marshall's brains were still seeping into the dirt while the killer filled his pockets. Then the killer dragged the body a foot or two to the pool at the base of the falls. Dumped it into the water. The corpse sank down to the bottom where it lay a pale, wavery phantom, never quite invisible. The hiker had been peering down to see what it was when the bloat of decay brought it up to the surface.

"Sit down, sweetheart, and I'll bring you your coffee," Marie said.

It was a moment before I heard her, then I shook my head. "I have an early meeting this morning. I'm already late. I have to go."

I began to move to the door.

"Well, gee," she said. "Not even a kiss good-bye?"

I came back. She was at the kitchen doorway, waiting for me. I was very near her now. There was no question: her eyes were quick and hectic.

I kissed her good-bye.

THE POLICE WERE OUT ON the road. Out by the public entrance to the Silver River Gorge Preserve. Hunnicut was there, towering over a couple of patrolmen and another man in plainclothes, a detective I guess. The detective and the chief were drinking styros of coffee, talking, laughing. The patrolmen were nodding and laughing too.

Just beyond them, the chief's SUV, a couple of squad cars and a couple of ratty sedans with official markings on the doors were lined up at the edge of the forest. Hulks against the dull-colored trees in that light, the beginning of a drab, colorless day.

One of the patrolmen saw me coming, stepped away from the others to wave me by. I had to ask myself: Would it seem suspicious if I pulled over to chat? Or more suspicious simply to drive on? Undecided, I passed the waving cop. But then, on impulse, I stopped and parked the Volvo at the end of the line of cars. I got out and walked back to the investigators.

"Well, Doc, you're out early," said the chief.

"So are you," I said in what I hoped seemed a natural tone. "This about Lester Marshall?"

I was surprised by the way he looked. Fresh and full of energy. The big body straight and easy. That fleshy rock of a face all wreathed in smiles. He seemed almost a new man. As if some burden had been taken off him, some pressure released. And if he held any grudge against me for our run-in at the clinic he sure didn't show it. He shook my hand. Made a jovial gesture at the forest with his styro. "Yeah, we been out here a while. Had to get our fellas on top of the crime scene down there before it gets tromped on by every-damned-body and his uncle."

I glanced into the woods. A faint morning mist hung in there over the dead leaves, among the trunks of the trees. "Come up with anything?" I asked.

"Not a whole hell of a lot so far. Bunch of slugs that went wild. Our shooter wasn't exactly dead-eyed Dick. God-damn bullets were flying all over the fucking place, it looks like. We're picking them out of the trees, out of the ground. Must've been a regular fireworks display. Pure luck our fellow caught one where he did."

I tried to give an amiable laugh. It sounded more as if I were strangling. "You have an interesting job," I said.

"We got our work cut out for us, that's for damn sure. Establishing time of death for one thing. Sometime yesterday morning it looks like but the water damage'll make it tough as hell to pin it down. And with all the hunters banging away in the woods it's gonna be hard to find anyone who heard these particular gunshots too, if you see what I mean." He went on, downright expansive. "Then, of course, the biggest problem we've got is figuring out exactly who our victim is. I doubt Lester Marshall was his real name. All his ID's phony anyway. Haven't even figured out where the little fucker lived yet so . . ." He shrugged. "We'll get his prints out to the feds this morning. Pretty good bet we'll have an ident by afternoon."

Later on, of course—later on, I would think back to the way Hunnicut acted that morning. The new energy. The friendly smiles. Later on, it was all clear to me what they meant. But at the moment I couldn't see it. I was too eager to end this, to get away.

And then another car, a Volkswagen, pulled up. Cassie Webber, the girl from the local radio station, unfolded herself from the front seat. Fishing her small recorder from her great cloth sack of a purse.

"And here comes the goddamned press," Hunnicut muttered into his coffee.

"Well," I said, "I'll let you get back to work."

"See you later, Doc."

"See you."

I could hear Cassie calling to the chief behind me as I went back to my car. I tried not to walk too quickly, not to seem as if I were running away. As I pulled open the Volvo's door, I even managed to glance casually up at the sky for a moment.

It was going to be a gray and heavy day, it looked like. The air felt chilly and full of rain.

AS SOON AS I REACHED the Manor, I went to see Peter. I wanted to be the one to tell him but it turned out he had already heard the news. The local paper had run the story of the body being found. The radio had carried the identification from an unnamed police source. When Peter understood what had happened, he left Cade House and went for a walk. I found him by the edge of the woods. Sitting on the bench there, gazing into the mist among the trees. I stood beside him.

"I'm glad," he said. "I'm glad he's dead."

"Well, that's understandable."

"Is it? Is it? To you maybe. Not to me." He frowned at the forest. "I mean, is this what you want me to be like? Hateful like this? I'm all just . . . just anger now. Just hate and anger. It's like . . . like some kind of tar—hot tar—bubbling inside me. Everything . . ." He brought both hands to his forehead, pressed his palms to his brow as if to hold his thoughts together. "My whole life. It's all just about this . . . this rage, isn't it? Against Lester. Against my father for leaving me. Against my mother for being a drunk. Just rage and hatred over everything. Ah!" With the exclamation, he tore his hands away. Crossed his arms over himself. "And now I can't feel God anymore. I can't feel God. Just this rage. Is that all He was too? Was he just this rage? Was everything just this rage?" Now finally he looked up at me. "Why did you do this to me?"

"The rage was always there, Peter. I just helped you to face it."

"And that's good?"

"Yes. It's better to know than not to know."

"*Why?*"

"Because then you can deal with it. Learn to live with it."

Still holding himself, he shivered. Shook his head. Turned away from me to the woods again. "Live with this? I don't want to live with this. To feel glad—happy—when a man is murdered. To feel this—rage—this terrible rage against my own parents. My father...I don't...I don't want this. I never wanted this. You think it's so good that I feel this? I would give—*anything*—everything—to feel God again instead, that perfect love again. Even just for a second. I would, I mean it. I mean...That's all I felt before. That's all. And now I don't feel any love, I don't feel any love for anything except..." This time, when he turned his face to me, I was the one who shivered. At the hollowness of his stare, the depths of his hurt and anger. In a tone almost of wonder, he said, "Except for you." A short laugh fell out of him. "What do you think of that? I feel love for you. And you're the one who did this to me."

I put my hand on his shoulder. He reached up and gripped my hand with his.

"It takes courage to face the truth, Peter," I told him. "Most of us never do."

We stayed like that awhile, our hands together. Then I left him there and went off to dispose of the murder weapon.

SIXTEEN

SHE HAD USED THE *AIRLITE*, of course. When I'd gone

upstairs to check it the night before, all eight of its bullets

were gone. She must've fired at Marshall again and again.

In panic maybe or desperation or maybe in a fury as all the

years of fear and falsehood exploded in her. She had no

more money to give him. He was threatening her children,

threatening me. So she fired and fired wildly. *Bullets were*

flying all over the place, Chief Hunnicut had said. *We're*

picking them out of the trees, out of the ground . . . I guess

my recoil had been a little too powerful for the wife.

I never doubted for a second that it was she who'd done it. The minute Hunnicut told me Marshall had been murdered, I was sure. It was like the shadow that trails behind you in the morning: you don't see it at all and then, at noon, it simply becomes part of you. Suddenly I just knew Marie had shot Lester Marshall; I knew it as if I had always known.

And I knew in the same way that I had to get rid of the gun. I never even thought about it, I just knew. After leaving Peter, I stopped off at the Manor and had a cup of coffee with my breakfast group. Then I told them I was going to drive over to Whitefield for a morning hike. It was a good alibi. I did that from time to time for exercise when I couldn't walk to work.

But I didn't drive to Whitefield. I went north along a winding two-lane highway. Up into the countryside. Past antique barns and quaint clapboard B and B's. Past speed-trap towns and rolling hills of hardwood forests, yellow and red and green. The day grew brighter over time but not by much. The sky remained leaden.

After about an hour, I reached South Salem and turned off onto a road I knew. There was a walking trail at the end of it, an old fire path. I'd taken the kids there once or twice for easy hikes. I parked and started down the broad dirt road carrying my day-pack.

A quarter of a mile in, the scraggly wood by the trail-side became swamp. The frogs, cicadas and crickets were suddenly garrulous and loud. I stopped and glanced around to make sure no one was watching.

The pistol was still in its box—I'd set the lock at its

combination numbers to make it easy to open. I took the gun out and threw it quickly over the water as far as I could. I held my breath as it spun through the air. In the drab light its chrome looked flat and dull.

The gun fell with a splash. Several frightened birds burst fluttering out of the surrounding trees. Startled, I stiffened, my eyes wide, my heart beating hard. I had to take a few breaths to calm myself. Even then my hands were trembling.

Anyway, that was the gun. But the box was another matter. It came to me all at once that the box wouldn't sink. I had been awake most of the night making plans but I hadn't considered this. The box had the Smith & Wesson logo on the top of it and the inside was contoured to the shape of the pistol. I had to get rid of the box as well.

"Okay, okay," I whispered aloud, trying to think. I felt a line of sweat roll down my temple.

But I was lucky in the end. As I drove nervously back to the highway, I noticed a Dumpster in an alley behind a row of stores. I pulled up close to it, jumped out of the car and shoved the box deep into an open trash bag. Then, as I was driving off, I passed the garbage truck on its way to the alley. I took a detour, drove round the corner and came back in time to see the Dumpster emptied into the back of the truck. I watched as the compactor crushed its contents. I watched, thinking about how hard it was to destroy evidence of a murder. Or evidence of anything if it comes to that. Nothing just goes away. Nothing just vanishes. Whatever it is, it's always there somewhere. It can always come back to haunt you.

When the truck drove off, I drove off too. Along the winding road again. Past the antique barns and the quaint B and B's, the speedtrap towns and the rolling forest hills. I felt strong and calm as I drove, a suprisingly cool criminal. It was only now and then that I heard a strained, pinched noise coming from not far away—as if someone near to me were crying.

AT 2 P.M. I MANAGED TO catch the local news on the radio in my office. Chief Hunnicut and his crew had now identified the murder victim.

The man who had called himself Lester Marshall was in fact named Billy Frost. He had recently been released from state prison in Missouri where he had served twenty years for his role in the murder of an elderly couple, the Whalleys. Frost was among what the newscaster called "a gang of youths" who'd invaded the Whalleys' farmhouse all those years ago. They vandalized the place, killed the old man and raped the old lady before killing her too. Three of the gang were arrested at the time and two more were picked up later. Frost—aka Lester Marshall—made a deal with the prosecutors and testified against his co-defendants. As a result, they'd been imprisoned for life without the possibility of parole while he'd received a lighter sentence.

After I turned the radio off, I logged onto the Internet on my computer. I ran a search for the Whalley killings and for Billy Frost. I couldn't find anything. I logged off and sat in the chair behind my desk swiveling slightly back and forth. The library, I thought. I'd better go to the library.

My pen was lying on the table. I picked it up to put it in my pocket. But my hand was shaking so badly the pen just flipped out of my fingers. I bent down to pick it up off the floor. And as I did, I felt something happen inside me. It's a difficult sensation to describe. It felt as if my self, my soul, the thing I am yawned suddenly open. Suddenly, where my center had been, there was a pit, a chasm, bottomless and black. I felt as if I were peering into it, peering deep, deep, deep into life's most dismal and intimate secret: its emptiness, its nothingness. I gasped out loud, clutched my chest. Sat up fast, my chair cracking as it rocked back against itself. In a kind of panicked act of moral terror, I willed the chasm shut. And that was it. It was over. The whole thing was over in a second. The sort of vague emotional non-event you just dismiss, shake off, forget. But I knew it was still there—that pit, that blackness—I knew I had only covered it because I would go crazy if I had to look at it any more. I would go crazy with despair.

When I could breathe again, I worked my way to my feet. I had to go. I had to. The newscast had pointed me to the last piece of the puzzle: Just what had Lester Marshall—or Billy Frost or whoever he was—what had he been blackmailing my wife about? What was the secret she was paying him to keep?

I canceled all my afternoon meetings and drove over to the library.

WHEN ALL IS SAID AND done, you know, it's easy to find the truth. All you have to do is give up your opinions. That's it. Once you're sure you believe nothing, know nothing, understand nothing, the truth will smack into you like an express train. Only twenty minutes after I arrived at the library I had found out as much as I could bear to know.

The library carried the archives of the *New York Times* on microfilm. There had been a few articles on the Whalleys' murder at the time it happened, a few more when the killers went on trial. Some of these were substantial pieces appearing on the front page of the national section. But none of them had what I wanted.

About a week after the first convictions, however, there was a feature story in the Sunday magazine. It was an overview of the case, one of those Tranquil-Community Shattered-By-Violence things that city reporters love to write. This writer had augmented trial testimony with interviews and visits to the important scenes. There were vivid descriptions of the victims and the police manhunt and the area where the crime took place and so on. Mostly though the story was about the killers. That's the stuff I was after.

Altogether there had been about twenty of them, twenty young people give or take a few. They had lived in a rundown house on five acres of untended land secluded amidst the vast farming fields of north central Missouri. Sometimes they thought of themselves as a commune, sometimes they talked about establishing a new, purer way of life as an example to the corrupt capitalist society around them. Now and then they entertained grandiose notions of instigating some kind of social change. But in truth those heady days in America were already finished and, anyhow, these were no revolutionaries really, just a dissolute crew of petty crooks and runaways. They spent most of their time shoplifting and taking drugs and passing the latest female recruit from bed to bed.

Some witnesses said it was Billy Frost who held the whole thing together, that he was the charismatic leader of the clan. Frost himself claimed to be a hanger-on and fingered one of his friends—the guy who owned the house— as the motivating force. In any case, the police said, someone had led nine or ten of the group to the Whalleys' farmhouse one April evening. They were stoned on hallucinogens and in the grip of one of their occasional grand delusions about bringing on a better world. They struck their first blow against capitalist tyranny by painting graffiti on the Whalleys' walls and stealing about seventy-five dollars from a kitchen cookie jar. When the old lady cursed them for what they were, they started taunting her. Things quickly got out of hand and a couple of them raped her. A few of the gang ran off at that point. But the bolder ones conferred and decided the Whalleys had to be silenced. They then proceeded to beat the old couple to death with some lengths of plumbing pipe they'd discovered in the barn.

After the murders, the clan of wannabe-revolutionaries panicked and scattered. What made it so tough for the cops to track them down was the fact that few of them had ever used their own names even with each other. They'd all been assigned commune names like Sunrise and Vision and Daffodil and such. In the end, the police said they were satisfied they'd rounded up the core of the group but the rest of them just faded back into the obscure, rootless lives from which they'd apparently come.

There were photographs accompanying the article. There was one of Billy Frost being led into the courthouse in chains. Even after all this time I recognized him as Lester Marshall, as the man who'd slithered around the quarry stone, smoking his cigarette and giving me the evil eye. Then there was another shot, a larger one, a black-and-white snap of the group in front of their house. About ten or so teenagers and twenty-year-olds posing around a beaten-up Volkswagen bus in attitudes half languid and half swaggering—as if they weren't sure whether they wanted to portray themselves as sixties-style hippies or twenties-style gangsters *a la* Bonnie and Clyde. The photo, grainy to begin with, had been enlarged to the point that details and faces were difficult to make out. But my eyes went at once to a girl in the background. Dressed all in white with a halo of white flowers in her silky blond hair. Behind the bus and off to one side, she was sitting cross-legged on the unmown lawn of the front yard. A refugee waif from another era and so unfocused a figure she nearly blended in with the grain of the grass and sky. A ghost, a shadow; she was hardly there. No one else would've recognized her, I told myself. I shut off the viewer quickly. Rewound the microfilm quickly onto its spool.

No one else could have possibly recognized her but me.

SEVENTEEN

MARIE SERVED CHICKEN FOR DINNER THAT night. Roast chicken with rice and broccoli. Tot was already in bed so it was just the four of us, Marie and I at the foot and head of the dining table, Eva and J. R. on either side.

"I have a solo in the autumn concert," Eva told me as we began eating.

"Do you?" I said. I cleared my throat. "Hey, that's great."

"She's going to sing a song from that French musical," Marie said proudly.

"It's not a French musical, Mom! It's *Les Misérables.*"

"Well, isn't that French? It sounds French. I always thought it was."

"Sounds French to me," said J. R. in his mother's defense.

"It's a musical based on a French novel," Eva drawled. "It's not a French musical. The songs aren't in French. God!"

"Gawd!" J. R. mimicked her with a funny face. "Idiot."

"Stop, J. R., don't be mean," said Marie. "Well, I guess I meant the novel, that's all."

I stared at the three of them. *Dear Jesus*, I thought. *Dear Jesus.*

"What's the song's name again?" Marie asked.

" 'Castle in the Clouds'," said Eva. "It's very French."

"Oh, that's that pretty one I hear you singing all the time."

"I don't sing it all the time."

"You do. It's very pretty. You were singing it while you were setting the table. You probably didn't even know it."

"She's too stupid to know she's even singing," said J. R.

"All right, that's enough, J. R. I mean it or there'll be no dessert."

She looked a little pale, I thought. Or maybe I imagined it. It seemed to me the corners of her mouth were pulled down tensely. But the children didn't seem to notice anything so maybe I was wrong. Maybe she was just the way she always was. Or maybe the signs were always there, at every dinnertime, and I'd just never seen them before. Maybe every evening of my marriage had been exactly like this one and I simply never knew.

"Why don't you tell what happened to you today," Marie said to J. R. "Didn't you say you had an assembly?" Her voice sounded whispery and gentle as it always did. Just as it always did.

J. R. rolled his eyes. "Mr. Wilkins. It's the same thing over and over. Don't take drugs, don't take drugs. It's so lame."

"He gave that assembly, like, every week when I was there," said Eva.

"Well, it's important," said Marie. "You know what drugs do to people."

I chewed and chewed on a mouthful of chicken. I found it difficult to swallow any of it down. I had to force myself to stop staring, to stop staring at Marie's hands. Her slender hands. I had to force myself to stop imagining her finger pulling the trigger of the pistol again and again and again. I thought if I couldn't get away from this table I might lose control of myself and cry out. I might just sit back and start howling.

"It's not like I'm gonna take drugs, Mom," said J. R. lifting a glass of milk to his lips.

"It's just that Mr. Wilkins is such a weasel," said Eva.

Surprised, J. R. laughed suddenly, shooting milk out through his nose.

"Oh, Eva," said Marie. "Now look."

"Well, he is," laughed Eva. "I can't help it."

"He is, Mom," J. R. said, coughing. "He's a weasel."

"Never mind. Wipe your face, sweetheart. You've got milk all over it."

"It's my new look."

She lifted a napkin to mop his chin. Her eyes were glistening with some hidden emotion. I thought they were anyway. "Your new look," she said. "I swear. Where do you get these things?"

I stared at her. I stared at her hands. I had to force myself to stop, to look down at my food.

I pushed a stalk of broccoli around with my fork. *Dear Jesus*, I thought.

LATER, STANDING AT THE LIVING room window, I watched the houselights through the trees. The evening was finally coming to an end. I had played with J. R. Helped Eva with some homework. Taken out the trash. It was oppressive, suffocating. Now the children were getting ready for bed. I was waiting for them to come say good night. I was standing there with my hands in my pockets, staring out the window. There were two houses within view of us. I could see the lights of their windows through the woods. They looked warm and inviting to me. It was funny, strange. I longed to be in those houses instead of this one. And yet I knew the people who lived there. Amy Stillman had recently lost her husband to a younger woman in the city. She was fighting to get support payments out of him and raise her three kids and find enough catering work to hold onto her home. As for the Wintersons, it was a second marriage on both sides. They worked all the time, he on Wall Street, she in publishing. His son was in drug rehab in Wisconsin somewhere and her daughter was being treated as an outpatient at the Manor for an eating disorder.

I confess I had always harbored slight, secret feelings of superiority over these broken families. But the yellow lights of their houses—lighted windows with the shadows of branches laced over them—made me yearn to be among them. I imagined them sitting at the dinner table, happy with each other, talking about their day and laughing. I ached to be there instead of here.

The awful minutes passed, too fast, too slow. Waiting for my chance to be alone with Marie; dreading it more than anything ever. Eva came and kissed me, then J. R. came. I stood at the window and stared out, my hands in my pockets. At last, my wife appeared, standing behind me, reflected dimly on the glass, a half-figure full of night.

"I'm still a little tired from being sick," she said. "You mind if I go up early?"

"I'll be right there," I told her.

I watched her image move across the pane and out of sight. I gazed through the window at the homey yellow lights. Then slowly, heavily, I turned to follow her upstairs.

SHE WAS ALREADY IN HER nightgown when I came into the bedroom. A nightgown of pearly silk I'd always liked. She was just turning from the mirror as I shut the door. She smiled briefly, kindly at me and I saw—or thought I saw—some lost and desperate something in her expression that'd never been there before. Maybe I just hadn't noticed it until now.

"Do you want to make love?" she asked me.

"I got rid of the gun," I said.

A thought, a feeling, flickered over her face. "The gun? Your gun? Well . . . good. You know I hate that thing."

"I dumped it in that swamp off the walking trail in South Salem."

She gave a puzzled little laugh. "Well, that was dramatic. But I'm glad you got rid of it one way or another."

I couldn't help it. I stared at her again. Her head was tilted to one side. She seemed confused, waiting for me to go on, waiting for me to explain. Even now—even now— I could almost believe I was mistaken, that I had somehow gotten it all wrong. "Marie," I said. "For God's sake."

"What, Cal? What's the matter?"

"What's . . . ?" I managed to keep my voice low, a choked whisper. "I know. I'm trying to tell you: I know."

Her eyes narrowed. "Know . . . ? Cal, are you all right? What's wrong with you these days?"

I felt the room swimming around me. Her face, sweet, kind, inquiring, seemed the still center of a dizzying blur. "Damn it," I said. "Damn it. Don't do that. Stop doing that. I looked at the bank accounts. I saw your picture in the paper. In the story about the murders in Missouri. I *saw* it." And she still stood with her head cocked, with a smile of half confusion on her lips. And the room spun. And I stepped forward. "Marie." I took her by the shoulders. "Marie, for the love of God! You have to talk to me."

"Cal . . . ?"

"I know Marshall was blackmailing you—Billy Frost, whatever his name was. Marie, I know you ki . . ."

"Mo-om?"

The words turned to ashes in my mouth as the call

came up to us, soft, plaintive. It was Eva, downstairs. And there we stood, Marie and I, staring at each other, she with her lips parted, I with my hands gripping her shoulders. And I felt as if our daughter's call had awakened me in some other place, some helter-skelter country where familiar objects and colors and dimensions were suddenly bizarre, foreign, askew.

"Mo-om?" Eva called again.

Marie blinked once and swallowed. "Would you mind going, Cal?" she said softly. "I'm not dressed."

I stumbled out into the hall, wiping my mouth with an unsteady hand.

Eva was standing at the foot of the stairs. She was wearing her valentine pajamas. Gazing up at me, woebegone.

"What . . . what's the matter, sweetheart?" I asked her.

"I need Mom," she said.

"Mom's getting ready for bed. What's wrong?"

"I need my white blouse for choir tomorrow. I can't find it."

"Well, uh . . . did you look in your closet?"

"I looked everywhere. I can't find it. Mom must've forgot to wash it."

"Well . . ." I tried to wet my mouth, tried to force down the ashes of what I'd almost said to Marie. "Well, I'll tell Mom and I'm sure you'll have it in the morning." That was good, I thought, that sounded good. That almost sounded like me.

"But it's gotta be ironed and everything and I need it," Eva insisted.

"Okay, I'll tell her. You'll have it, sweetheart. I promise. Okay?"

"Okay."

"Go to bed now."

"Okay. Love you."

"I love you too."

I stood and watched as she padded off toward her room.

Marie was drawing back the covers of the bed when I returned. Her face was serious, thoughtful. She looked up as I closed the door behind me.

"She needs..." My voice was hoarse and dull. "She needs her white blouse for choir tomorrow."

Her gaze seemed to pass right through me. She answered in her gentle whisper, "I washed it yesterday. It's already hanging up in her closet."

"She says...she says she looked everywhere."

"Oh, it's right there in front of her. She can never find anything," she said.

For another weird moment, we stood confronting each other like that. Then Marie began to tremble, her whole body. A violent shudder went through her and turning she sat down hard on the edge of the bed. She was hugging herself as if she might come apart. Her mouth had fallen open, her eyes had gone terribly wide. "I'm going to Hell," she gasped. Her hands flew to cover her mouth. Her wide devastated eyes stared out above them.

"Marie..."

"I'm *in* Hell," she whispered through her fingers. "*This* is Hell."

It was not until that moment that my life tumbled

down on top of me. Even though I had known the truth, I hadn't really known anything till then.

"I thought it was what God wanted." Her whisper had become high and squeaky. "But it couldn't be. It couldn't . . ."

I made myself go to her, made myself sit on the bed beside her. I wanted to take her hands but I couldn't bring myself to touch her. They fell—her hands—they fluttered down into her lap like leaves. She turned her nightmarish stare my way but it was all unseeing. "He wanted me, Cal. He said he just wanted the money at first but he wanted me. He wanted us."

"The bastard . . ." I heard myself say.

"He just wanted . . . just to hurt us. Just to destroy us, just to do it. He . . . He said it wasn't fair. I had everything and he went to prison all those years. He said he was going to destroy us unless I'd be with him again. He said . . ."

In a convulsive movement, she reached for me. Without thinking, I took her hand. I held it fast in both of mine.

"And when he drove his car at Tot—at Tot! . . . I didn't know what to do. I prayed," she said. "I prayed so hard. And I thought God wanted me to tell him, to tell him he had to go away." I remembered her in church, praying to the wooden Christ, that expression on her face of transcendence and gratitude. I remembered thinking that Christ was answering her prayer. "I don't know why I took the gun. I hated the gun. You know I did; I hated it! But I was afraid of him. At first he just wanted the money—he wasn't mean at first, he said he just wanted the money—but now he was different, awful, I was afraid. And it was like a dream, it was like I was being told what to do. I thought it was God telling me to take the gun. He drove his car at Tot! He drove his car . . . And I thought God was telling me . . ."

I held her hand tight. "Ssh," I said. "Ssh."

"I told him. I told him he had to go away," she said, still with that horrifying stare, that bright unseeing stare. "And he laughed at me. He laughed at me, Cal, and I just . . . I took out the gun. I didn't even mean . . . I just wanted to tell him if he came near any of you again . . . But then . . . it was like I was in a tunnel. Wind . . . All this wind was blowing past me. This wind, and I was rushing down this tunnel. And I could see that it was evil, I could see then it wasn't what God wanted at all, it was evil but . . . it just kept happening." She winced—as if she heard the shots again, as if her finger were pulling the trigger again. Again and again. "It was too late. It just kept happening."

I swallowed hard, too sick to think. I went on holding her hand but I didn't like to. I wanted to move away from her, catch my breath.

"Do you hate me, Cal?" she said. She was staring through me at nothing. "You don't hate me now, do you?"

". . . No." It took me a moment to get the word out. "No, of course not but . . . Dear God. I mean, why didn't you come to me? Right at the start. You could've come to me, told me, why . . . Why didn't you?"

Now, finally, she looked at me. The brightness of her wild stare dimmed and she focused. I think the question had taken her aback actually. I think the answer was so obvious to her she couldn't imagine I would have to ask. To her, I think, it was the most obvious thing in the world.

"Because we were so beautiful," she said. "You and me and the children, the way we all were. All these years, whenever I was afraid he might come back, he might get out and find me, I would tell myself that God would never . . . God would never make us all so beautiful and then let something so terrible happen. He might bring him back to punish me but . . . not you, not you and the children."

I had to let her go then. She was talking too crazy. It made me too ill to stay by her. I stood up, sucking in deep breaths. I took a step or two away.

"When he came . . ." she said. "When he did come, I thought: if we can just be good . . . If we can just go on being so perfect, the way we were, everything so perfect, then God would see, God would make him go away . . . I thought if we could just go on, Cal. If I could just keep it in a separate part of my head just like always, in a separate part of my head and we could just go on and be like we always were then God would make him go away again."

"Go away . . ." I pressed a palm against my forehead, my back to her. *Goddamnit*, I thought. *Goddamnit, Marie. Nothing goes away. Nothing! That's the whole goddamned point!*

"I never thought God would punish you and the children."

And God! I thought. If she mentioned that fucking God again . . .

"Billy said I would go to jail," she raced on. "For what happened to the Whalleys. Even though I was only there at the beginning. I was only there at the beginning, Cal, I swear and then when they started to paint things and break things and be mean to the lady, I ran away. I ran away. But he said it didn't matter. He said I was a murderer too just because I was there and I would go to jail. And the children . . . Eva. J. R. And Tot's still so little . . . How would you even explain to her?"

"I don't know." I pressed the palm hard against my brow. "I don't know. You were so young at the time. If you'd just come to me. There might've been some way out. I don't know. If you really weren't there . . . The statute of limitations may be . . ."

I could feel her helpless gaze on me. "Well, I don't know what that is, Cal," she said softly. "I don't even know what that is."

Still turned away, I nodded.

"And that wasn't it," she went on. "That wasn't it anyway. I mean, even if it just came out . . . Even if I didn't go to jail and it just came out and you and the children knew about it . . . We were so beautiful and you loved me so much . . . It would've all been ruined. You see? We were so perfect and if you found out it would've all been ruined." I heard her begin to cry. "Why did I ever know him, Cal? Why did I ever know him?"

"Oh, you were fourteen," I said. "Fifteen. You were a child . . ."

She was crying now and I spoke as gently as I could, as kindly as I could. But I did not feel gentle. I did not feel kind. This is a confession and I promised you the ugly truth and, at that moment, I did not feel gentle and kind at all. I was revolted. I tried to fight it but I was revolted by what she'd done. More than that. I was furious with her. Furious.

With her stupidity and her ignorance. With her simplistic, blithering faith in her wooden God. With her idiotic assumption that she could stumble through all this lying and lying and it would somehow go away. Go away! I mean, Christ! What had she done? What had she done to the children, to me, to all of us? Murder? Jesus! She'd committed *murder* out there in those woods. She would be found out. These things were always found out. There'd be a trial, headlines, prison. Prison! My children. My children's lives would be shattered. They would never recover from it. Eva, who needed her so much; J. R. and Tot—they all needed her. And their lives would be shattered. I mean, Christ! Christ!

"I was fourteen," she echoed me, still crying softly. "I had to run away from home, from my father. I was alone, Cal. I was so scared. I just . . . I wanted someone to love me, that's all. And Billy came along and . . . I was fourteen. I didn't know it could be like this, like it is with you. I didn't know there was anyone like you who would be so nice to me."

Well, I faced her finally somehow. Saw her sitting where she was on the bed all forlorn. Her shoulders slumped, her hair disheveled, her face mottled with tears. Lost, looking up to me. My anger began to ebb a little. Hell, I'd married her precisely for what she was, hadn't I? Even in my fury, I knew that. I knew that. I'd loved her for what she was and I'd refused to see what was happening because I wanted her to stay the way I loved her. And so we had come to this together, the two of us. I was as much to blame for it as she.

"Could you hold me, do you think, Cal, a little while?"

she said. "Could you come to bed a little while and hold me?"

I did. Of course I did. I forced my stomach down, my anger down, and I went to her. I put my arms around her. I pressed her against me and made myself kiss her hair. I closed my eyes and tried to think of her as she had been to me throughout the years. And finally I settled on a memory of a vacation we had taken once by a lake in Maine. There was only Eva then and she was very little and afraid of the water. And Marie had coaxed her into the lake with that endless sweetness and patience of hers. I had watched them splashing and laughing together and my wife was young and slender and pale in her bathing suit and so kind and happy with our child that my joy in them both felt fathomless. Later on in the night we had slipped out of our cabin and made love by the lakeshore while the Perseid meteors fell: white streaks of light in the sky and on the water and Marie's hands clutching at me and her muffled cries.

After a while, remembering that, I managed to get myself aroused. I found, despite my anger and my revulsion and my fear, I could make love to her now too, which is what she wanted. It wasn't much but I went through the motions as best I could for her. All I had to do was keep my eyes closed and pretend she was Marie.

E I G H T E E N

THEN CAME THE NIGHT, THE MOST hellish night. My

conscience tearing at me like ravens at a corpse. Marie cried

herself to sleep but I lay awake for hours. I remembered

everything, every incident I've set down here, every mistake

I made, every moment of self-deception. After a while in

fits and starts I dozed. And then I dreamed about it. The

wavery figure at the bottom of the pool. Rising, rising to

the surface. Frost. I woke in a sweat. I lay awake. What

was I doing to do? I kept asking myself. What was I going

to do?

———

BY DAYBREAK I KNEW THE answer. Or, to be more exact, I faced the fact that I had always known, that there had never really been any doubt. I was exhausted, but weirdly calm, weirdly clear. Everything seemed distant to me but crisp and brilliant too. I sat over my second cup of coffee at the dining room table. I watched Marie tying Tot's sneaker laces. She knelt on the floor in front of the child's chair, singing to her tunelessly as she made the knots.

". . . and then this snake turns around," she sang, "and this snake turns around, and both snakes twist together. And then a giant crab comes and bites you on the toe! Eek!"

Tot giggled as Marie pinched her foot.

I watched them from far away through the lens of my clarity and exhaustion. When on earth had she done it? I wondered, raising my mug to my lips. Between dropping Tot at pre-school and serving on the church fair committee? When on earth had she ever found the time? *Sorry my cake for the bake sale is late, but I had to stop off in the woods to blow a blackmailer away and sink his body in a murky pool.* I mean, you had to hand it to her: the woman was just never too busy to get something important done.

"All tied, all finished," Marie said. She pushed to her feet, kissed Tot on the head. The child said, "Thank you, Mommy," and scampered off to her room.

Marie turned—and her tenderness for her baby lingered on her features—she turned and saw me watching her; and she blushed. I think she felt ashamed a little—to be caught in a moment of thoughtless pleasure like that.

But it was amazing. It was as she said. Somehow she could stow it away in one corner of her mind and just go on as always. We found ourselves looking at each other awkwardly.

"Mo-om," called Eva. "Now I can't find my black shoes!"

Marie quickly averted her eyes. "That child!" she murmured. "She couldn't find her head." Then gently she called, "I'll be right there, sweetheart," and went to help her.

I sat and watched her go. Everything seemed very clear. There was no doubt or confusion anymore. I knew exactly what I was going to do.

I was going to help her. I was going to do everything I could to help her hide her crime. In the first shock of knowledge, I had already thrown away the murder weapon. I had done that automatically, without thinking. I would go on with it. Do anything. Lie, if I had to. Falsify evidence, give her alibis. Hell, if I had to barricade myself in the house with a Tommy Gun shouting, "Eat lead, John Law!" while the cops closed in I would do that too. Morality be damned. My conscience be damned. There weren't going to be any guilt-wracked confessions. We weren't going to "get anything off our chests" to the police. We were going to brass this thing out, she and I, one way or another. For the sake of our children and to preserve our marriage too. That was what mattered, all that mattered. This marriage, these children, this house. And as for the late Billy Frost— well, he was a murderous, blackmailing ratbag who had tried to steal my woman and destroy my family. I'm not saying he deserved to die. But fuck him. Fuck him. Marie was my wife.

It was all clear to me. Cold and hard and dazzlingly clear.

It remained that way until approximately 10:15 that morning, when Chief of Police Orrin Hunnicut arrived at the Manor and arrested Peter Blue.

THEY CAME IN FORCE, A parade of them. Hunnicut's SUV in the lead, two patrol cars with their lights flashing, two municipal junkers with plainclothesmen inside. Oakem was there to meet them, expecting them, strutting at the base of the Manor stairs, preening his goatee. The chief had displayed his warrant and was marching off to Cade House before I even knew he was on the grounds.

Then the receptionist burst into my office babbling the news: "They're going to arrest Peter—Peter Blue for killing that man, that man out in the woods, they..."

I was off and running as fast as I could across the grass. So much for my clarity. It was gone in an instant. There was just a light, dizzy, floating feeling and thoughts racing by too quick to grasp. I was dimly aware that Gould and Karen Chu were also running to Cade house along different paths. We converged on the southern door together. Tumbled into the lounge, all three of us breathless. Gould and Karen were at my shoulders as I stared with my mouth open, my mind reeling.

Hunnicut. He came swaggering out of the residence hall, sailing magnificently across the lounge with his gut

for a prow. The two patrolmen followed, holding Peter Blue
between them. Peter's hands were cuffed at his back. His
legs were rubbery with terror, his eyes quick and desperate
with it, looking everywhere, at everything as if for the last
time. The patrolmen had to support him as they hustled
him along, each one gripping him under an arm. And two
more patrolmen flanked these two and two plainclothesmen
brought up the rear.

And with them, all around them, harassing them on
every side, were the children of Cade House. The inpatients.
Nora and Angela, Austin and Brad and Shane. They were
shouting. Lamenting. One of them even wailed—poor Nora,
no longer the starving waif, stouter now, stronger—she
wailed in hoarse, high gasps, clutching in supplication at
one of the patrolmen's elbows. Brad, whose violent temper
hadn't shown itself in weeks, was angry now again, shaking
his fist at the detectives, his face crimson as he screamed,
"You bastards! You bastards!" Angela was weeping, her
scarred hands clutched together and Austin was frantic with
helplessness running his fingers again and again through
his hair. Only Shane, the depressive girl who had laughed
and smiled when Peter talked to her, stood still, hanging
back at the hallway entrance and staring dully after the
procession like some statue in a graveyard.

Oakem, the wonderful Wizard of Odd, danced among
them all uselessly, flitting first to one and then another.
"Now people . . . Now people . . ." he kept saying.

"My God!" whispered Gould.

Both he and Karen Chu moved forward, toward the
kids. Gould took hold of the hysterical Nora. Karen gently

grasped Brad's fist in her two hands. Trying to calm them, soothe them, as the police marched Peter across the lounge.

I could only stand where I was. Stunned. Watching Hunnicut come on. Right to me, right at me.

Oakem flitted to my side. "Cal," he clucked. "You have to understand. This is police business now. There's nothing we can do."

I ignored him. Hunnicut reached me. Stopped. Didn't try to get around me or muscle me aside. Just came to rest right in front of me, enormous, his little, black eyes glittering with satisfaction. With triumph. Of course. This was why he'd been so happy. So friendly. No hard feelings. A handshake and a smile. Somehow—I didn't know how yet but somehow he had worked it out in his mind: Billy Frost was dead and Peter Blue had killed him. Victory—over Peter, over the bleeding heart courts, over the little shrink who'd thwarted him—victory was at hand.

He'd even brought that same young cop along, the one who'd been watching while we argued last time. Right there: the sandy-haired lad holding Peter under his left arm. Now the kid could watch me be humiliated as I'd humiliated Hunnicut. Now he could see what happened to people who tangled with the chief.

"Now, Cal," Oakem was still going on, "you understand the chief just wants . . ."

"Come on, Chief," I said, cutting Oakem off. I hooked my thumbs in my pockets to keep my hands from trembling. But I couldn't keep the tremor out of my voice. "What's this all about?"

"What's it all about?" Hunnicut answered loud enough

for all to hear. "Well, Doc, it's all about the fact we're arresting your boy here for murder. For the murder of Billy Frost."

I could only just get the words out. "You know that's ridiculous."

"I'm afraid I do not know it," said Hunnicut. "I know no such thing." He allowed himself the trace of a smirk here, a glance at his smirking colleagues. "It's come to my attention that your patient recently escaped from these grounds without the authorities being properly notified. Isn't that right?"

"Oh, so what? He wandered off . . ."

"And it's also come to my attention," he steamrollered on, "that that escape occurred at the approximate hour of Mr. Frost's untimely and violent demise."

I opened my mouth to protest again but nothing came out.

"And it has further and finally come to my attention, Doctor," said the chief heavily, "that Mr. Blue and Mr. Frost were engaged in what I believe you would refer to as an *alternative relationship*. Which is to say they were getting up to a little bone-smoking out in the woods there, weren't they?"

Peter groaned at this, to have it said out loud like this in front of all his friends. My glance flickered toward him. Supported by the officers, he had sagged, his knees buckling, his lips trembling, his gaze rolling up to the ceiling. His sensitive face had lost all its dignity, had assumed an expression of dumb, childlike suffering.

And I—I couldn't think. I wiped my lips with a shaking hand. All around us, the Cade House patients continued to keen and sob. I couldn't think for all the noise they made. I couldn't think of anything except . . . Except that I could end this now, right now, with a single sentence. A single sentence I couldn't speak.

Chief Hunnicut went on, "Which anyway speaks to motive, as the lawyers say. Mr. Blue here's mother was kind enough to share with us some of her son's notebooks which not only include some veiled references to the aforesaid relationship with Mr. Frost but some very interesting drawings of Mr. Frost aka Lester Marshall being hanged and stabbed and shot to death which lo and behold he eventually was. I guess Hell hath no fury like a woman scorned, eh, Doc?" The plainclothes detectives laughed out loud at this. "Now, sir, if you'll excuse us, we have to be about the performance of our duties."

"If you put him in a cell, he is a severe suicide risk, you know he is," I said.

"Precautions will be taken," said Hunnicut. "You can be sure of that."

I stood there. I couldn't think. I didn't know what to say. "I'll have a lawyer at the station in half an hour," I finally managed. "I'd like a moment with my patient before you go."

Hunnicut shrugged and waited. I stepped past him to Peter's side.

The boy was terrified, just terrified. He hardly seemed to know where he was. When I approached him, he seemed barely to recognize me at first. Then his eyes grasped at me as if I were all his hope of salvation.

"I didn't..." he said. "I didn't...I..."

"I know, Peter. It's all right," I said. I made my voice cool and authoritative. "Just take it easy. This is just a mistake."

"It's a mistake," he said. "It's..."

"I'm going to call David Robertson. Remember? The lawyer who helped you before."

"I can't...I can't go back..." He fought tears.

"Ssh. You have to stay calm now. No one's going to hurt you. I'll have you out as soon as I can. By the end of the day. Just don't do anything foolish."

That was all I had time for. At a gesture from Chief Hunnicut, the procession started again. Peter frantically tried to brace his feet under him, to stave off the moment. He cried out to me, "No, don't let them, don't let them!"

"It's going to be all right. No one will hurt you. I will get you out."

Taking a fresh grip on his arms, the patrolmen began to drag Peter away.

"Please!" he cried.

On every side, the Cade House patients set up a fresh set of wails and lamentations.

But the police marched on inexorable.

"I hold you responsible for his safety, Chief," I called after them.

Peter strained to turn back, to keep his eyes on me. Tears poured down his cheeks. "Please help me!"

"I will, Peter," I said. "Just..." Oh God.

The police angled him out the door. He went on craning his neck, trying to see me. Trying to keep me in sight till the very last moment. I watched through the doorway as the patrolmen pulled him across the lawn. The Cade House patients went on crying, wringing their hands, clutching their heads in anger and despair. I heard Gould murmuring to them and Karen hushing them, trying to comfort them, trying to calm them down.

But I went on looking through the open door at Peter—at Peter receding, receding, till he was out of sight.

NINETEEN

THE NIGHT MY SISTER DIED—THE rainy autumn midnight she drowned herself—she phoned me. I was the very last person she called before she dove into the grip of the harbor tides. It was late and she dialled my office though she knew I wouldn't be there. I guess she wanted it that way. She wanted to leave a message on my machine.

But I didn't get the message until late the next day. Mina's body was recovered quickly and I was summoned down to the city to identify her in the early hours of the morning. I remember the long drive south through miserable mists, the darkness lingering until I nearly reached Manhattan. I remember gray daylight seeping painfully into the sky above the East River as I headed down the FDR.

There was a woman at the medical examiner's office. I can't remember anything about her. She was black I think. I think. I can't recall. She handed me a photograph. A polaroid of Mina lying dead on a gurney.

"I want to see her," I said.

"Come with me," said the woman.

I followed her down a hall.

Then there was a room, a green room brightly lit and divided by a glass partition. I stood on one side of the partition and on the other side a man wheeled the gurney in and pulled down the sheet so I could see my sister's face.

"Let me through to her please," I said.

The black woman pulled back the glass partition to let me through. That was how they did it. First the photograph, then the glass, then I could go to her, touch her. You had to ask to get to each new stage. Some people just wanted the photograph, I guess.

I stood beside Mina's body, my hand on the shape of her arm beneath the sheet. I looked down at her face. It hadn't been damaged much. A few scrapes. She wasn't all torn up or anything. In fact, my first thought was that the troubles of her adult years seemed to have left her. Her features were so relaxed. She looked young again, the way she used to look when we were kids. I could almost see her girlhood self again. Man oh man, I had looked up to her then. I thought she was the soul of wisdom and sophistication. But of course I had changed. I was not a boy anymore. As I looked down at Mina in her girlhood now she just appeared baffled to me and afraid and defenseless the way children do when their lives are sad. And then that passed, and I saw her as she was. The corpse of a woman in her forties. I patted her arm for good-bye and left the room.

My memory is sketchy after that. I checked into a hotel at some point. Around five or six that evening I remember sitting on the edge of the hotel bed with the phone to my ear. That was the first time I had thought to call my machine for messages.

Hers was the first. The machine's recorded voice—staccato, soulless—announced, "Call received twelve forty-five A.M." and then there she was: "It's Mina, Cal." It was a macabre little moment. Three separate witnesses had seen her jump just before midnight. She couldn't have called at 12:45. The machine's clock must've been mis-set, that's all. Still, it was macabre.

She spoke quietly. Her voice vacillated, as it often did at the end, between a cool drawl of irony and a sentimental drunken slur. I sat on the edge of the hotel bed and listened and thought of the baffled little girl I'd seen on the gurney.

"It's Mina, Cal. I don't know what I'm calling to say exactly—besides good-bye, I mean. I suppose *I'm sorry* would be appropriate. I am sorry, Cal. I am. I know you'll be unhappy about this, you're such a sweet baby. But I don't know..." I could hear her weary sigh. "It's just all too fucked at this point, too fucked-up. It's just all gotten so awfully—fucked, you know, one way and another. Bit by bit. There's just this—art—this fine art of lying to yourself that I never mastered somehow. Like when you were little, you know, and I was maybe thirteen or fourteen. And there we were in the same house at the same time with the same parents? And for me, it was, like, I was living with Mrs. Drunk and Father Depressive of Chateau Despair. And for you, it was one big happy suburban family with Happy Suburban Mom and Happy Suburban Dad and everything was fine. You know? I mean, you've got to do that, haven't you? You've got to be able to do that, otherwise it's just all abyss, abyss, abyss. I probably should've had religion like Daddy. Or a family like you and your science or whatever you call it . . . Realism. Any lie like that, you know. Any lie would do. But to just live and live and live every day in the nightmare of God's love like this . . . no. No. That's just . . . uh uh. I can't. I'm sorry. Really. I mean, I sometimes think . . . Sometimes I think maybe . . . But I can't, I can't, I can't just walk on water. Oh me of little faith." She tried to laugh but her voice broke and I heard her swallow tears. Then she said quickly, "Good-bye, baby brother. I do love you, you know that. Kiss the kids for me, okay? And Marie. You hold onto her, baby. I mean it. Don't you ever let her go. Trust me on this. There's nothing else out there but the whole fucked-up truth. Just . . ."

Then there was the sound of a kiss and it was over. Minerva's last oracle. As delphic and incomprehensible as all the rest. To me, at least. To me at the time. Well, I thought, she was on the verge of murdering herself. Some of what she said—all that stuff about walking on water and "the nightmare of God's love,"—that probably didn't make much sense anyway. Maybe none of it made any sense at all.

But it didn't matter. Hers was always the voice that haunted me. It haunted me the day they arrested Peter Blue. It haunted me as they dragged him away screaming, as I stood there silent. It haunts me now. It haunts me every day, damned as I am to the whole fucked-up truth at last.

IT WAS GOING TO RAIN. The gray sky of the last several days was darkening, blackening. The air was still and expectant. The weather was building to an autumn storm.

I walked to my car, the Volvo. Lowered myself in. I had called David Robertson, Peter's attorney, and Father Fairfax too. They had both said they would head for the police station right away. I said I would meet them there as soon as I could. But first I had other business. I drove out of the Manor parking lot and turned toward home.

The house was quiet when I arrived. The edges of the day had grown greenish and the birds had stopped singing the way they will before a downpour. Now and then a gust of wind rattled the dying leaves in the treetops. But it never seemed to reach the surface. As I walked up the front path nothing stirred.

It was quiet inside too. I stepped through the door and the room seemed silent at first. I could've believed Marie was out even though the minivan was in the garage. Then, before I could call for her, I heard a noise coming from the kitchen. A steady scraping sound, soft, like the whisper of fabric on skin.

I moved through the dining room to the kitchen doorway and saw her. She was on her knees. The oven door was open and she was leaning forward, reaching into it. She had those gloves on, those yellow plastic kitchen gloves. She was scrubbing at the oven walls with a sponge—that's what made the scraping sound. After a moment, she brought the sponge out and wrung it over a metal bowl that was already sloshing with dark, soapy water. She hardly glanced up at me before she began scrubbing again.

"These things are supposed to clean themselves," she said. "But after a while, they get so dirty. All the crud just builds up."

"Patsy can, uh . . ." I tried to concentrate. "Can't Patsy do it when she comes? That's what we pay her for."

"Oh, you know, then I just have to do it again," she said, working the sponge. "If you want something done well . . ."

I nodded and my eyes filled with tears. I leaned against the jamb of the kitchen door. I watched her, working and working the sponge in the oven. She was wearing jeans and a sweatshirt. Her right sleeve was rolled up. Her arm was very slender, very pale. Her hair was tied back sloppily but that one curl, yellow and silver, kept falling in her eyes. She would try to blow it away and then brush it back with one of the clumsy gloves. I watched her. A long time. The curve of her hip to the movement of her breasts in the loose shirt to her face, her gentle face. I was not revolted at her anymore or angry at her anymore. I was not cool and de-tached as I had been that morning. God help me, but I loved her. I had never loved any other woman and I loved her beyond telling, beyond everything.

"I guess . . ." It was another moment before I could speak. "I guess you heard about . . . They arrested someone."

"My friend Melissa called me." She sat back on her haunches to rest, brushing at the strand of hair again. "Since it was at the Manor, she thought I'd want to know. Then I listened and it was on the radio too. That boy, they said. The one who burned the church." For the first time she turned to me. "Oh. Oh, look at you," she said. "Poor Cal."

I swiped my sleeve across my eyes. "Yeah. Poor Cal."

"No," she said gently. "Don't, sweetheart. It's going to be all right."

"He's . . . frightened," I told her. "He's frightened of being in jail. He tried to kill himself before, when he was in jail before. He tried to hang himself."

"Oh gosh," she said. "The poor thing. You should've told them, Cal."

I shook my head. "I couldn't. I didn't think . . . It wasn't for me to tell. I couldn't."

With her hands on her thighs she examined the stove a moment. "It's just about done." She leaned forward and began scrubbing again. "I don't want to leave the place a mess."

I had to cover my face then. I spread my hand across it.

"Your shirts will be back from the dry cleaner's Thursday," Marie went on. "I sent in an extra load. You should have enough till then. And you have all clean underwear, all right? That'll get you started." She kept scrubbing and scrubbing. I could hear the soft sound. "I'll arrange to have Patsy come in full time. She can cook for you but Cal . . ." For the first time her voice weakened, faltered. "Don't use her too much for the children, all right? They'll need you to be there and I'll give you the name of the agency that sends the nice babysitters from the college ..."

"Stop," I said.

She sat back again and looked up at me. "Now, we're going to have to lie about the gun, okay? That's just the way it is."

I went to her. I went down on my knees next to her.

"I'll tell them I threw it away," she said. "That way you can't get in trouble."

"Listen ..."

"I know it's wrong but it would be too much for the children to lose both of us. The police don't need to know anything about the darned gun. That's just all there is to it."

I wrapped my arms around her, buried my face in her shoulder. She held me. I smelled the sour oven cleaner and the shampoo in her hair. "I can't do this," I said.

"It's all right, Cal," she whispered.

"Marie."

"It's all right. We have to. We can't let anything bad happen to this boy."

When I could, I drew back from her. I sat on the floor, dazed, my back against a cupboard, my knees drawn up. "I don't know if I can live," I said. "If I can live without you."

"Oh, sweetheart, no. I know it's hard to believe right now, but God is going to take such good care of you. He will, you'll see. Because you're such a good man. You're the best man in the whole world and He'll watch over you every day while I'm gone. The children too. You'll see. It's going to be all right." She leaned over and kissed me very softly on the cheek. "You better go now, okay? Go and talk to the chief. You'll do that better. You'll know what to say."

I tried to hold her gaze, to look into her eyes, her blue eyes, to keep looking. But she turned away. She examined the oven again.

"I'll finish up here," she said.

THE POLICE STATION WAS A three story brick building just off State Street. There were reporters standing outside when I got there, nine or ten of them, a lot for our little corner of the world. I didn't even think about them at first. I mean, I was there to turn in my wife. I had a lump in my throat the size of a fist. I didn't care about the reporters or about anything. But as I climbed the steps to the front door, one of the locals recognized me.

"Dr. Bradley," he called out, "do you think security at your facility needs to be beefed up?"

The cluster of journalists oozed toward me like a single organism. Microphones were stuck out at me. Voices called.

"Do you regret your recommendation to the court, Doctor?"

"Are there other patients at your hospital who could be considered dangerous?"

"Did Peter Blue ever discuss any homicidal impulses with you?"

"Did you know about his relationship with Frost?"

The media glob surrounded me like an amoeba engulfing lunch. I said nothing. I shouldered through them. If they thought they had a scandal now, let them wait till they got their pods on the truth. I reached out and pulled the police station door open—roughly, to clear the journalists out of my way. I went inside and let the door shut on their faces behind me.

I crossed the foyer to where a civilian receptionist sat in a glass booth. I told her who I was. "I'm here to see the chief," I said. "Tell him it's important." My voice was steady now. My eyes were dry. I was past all that. I was past everything.

The receptionist buzzed me through a gate. A polite young patrolwoman led me up a stairway, down a hall. She opened a door for me. "Wait here," she said. I went into the room.

It was one of those awful, cheery places you always find yourself in when the roof of the world collapses. Shiny tiled walls and brightly colored plastic chairs. You could see the town hall's grassy yard through the open venetian blinds. There were lots of pink, yellow and blue fliers hung up everywhere. MAKE YOUR HOME OFF-LIMITS TO BURGLARS. HELP YOUR CHILDREN SAY NO TO DRUGS. NEVER TALK TO STRANGERS. A table with stacks of similarly useful pamphlets sat against one wall.

And here was Father Fairfax murmuring to David Robertson in a far corner. And two women seated beside one another in the red chairs to my left. I recognized the older of the women. She was Peter Blue's mother. She had come to visit him at the Manor once or twice. She was a blowsy creature, in her forties but leathery with booze. Hair dyed blond. A skirt too short for her mottled legs and too tight for her bulging middle. Her blouse was a concoction of jarring shapes and colors—gold, black, gray—and it was also too tight for her. Her heavy breasts crowded the neckline as she leaned forward to cry into the ear of the teenaged girl next to her.

I didn't recognize her, the teenager. Dumpy, plain. Bad, swarthy skin. Straight brown hair. Shapeless in a pink sweater and black jeans. She was half frightened, it looked like, and half excited by the situation. Mrs. Blue was pressing close to her, sniffling in her face. "I don't know what else to do. I'm at my wit's end," I heard the older woman rasp. She dabbed the mascara from her cheeks and the snot from her nostrils with a ragged Kleenex. The younger woman nodded, trying to look sympathetic and mature.

With a small shock, it occured to me that the teenager was probably Jenny Wilbur, Peter's girlfriend. I don't know why this should've surprised me exactly. I guess there was just something so slack and charmless about her. When I thought of Peter—Peter at his best—with his good looks and his quick mind and his big laugh—and when I thought of how passionate he'd been about her, how much trouble he'd caused in his passion . . . well, I guess I'd pictured her differently, that's all.

I made a small gesture of greeting to the two women. But Fairfax was beckoning me over. I joined him in the corner with Robertson. We spoke in low tones.

"Thank God you're here, Cal," Fairfax said. "We're gonna need you on this. Listen to what David has to say."

The attorney was a lean, hyped-up guy. Bald and bearded with sharp eyes and a way of nodding quickly when he listened that made you feel he understood your sentences before you finished them. He had a choppy, precise voice.

"The sheriff's department is on its way to take Peter over to Gloucester for his arraignment," he said. "In terms of bail? I can't hold out all that much hope. Given the charge and the circumstances, the judge is almost sure to hold him."

I glanced out the window. I didn't answer. None of this was going to matter soon.

"Actually though?" Robertson went on. "The overall situation isn't as bad as it could be. I had a preliminary conversation with Larry Wallace over at the state's attorney's office. The investigation is still ongoing. Right now? The police are searching through Billy Frost's apartment up in Garland. They're apparently recovering all kinds of guns and drugs—I don't have all the details. But the point is it's pretty clear Frost was not exactly a reformed character. Now it's too early for Larry to start any deal-making—but off the record? We were discussing a possible scenario where maybe the murder weapon belonged to Frost and he and Peter got into some kind of lover's quarrel or whatever, the gun went off. Something of that nature."

Still, I didn't answer. I didn't have the energy.

Robertson continued: "In that case? State's attorney might be willing to entertain a plea of second degree manslaughter, with maybe a five year sentence. The problem then, of course, is the arson . . ."

"Look," I said dully. "We're not doing any of this. Peter's innocent. There was no lover's quarrel. He didn't kill anyone."

"Cal. Cal." This was Fairfax now. The silver-haired

priest was firing on all deal-making cylinders, I could tell. He had those Onward Christian Soldier features leveled at me like a weapon. "We have to focus now on the realistic possibilities. We have a genuine situation on our hands. If this gets dragged out it's going to be very bad for the community."

I blinked at him. "Bad for the community. What the hell does that mean?"

Now he started gesticulating too. I mean not only was his face in my face but his hands were in my face as well. "Do I have to spell this out?" He had to hiss to keep the volume down. "By all rights this boy should've been in jail. Or at least awaiting trial instead of living large at your clinic, roaming around the woods at will. The longer the press has to play with this the more of a scandal it's going to be. And if there's a trial... Well, what do you think is going to happen to the Manor when people find out you let a murderer escape?"

"Well, yeah, that would be a problem except he didn't escape, I didn't let him and he isn't a murderer." I was too depressed to be patient with this crap.

"Cal," said Fairfax urgently. "Cal. People put their reputation on the line for this boy. Not just you. The judge, the state's attorney. I put my reputation on the line. With Hunnicut feeding the media who knows what, they'll tell it all his way... Damn it, couldn't you have seen this coming? You knew the boy was unstable. Couldn't you have at least provided some security?"

I couldn't answer him. I couldn't. I could only go on looking at him, looking at him. Where was the concerned soul who had come to me after church begging for my help? *There's something extraordinary about this boy. Very spiritual; extraordinary.* Yeah but oops, hint of scandal, fuck him, cut him loose.

"You've got to convince him to plead to manslaughter," Fairfax said.

"What?"

"He trusts you. You're the only one he does trust. David and I both told him how it had to be but he just kept asking, 'What does Dr. Bradley say?' He'll do it if you tell him to, Cal."

"Michael—he's innocent."

"He's not innocent." The priest's voice had grown a little louder. He brought it down again. "He's not innocent. He set fire to my church. He held the chief at gunpoint. If David here can bargain the prosecutor down to five years for manslaughter the boy'll be getting off easy."

I finally turned away from him. Turned to the window. There was water running down the glass now. It had started to rain.

"He'll do it if you tell him to," repeated Fairfax in my ear. "Then it'll be over. Then it'll all be over."

The funny thing is: he was probably right. Given Peter's hysteria, his confusion, his trust in me. Eventually I probably could convince him to plead to manslaughter. Maybe I could even convince Marie that it was for the best that way. I thought I could. I thought I could probably do that too. Then it would be over. Then Marie could stay with us. My children would never have to find out. Then it would all be over.

"Come on, Cal," said Fairfax. "It's the right way to go for everyone."

The waiting room door opened. I turned and saw Chief Hunnicut filling the frame. "Hey, Doc," he said. "Let's go get ourselves a cup of coffee."

It took me a moment, but then I glanced at Fairfax. "No," I told him.

"Cal . . ." said Fairfax.

"I won't do it. No."

I walked across the waiting room to the chief. My heart weighed a ton.

THE RAIN FELL HARD. STREAKING silver lines of it then sudden gusts that splattered on the pavement. The journalists were a cluster of black umbrellas now at the edge of the sidewalk. They saw us but the chief waved them off. They let us pass without a word.

I cinched the belt of my raincoat and turned my collar up as we hurried across the street to the coffee shop on the other side.

"Shit day," the chief grumbled.

We went into the cafe.

It was nearing noon. The lunch crowd had not yet come. There was only one other man at the counter, a home oil trucker seated right up front. At the tables, only a few other suits and civil servants were reading their menus. They all waved to Hunnicut as he came in.

The chief led me down to the counter's far end. We had a private place for talking there if we kept our voices low. The waitress was setting our coffee in front of us even as we sat down. Hunnicut surrounded his cup with his huge paws, meditated into the steam. I took a sip of mine. Trying to think through my sadness, trying to find the right words. I didn't know if I was going to be able to do this.

"So you see your patient?" Hunnicut asked me.

"What? No. Not yet. I wanted to talk to you first."

"Too bad. I was hoping you'd beat a confession out of him."

I paused. I studied him. His slab of a face was turned down, unreadable. All the same, some confused notion of hope went through my mind. "What does that mean?" I said. "You have doubts?"

He sat up on the stool, casually stretching his back, running one palm up over his angry white crewcut. "Hell no," he said. He broke from the stretch. "No doubts he's a criminal anyway. Man set a house of worship on fire. Pulled a gun on an officer of the law. No doubts on that score whatsoever."

"What about Billy Frost?"

"Well . . ." He settled heavily around his coffee cup again. "You know. It's an ongoing investigation. And justice will be served, believe me. But there have been a few interesting developments this morning, I will say that. I will say that."

The rain washed loudly against the cafe storefront. The glass shuddered with the sudden blow. The town's first selectman, Tony Frazetta, fought his way inside. He clapped a hand on the chief's shoulder as he passed by on his way to join a colleague. Hunnicut waited until he was out of earshot before going on.

"We located the late Mr. Frost's living quarters for one thing. Little rathole apartment over in Garland. Had enough guns lying around the place to supply an army. Marijuana, cocaine, shit you'd pretty much expect. What we didn't expect was all the money."

"The money," I echoed back.

"Yessir. Big old cardboard box just chock full of it, hidden right under the floorboards. Over fifty thousand dollars in small bills. I have to admit it has me wondering. I mean, where does a man just out of prison land himself that kind of swag? You see what I'm saying? Especially up here, middle of nowhere. He was into something, that's for sure."

It was odd hearing that, an odd sensation. On the one hand, it sickened me. Marie's money, the blackmail money, discovered by the police. The investigation closing around her. But on the other hand . . . Well, why was he telling me? Was it a signal? Something I could pass on to the lawyer? Was it possible, I mean—was there any chance—that I could get Peter out of this without incriminating Marie?

The chief's huge neckless head went back and forth. "And then I had a conversation with the medical examiner a short while ago. Seems he's concerned about the bullets going all over the fucking place. Says a man wouldn't do that—even a little girlie-boy like your guy—wouldn't shoot so wild. More like a smallish woman, no upper body strength, pulling the trigger real fast, can't control the recoil. I don't know." He grimaced down at the counter, out of sorts with the world. "Another party heard from. What can you do?"

I shook my head slowly. "I don't understand," I said. "Why are you telling me this?"

"How's it hanging there, Orrin?" A man, a business-man I didn't know, just in, dripping with the rain, had paused to slap the chief on the back.

"At my age, it hangs pretty low," the chief told him.

The businessman continued on to the tables.

"The reason I'm telling you, Doc," Hunnicut said to me the moment he was gone, "is I don't want you to take it wrong, what happened at your clinic today, what's hap-pening here. This may be a little hard for you to believe, but I got a lot of respect for you. A lot of respect. A lot of people nowadays, they think a fellow has to share their opinions or their politics to be a good person. But me, what matters to me is the man, his integrity. You have integrity, Doc. I admire that. I do. I understand what it is that fine wife of yours sees in you. And whatever has passed between us in this matter and whatever my feelings are about Mr. Blue, I want you to rest assured that I will not see justice miscarried against him or any man. I want you to be easy in your mind, Doc, knowing that I will do everything in my power to find out the truth."

"But what about now? Are you still going to arraign him? Are you still going to send him to jail?"

"Hold on a second," he said. And he got up and walked away from me.

I SWIVELED ON MY STOOL to watch him move to the door. I could see past him, through the storefront, what was going on.

There was an alley to one side of the police station.

There was a van turning into it. I caught the marking on the van's side: GLOUCESTER COUNTY SHERIFF'S DEPART-MENT. As it made the turn, it's brake lights burning red through the silver rain, the photographers out front moved to meet it. I could see the flashes going off behind the ridged black circles of their umbrellas.

"They're gonna take him to court," Hunnicut said to me over his shoulder. "I gotta get out there."

And he pushed out into the rain.

"Chief." I went after him.

What was I going to do, I wonder. Would I have told him? Would I have told him then, right out in the rain like that, with everyone around us? I don't know. I really don't. I like to think I would've done the right thing at some point. But the way it turned out, I never got the chance.

By the time I reached the sidewalk, Hunnicut was already halfway across the rain-black street. I had to stop to let a pickup truck go by. Then I followed him to the alley.

The alley was wide. A lane nearly. The photographers were gathered at the mouth of it, held at bay by three uniformed officers in plastic yellow ponchos. The officers shunted the flashing umbrellas to one side to let the chief pass through. I was several steps behind him but I passed the yellow cops in his wake.

Now I could see the van parked halfway down the lane, right beside a large metal door in the ground level of the brick station. Two sheriff's deputies had come around the rear of the van to open it. They weren't wearing ponchos and their khakis were turning dark in the downpour.

As I passed the photographers, there was a fresh flurry

of flashing bulbs. The metal door of the station house had come open. Two town officers were bringing Peter, handcuffed, out into the rain.

I was just at the mouth of the alley when this happened. A good way away—I don't know—maybe twenty yards. The chief was closer, a few yards ahead. I called to him. "Chief." But he continued toward the van. I continued to follow him. One of the town cops was conferring with one of the county deputies now. The deputy nodded and climbed up into the van. And then, to my surprise, the town cop moved behind Peter Blue and undid his handcuffs.

I heard Hunnicut, a step in front of me, mutter, "Aw, what the hell...?" And then he barked loudly, "Hey!"

But it was too late. Everything happened too fast. I was close now, coming abreast of the sheriff's van. Almost beside the chief. Ten yards away from Peter, if that. And it was so fast even I couldn't follow everything that happened. All I know is that Peter moved. Turned. Swiftly, gracefully. I saw him clearly for a moment as he came around. His black hair was plastered wet on his forehead, his face was white, set, grim, wild. His eyes were burning, terrible and bright. One of the police officers seemed to stumble forward, his hands up in front of him as he went down hard to one knee. And when I looked again, Peter was backing up, backing away from me, wheeling this way and that, focusing those burning eyes—like beacons in the gray weather—on one of us then another then another as all the cops fell back from him. I was so transfixed by that stare when it lasered into me that it was a second before I could shift my gaze, before I saw, before I realized that

Peter had stolen the patrolman's pistol, that he had it up-raised, gripped hard in his two hands.

All this took place in a moment—and in a moment more, Peter pivoted around and took off, running fast toward the parking lot at the other end of the alley.

"Peter!" I shouted. "Don't!"

I was dimly aware that one of the county deputies had drawn his pistol. That he was bringing its barrel down in a line with Peter's back. I was still shouting when Chief Hunnicut threw his arm out across my chest and swept me back behind him to shield me with his big body. But he himself kept charging forward and when he moved I saw around him. For one instant, I had a glimpse of everything. I saw the deputy with his leveled gun. Peter running, the puddled water splashing up from beneath his feet. I saw cars in the lot at the alley's end, the green and maroon and white of them dimmed to almost nothing in the rain. There was a woman there, in the lot, a woman in a kerchief hurrying past the far end of the alley. She was searching in her purse for her car keys and wholly unaware she had stepped into the line of fire.

It was only an instant but I had time to imagine the sound of the gunshot, time to imagine the bullet cutting through Peter's spine. And I had time to realize, time to know that something—some dark something in my heart was glad. *It would all be over then,* I thought. *That would be the end of it.* But I was still shouting, "Don't!"

And then the instant was over. Chief Hunnicut swung around—amazingly fast for such a giant. Pivoted and swung around in front of the deputy—right in front of his gun so that his huge gut was nearly flush to the barrel of it. In the same motion, his hammy hands clapped shut over the weapon. He snapped it right out of the startled deputy's grasp.

I heard the splash, splash of Peter's feet as he rounded the alley corner and disappeared from sight.

And that was it. Hunnicut cast an irritated glance at the vanishing prisoner. Then, with an angry grimace, he gave the weapon back to the deputy, shoved it against the deputy's chest so hard that the deputy grunted as he instinctively took it back.

"You could hurt someone with that thing, sonny," the chief said. "Just don't do it in my town." He turned to his own officers. "All right," he said. "Don't just stand there. Let's goddamned go and get him."

TWENTY

THERE HAD BEEN SOME MIX-UP IF I understand it right.
Some idiot thing about the police handcuffs versus the sheriff's shackles. The sheriff's department was a relic of the old county system, destined for extinction, and proud and particular about such matters. They had insisted on changing from one to the other and that's when Peter had made his break. He can't have planned for such a thing though he must've been watching for his chance. I suppose it was only a matter of time before he did something like this anyway.

After he ran away, he stole a car in the parking lot. The lady with the kerchief. He caught her as she was opening the door to her Toyota. Snatched the keys from her hands and slipped in behind the wheel. "I'm sorry, ma'am," he said to her. He was driving away before the police made it to the end of the alley.

Hunnicut had the description and license plate of the car out over the radio in minutes. If Peter had tried to leave town he probably wouldn't have gotten ten miles. But within the hour, the Toyota was found again, abandoned by the side of the road at the southern border of the Silver River Gorge Preserve. By that time, although the rain kept falling steadily, the winds had died down so the chief asked the state police to send up one of their helicopters to see if they could spot the fugitive among the trees. Hunnicut and his boys, meanwhile, went into the forest on foot. They brought K-9 with them too, a German shepherd tracker specially trained for police work.

But Peter knew the woods. And he was smart enough to travel in the streams and the running gullies—and the river once he reached the bottom of the gorge. And, of course, the rain was on his side as well, washing his scent and his trail away. There's no telling how far he might've gotten if he'd actually been trying to escape.

But no, he was just trying to get back to the overlook, back to the place above the falls where God had once gone flowing through him. I knew that. I knew it the second I saw him run for it. And so I was the one who found him in the end. And so I'm the only one who knows what really happened.

I DID NOT WAIT AROUND in the alley. I knew that no matter what I said now, Peter was a fugitive with a gun and could be killed if the police got to him first. He might kill himself even before that. He probably would. So as the chief dispersed his people this way and that, I ran, unnoticed, to my car. I drove quickly back to the Manor. Dashed down the hill and over the lawn. I could already hear the chopper above me as I reached the trail head. I stopped, glanced up and saw it hovering insect-like above the trees. A spotlight was shining down from it etching a cone of rain against the colorless sky.

Then I was in the woods myself, rushing along the path to the overlook. It was a miserable trek. The mud sucked at my shoes. The rain pelted my head. My clothes grew damp and stuffy with sweat beneath my trenchcoat. The throbbing of the chopper blades above me made my pulse race, made me frantic. And when the machine pulled higher and its noise dimmed, I could hear men shouting in the distance: the chief and his minions on the hunt.

I stumbled, cracked my shin against a humped root. Clawed my way to my feet, groaning with the pain and staggered on. I could feel the minutes racing after me. I could almost hear the ticking time bomb of Peter's despair. The dog barking. The men shouting. The chopper over the trees.

Finally there I was. Above the hissing waterfall. Breathless and sopping and caked with mud. Climbing that hidden ladder of roots and footholds up to the little grove again. I pushed through the surrounding circle of birches and evergreens, staggered into the open space.

Peter was sitting quietly on the altar stone. His head was lowered, his arms rested on his raised knees, the policeman's pistol dangled from his hands. The cross formed by the birch trunk and the hemlock branch hung above him. The rain drenched him, falling steadily down.

The chopper had veered off now to some other part of the preserve. Its dim thudding whisper melded with the whisper of the falls. Beneath that white noise the cries of the dog and the men sounded faint and far away. But they were moving to the river it sounded like. Coming closer all the time.

Peter lifted his weary eyes to me. He gave a tired laugh. "Welcome to my suicide," he said. "We have to stop meeting like this."

I had to raise my voice a little over the sound of the cascade. "This was foolish, Peter. Give me the gun. Come on back. Everything is going to be all right."

"I had a dream last night," was all he said. "You want to hear it?"

"Sure. But first give me the gun."

"I dreamed that I saw paradise." He smiled to himself and looked away into the trees. "It's funny: It wasn't really all that different from here. From the world, I mean, from this. It was just—white, that's all. Everything. Everything was this—beautiful, this perfect white." He rested his cheek on his knees, narrowed his eyes dreamily. "There were trees, there still were trees, and the grass and the hills, you know? All the good things were still there. But they were white.

Everything perfect white. Except for the angels. There were these angels and they were all different colors. Bright colors. Red and yellow, blue. And they were just waving their wings. Out in the whiteness. Waving, waving their wings very slowly, very easily, lazily ..." He looked up at me. "And all the time they were there, the whole time, just above them, I could see—I could sense—this spirit—this beautiful spirit of perfect love. Watching over them. Watching the angels waving their wings in all the whiteness." He brushed the wet black forelock from his brow as if it obscured his view. "Perfect love. It was just—beautiful."

"Peter," I said.

He came back to himself slowly. His dreamy little smile turned wry. "So what does it all mean, Doctor?"

With both hands, I wiped the rain from my face, from my hair. "I don't know." I stepped closer to him. Closer to the altar stone. The stone rose nearly to my knees so Peter was just below my eye level. I looked down at him. "I don't know what it means, Peter," I said. "Maybe God granted you a vision of Heaven. I don't know."

He liked that. He nodded, the water running down his cheeks, dripping off his chin. "Maybe He did. Maybe He did."

The whisper of the falls surrounded us. The whisper of the rain pattering down on both of us. The whisper of the chopper—it was headed back this way again. Below us somewhere, the dog barked dimly.

"My wife killed Billy Frost," I heard myself say.

Peter straightened slowly. His cheek came off his knees. His lips parted. "Oh no. Oh my God."

"They were together a long time ago. When Frost killed those people at their farm. Marie—my wife, Marie— was there, part of the time anyway. When Frost found her he started blackmailing her, telling her she'd go to jail for the murder. She tried to pay him off. But he wanted more than that. He wanted her back. He threatened her. Threatened me, our daughter. She tried to scare him off with a gun and she killed him."

"Oh. Oh," said Peter Blue. He shook his head. "He was so evil. He was such an evil man."

The chopper was getting closer, louder. The sound of the falls was disappearing into it. The sounds of the men and the dog were already gone.

"I love . . ." I had to fight the tears back. "I love my wife—Marie—I love her—our children . . . I don't know how to say how much. And because—of that—of how much I loved them, I didn't see what was right in front of my eyes and that's why . . . That's why this happened to you."

I don't know what I expected. Forgiveness, revelation, rage. He just sat there, gazing into space, thinking it over. A long time it seemed like. Thinking it over. And then he nodded—smiled a little and nodded—as if this were the solution to a puzzle he'd been pondering a long time.

"I'm sorry, Peter," I said.

He kept nodding, nodding. And then with a sigh, he lifted out of his reverie. "What?" He looked at me, surprised. "Oh. Oh no. No, no. You don't understand." He pushed to his feet. Came to me, standing high above me on the stone. He reached down, gripped my shoulder. "This is fine. This is better. You've been so much to me. So good. This is perfect now."

"If I'd seen faster, acted faster . . ."

"No. No one was ever like you are, not to me. This is just right."

The air was pulsing now, pulsing as the chopper came hovering near. Even with Peter right there, right there above me on the stone, I nearly had to shout.

"It's time to come back with me, Peter. Come back and we'll straighten this all out. This is our debt to pay, Marie's and mine. I'm sorry you had to suffer for it."

"No, no, you don't understand. That's just it. That's what makes it so good."

"What do you mean? I don't . . . I don't understand what you're saying."

He didn't seem to hear me. I mean, he only smiled. He smiled that radiant smile of his. It flashed full cross his face and made it beautiful. He let my shoulder go. He stood up straight. He also had to shout above the chopper and the chopper noise grew louder as he spoke.

"Because it's still there," he said as if this explained everything. "I thought you'd taken it away from me. But you didn't. It's still there. I saw it in my dream. I saw it right in front of me."

And now the helicopter was just near—must've been just behind the low hemlocks. Its whipping whisper overwhelmed everything. The falls' whisper was gone into it and so was the whisper of the rain. Everything was gone into that pulsing air so that when Peter spoke again I couldn't hear him—or I misheard him—I must've misheard him because what I thought he said was, "You just have to walk there on the water, baby."

"What?" I shouted. "What did you say?"

The rain still fell. The clouds still hung heavy and low. But I saw then—I swear I saw—that light, that golden light, suffuse his face again. Again his arms lifted up from his sides, his form went taut, went rigid. He threw his head back to the weather, to the storm. The chopper sailed into view above us. The treetops shook. The cross—the birch and the hemlock—shook and rattled. The rain whirlpooled wildly. Peter stood there with his arms spread wide and the air around him throbbed in rhythm to the rhythm that seemed to course through his veins.

I couldn't hear him but I know he laughed. He laughed that big, that child-like laugh of pure delight.

And then—then finally—I understood.

I threw myself at him. "No, Peter, no!"

But he was already bringing his arm around, bringing the gun around to his temple. My hand swiped at where the gun had been and touched nothing. Peter pulled the trigger as I tumbled to my knees.

I stayed like that, kneeling, my head bowed down. The chopper hung deafening in the charcoal sky. The young man lay dead on the altarstone.

FIVE

AT THE END OF JANUARY, THERE was a heavy snowfall.

It began on a Friday evening around 8 P.M. By midnight it

had blanketed the town so completely that the white forest

and the white pavement seemed to blend into one another

and the deer wandered out to graze along the road.

When Saturday morning dawned crystal clear, the kids

couldn't wait to get outside. Eva and J. R. were in their ski

clothes minutes after they finished breakfast. They were

already throwing snowballs at each other while Marie was

still wedging Tot into her boots. "Wait for me, wait for

me!" Tot kept shouting at them until Marie guided her gently out the door.

I was sitting in the breezeway drinking my morning coffee. I'd put the storm windows up in there at the end of autumn. I had the baseboard heater going. It was a cozy place to sit and watch the kids at play.

I heard Marie come in after a while. I felt her standing at my shoulder. "Let me warm that up for you, sweetheart," she said.

"Thank you, darling. That's very nice of you." I heard the sound of the pouring coffee as I watched the children. "Look at them out there."

"I know," Marie said happily. "They really love the snow."

Eva and J. R. were building forts now at the base of a little hill. Tot had her plastic sled with her and wanted someone to pull her around.

"I better go out and help with Tot," Marie said. "Do you need anything else?"

"No, I'm fine. Thank you though."

I heard the whisk of her jeans as she went out the breezeway door.

There were still days like this when I found it hard to look at her. There were fewer of them as time went on but there were still occasional days. Her smile was just so endlessly sweet, her eyes so endlessly kind—I don't know—it was painful for me to see somehow. Other times it was better. It was always better at night. In some ways it was even better at night than it had been with us before.

At first, I had been unable to touch her. I would sleep on the edge of the bed with my back turned, staring into the dark. But soon she began to move close, to curl her legs into mine, to lay her hand on me. One night, finally, I rolled over and she was in my arms. And it was strange. It was the way it was when we first met. It was every night again and with the old feverish intensity. We were quick and hard, almost harsh, desperately urgent. Breathing into one another's mouths as if we were sharing the last breath in the world. It was almost embarrassing—exposing our hunger for each other, our capacity for pleasure in each other no matter what. For a while, in fact, I think we actually were embarrassed, even ashamed. In the light of morning we would act like strangers after a one night stand, impatient to get away. But we were not strangers, after all. There were mornings now when Marie would glance at me and smile and I would smile. And for a while, things would almost be as they had been in the old days.

Marie especially, I think, had a way of forgetting about it. She'd been living with her secrets now for more than twenty years. I guess she'd developed a knack. For one thing, she sincerely believed that God had saved her from prison for her children's sake and mine. She had the sure and certain faith that He would forgive her her trespasses— all her trespasses—if she was very good to us and worked for the church and prayed on Sundays very hard. But also, I think, her talent for devotion, for devoting herself completely to the people she loved, turned her mind naturally outward. It was a trait that had brought her to grief in her youth when she devoted herself to Billy Frost. But it helped her now. At times, it even seemed to lift her into a sort of state of grace.

It was not so easy for me. I don't think a waking hour

went by when I didn't think about it, some angle of it, when some angle of it didn't come back to haunt me. Certainly there was never a day—there has never been a day yet— when I didn't think about Peter Blue.

I think, of course, about all the times I might have saved him, all the chances I had and missed. If I'd only spoken up in the coffee shop. If I'd only spoken up when Hunnicut came to arrest him. If only I had seen through Marie's lies earlier. If only I had loved her less.

But then sometimes too I wonder if any of that would have mattered. I don't know how to put it exactly. It just sometimes seems that from the first moment I met Peter this was what he had in mind. *Welcome to my suicide.* As if it were inevitable. As if I were merely the audience for a story already written into the nature of things. I know I felt something like that when I convinced Marie that we had to keep silent afterwards. She still considered turning herself in, even after Peter was dead, even though the police were now convinced that he had done it. But he was gone, I told her, our children were here and they needed her. We couldn't let Tot and J. R. and Eva pay with their happiness for the life of a man like Billy Frost.

I don't know whether I believed that or not. I don't know much about what I believe anymore. And I'd be the first to say it was a selfish argument, that it served my selfish ends. But what I'm trying to tell you is: I had a sense that that was how Peter wanted it, how he meant for it to be all the while. And I owed something to that, I think. Or that's what I tell myself anyway in the awful hours before dawn.

In any event, the case of Billy Frost's murder was declared closed by the Highbury PD. Chief Hunnicut announced his retirement shortly afterward and stepped down at the end of the year. I'd heard he was planning to move to Florida sometime in the near future. I resigned too, gave up my presidency of the clinic. After Peter's death, the local newspaper started gearing itself up for a long-winded scandal with the Manor at its center. How could such a violent kid have ended up in a place with no security? How had he been allowed to escape and commit manslaughter and then suicide? Just what sort of evil dwelled in this Manor that sat like a canker on the rose of our community? And so on. I immediately issued a statement accepting all responsibility for Peter's case and stepped down. Delightfully enough, the Board of Directors also fired Ray Oakem for good measure. Gould was appointed the new director. And the newspaper, deprived of targets, pretty much let the scandal fizzle out and die. My reputation didn't even suffer very much from it, if at all. The important people in town—they all knew me—and they all assumed my resignation was an act of honor, that Oakem, an outsider, was really the one to blame. All of my personal patients decided to stay with me—Gould referred more—and soon I opened an office near the center of town. I feel I've done a lot of good work there.

As for the inpatients of Cade House, they had all moved on and been replaced by others. I've seen the follow-up reports and spoken with one or two of the kids themselves. Happily, I can report that they've all responded to treatment remarkably well. Nora eats normally now, is starting college next September, has a boyfriend. Angela has stopped scarring herself and is happily working at a TV station in Hartford. Brad is off drugs, doing nicely in high school. Austin and Shane have both defeated their depression and—despite medical advice—seem to have gone off their medications with no signs of setbacks at all.

Which pretty much brings things up to date until January. Until that Saturday late in January after the big snow.

AS I SAT IN THE breezeway drinking my coffee, watching my children play in the yard, a modest little Dodge pulled into the driveway. For the first few weeks after Peter's death, I would feel a little seizure of fear every time I saw a police officer approaching. That period was passing now. I didn't really feel much of anything when I saw Orrin Hunnicut unfold himself from the car. I went to meet him as he rumbled up the path to the door.

He looked different these days. The effect of retirement, I guess. Maybe getting over the death of his wife too, I don't know. But his expression was somehow blander than it had been, less threatening. His smile was gummy and harmless. He was beginning to look altogether like a harmless old man.

He joined me in the breezeway. He took no coffee; he said he couldn't stay. He wouldn't even remove his winter overcoat, which made him even more enormous than usual, made him look even more than usual like a bald-faced bear.

We sat side by side with just the small coffee table between us. He was holding an envelope in his two hands, a large manila envelope that was bulging, full.

We looked out the window at the children playing on the hill. Marie had joined them now. She was wearing her white woolen sweater and a fur cap that let her hair hang free. She looked very beautiful, old fashioned and wintry. She was pulling Tot on the sled and the other kids were bombarding her with snowballs from their forts. Even through the storm windows we could hear them screaming with laughter.

Hunnicut gave a grandfatherly chuckle. "Look at 'em go, huh. Look at 'em. That's a fine family you have yourself there, Doctor. A fine family."

"Thank you."

"That wife of yours—I know I've said it before. She is one of the best and kindest women it's ever been my honor to know." A sentimental shake of his head and he said, "That's what makes it happen. Isn't it? A woman like that. Believe me. I got myself two of the finest children on earth though I say it myself."

"Your son is in the Air Force, I remember."

"A full colonel now, yes sir. And my daughter's a teacher, got a fine family of her own. And every time I look at those two I thank God my wife was the woman she was, a woman like your wife. Believe me. That's what makes it happen. I know what I'm talking about."

"I do believe you," I said.

He chuckled again watching the kids. "Just look at 'em. Damn it's nice to be young, isn't it?" He shivered in his overcoat. "Brr. I know I won't miss this cold."

"So when are you off for Florida?"

"Oh, few days, end of the month probably. That's the plan. Probably wait to sell the house in the spring. That's when you get the good prices. I'm ready though. No one has to convince me." He laughed.

"You're enjoying retirement then."

"Yes I am. I most certainly am. It's a burden to lay down. A helluva burden. I was a law officer one way or another more than forty years, Doc, but... Well, I don't know. Once the wife was gone and all. It was just too much for a man alone. No one to talk to, share the troubles of the day. That's what it's all about, isn't it? Having someone to share the troubles of the day. Can't go far with things all locked up inside you. Why people marry, why people pray. Why criminals confess, if you ask me. Why people come to you too, I imagine. It's a rare person who can live with the truth alone, that's a fact." He sat silent only another moment. Then: "Well..." He held up the manila envelope. "I won't waste your Saturday with old fart rambling. Just wanted to drop this off with you. Stuff I gathered on the Peter Blue case. Just unofficial. Mopping up. Satisfying my own curiosity, if you like. Nothing the force would be interested in but I thought you might like to have it, seeing as you had a connection."

I felt a little twinge of anxiety but only a little. I took the envelope from him. "Thanks. I would. I'll take a look."

He groaned to his feet and I came up with him. We shook hands.

"You're a good man, Doc. It's been nice knowing you. You take care of that family of yours, y' hear me?"

"Keep in touch," I said, hoping with all my heart that I would never see or hear from him ever again.

He insisted on showing himself out. I settled into my chair again, the envelope in my lap. As Hunnicut walked to his car, I saw him lift one big hand to Marie. I turned and saw her wave back—hesitantly, I thought, with a hesitant smile. She seemed to stand very still and look after his car as it backed out of the driveway and motored off along the road.

I looked after it too. I waited till it was out of sight before I opened the envelope. Then I reached in and drew out the first piece of paper I touched. It was a copy of the article I had read about the Whalley murders in the *New York Times* Sunday magazine. It was the photo of Billy Frost's gang standing outside their house in Missouri. Attached to it with a paper clip was a section of the photo which Hunnicut had had enlarged. It was the woman sitting on the grass in the background. That is to say, it was Marie.

I slipped the papers back into the envelope. It was a generous gesture on the big man's part, I thought. His business was confession too, after all. He wanted me to understand that I was not alone.

But of course it wasn't enough. It couldn't be enough. Because he didn't know all of it. I was the only one who knew all of it—the connections, the inexplicable coincidences, the secret thoughts, the dreams—and even I wasn't sure exactly what it was I knew.

I can tell you this though. What I think about most now when I think about Peter Blue is the moment he broke away. I think about when he was running down the alley and the deputy drew his gun. I remember that single second when I thought that Peter would surely be shot dead. And I remember my gladness, the way my heart leapt up, the thought that had flashed through my mind, *It would all be over then.* I remember those things and then I remember standing with him in the rain in the little grove and I ask myself: did I know—in some part of me? I mean, I knew him. I knew him well. Did I know what he would do if I confessed to him about Marie? Even if I didn't, even if I couldn't have forseen it, couldn't I at least have understood a second earlier what he was planning? Couldn't I have leapt at him a second earlier and grabbed the gun?

I don't know. I don't know the answer. It's bad enough to have to ask. It's bad enough in the night, awake, alone, to share the darkness with those questions.

So I've written this, my confession. And it's been some comfort to me, all in all, to imagine you, my reader, taking it in. There have been times when I've seen you so clearly as I wrote that it actually seemed to me these words were linking us, life to life, and the burden of solitude grew a little lighter. But it's illusory, of course. I can never show this to anyone—to anyone real, I mean. I'll have to burn it when I'm finished just as I burned the contents of the envelope Hunnicut gave me. I'm afraid that you, my friend, will never be anything but a figment of my imagination. The moment I complete the final sentence of this story, you will vanish into thin air.

ANYONE WHO THINKS THAT BLISS *is shallow*, my sister Mina once told me, *doesn't understand the tragic nature of bliss.* It was always difficult for me to understand her mystical pronouncements but I think I do get this one a little better now. Because our bliss is built on water. Everything we are is built on water. And once you see that, once you know that, you begin to sink, to drown. But what Mina never understood—or what perhaps she understood too late—is that once you know, once you really know, you can *not* know again. You can know and somehow, even knowing, you can not know. And then you can walk on the water. There are moments still when I am very happy.

I was happy for a while that January day. Watching my family through the breezeway windows. I had closed Hunnicut's envelope again and set it on the coffee table. I sat easily with my hands folded on my waist and gazed at the children playing in the snow. The snow was smooth in the big yard. Smooth and pristine and very white in the sunshine. Off to the side, it sloped gently down to the edge of the woods and there the trees stood decked with it, decked with white, guarding the tangled pathways and distances of the white forest beyond. In front of me the whiteness rose up into the little hill where the children were. They had left their forts now and their sled. They were lying on their backs on the white incline. They were making snow angels, slowly moving their arms up and down, up and down to carve the shape of wings into the white surface. Tot in her red snowsuit. J. R. in his blue parka. Eva all in yellow. Vivid against the endless white. And Marie. I raised my eyes to her. She was standing on slightly higher ground with the white hillside behind her. She was standing with her arms crossed under her breasts, smiling down at the children where they lay.

I sat in the breezeway looking out and I was happy. To see my children in their colors making angels in the snow. To see Marie above them, smiling down on them. Watching over them. Like a spirit of perfect love.

ACKNOWLEDGMENTS

I'M VERY GRATEFUL TO THE PEOPLE who helped me with this book; they were all of them incredibly generous and kind. Dr. Richard C. Friedman not only instructed me on psychiatric methodology but actually took the time to give me his insights into the minds of my fictional sufferers. The Reverend J. Douglas Ousley, likewise, not only advised me on Episcopal practices and beliefs but, along with his wife, Mary, gave me an excellent reading of one of the book's early drafts. Waterbury State's Attorney John A. Connelly spent a long lunch during his successful prosecution of a murder case to teach me the ins and outs of Connecticut law and government. Information Director Pat Russo gave me an excellent and instructive tour of Connecticut's Silver Hill Hospital. The good and friendly folks at the Sharon Audubon Society instructed me on the care and feeding of owls. Casper Ultee of the Connecticut Botanical Society answered my query on wildflowers. Ellen Borakove of the New York City Medical Examiner's office told me about procedures there. And Astrid Miano did a fine job as research assistant. My more personal thanks go to agents Robert Gottlieb and Dan Strone in New York and Brian Lipson in California for their help and support, along with Tom Doherty and Bob Gleason at Tor/Forge. And, as always, my humble gratitude and slavish devotion are due to my wife, Ellen, my best and most tireless editor.

ACKNOWLEDGMENTS

I won't bore the reader with a lengthy bibliography but I do have to mention the works of Anthony Storr, which informed my sense of the psychiatrist/patient relationship; *DSM-IV Made Easy* by James Morrison, which remained open on my desk throughout the novel's development; and *In a House of Dreams and Glass*, a wonderful memoir by Dr. Robert Klitzman which gave me an idea of Cal's training and from which I garnered a description of shock therapy.

Having mentioned all the above, I hasten to add that they are in no way responsible for the errors of fact or licenses of fiction that the book no doubt contains.